THE ROOKIE'S SECOND CHANCE

The Silver Creek Series

Book 2

JENNIFER RIVERS

This is a work of fiction. Names, characters, places and incidents either are the product of the author's imagination or are used fictitiously. Any resemblance to persons, living or dead, business establishments, events, or locales is entirely coincidental.

The Rookie's Second Chance

Copyright © 2024 by Jennifer Rivers

All rights reserved.

No part of this book may be reproduced in any form or by any electronic or mechanical means, including information storage and retrieval systems, without written permission from the author, except for the use of brief quotations in a book review.

❦ Created with Vellum

Introduction

Rodeo bad boy turned rookie cop, and now I'm his Boss.

Jake is my ex, and now my rookie.

Forced to partner on a new stalker case the tension is unbearable.

He still has the same piercing blue eyes that give me butterflies.

And seeing his broad shoulders in his uniform has me buckling at the knees.

But I am his superior officer, and it's strictly forbidden to be involved with a rookie, no matter how good he looks!

When his sister's friend enters the scene, I can't help but want to give Jake a second chance.

Introduction

With an unhinged stalker from the past threatening Silver Creek. Jake and I must navigate a dangerous dance, as our history and present collide.

As a detective, my job is to uncover the truth. But in this small town, rumors spread like wildfire.

Has forbidden desires clouded my judgement? Is the true threat closer than I think?

Chapter One

JAKE

The early morning mist hung low in the streets of Silver Creek, softening the edges of the world. The usually bustling main road was nearly silent, save for the distant crow of a rooster and the soft hum of vehicles. I pulled up to Rosie's Diner, a Silver Creek staple, for a caffeine fix. The bell overhead jingled as I pulled the door open, announcing my arrival.

"Jake Barrows! Look at you in that uniform!" Rosie, a stout woman with silver hair pulled into a tight bun, stood behind the counter with a huge grin. Her hands, chapped from years of hard work, expertly poured a fresh cup of coffee.

"Yeah, yeah, don't make a big fuss," I mumbled, feeling a tad self-conscious. The badge on my chest was unfamiliar, and the glinting metal seemed to catch everyone's eye.

"I remember when you'd come in here with mud on your boots, fresh from the rodeo grounds. Now look at ya, all cleaned up and official-like!" She laughed, sliding the coffee cup towards me.

"Thanks, Rosie. Those days are behind me now." I

took a sip, welcoming the bitter warmth. "Needed a change, especially after what happened to Lexi."

She shook her head, sympathy darkening her eyes. "That was a damn shame. Your family's been through hell and back."

"Yeah," I sighed, avoiding her gaze. Every corner of this town seemed to echo with memories of that time. "Just wanted to do something right by the town, you know? After everything."

"You always were the protective type," Rosie remarked, her gaze softening. "But remember, it's not just about wearing the uniform. It's about what you do in it. Don't let it change you."

I smirked. "Always the philosopher, huh?"

She gave a hearty laugh. "Someone's got to keep you young ones in check."

A chime from the door interrupted our chat. In walked Kayla Green, her dark hair pulled into a messy bun and her cheeks flushed from the morning chill. Our eyes locked for a split second, and a flood of memories rushed back—the stolen glances in high school hallways, the summer nights on the town's outskirts, and the painful parting.

I hadn't seen her in years—in fact, I'd heard she moved for work, so it was a little jarring, running into my high school sweetheart right before my first day of work.

"Morning, Jake," she said curtly, not waiting for a reply as she hurriedly placed her order with Rosie.

"Morning, Kayla," I responded, though she was already engrossed in a conversation about some town gossip with Rosie. Taking the moment, I finished my coffee, relishing the last few drops. The warmth of the diner, with its familiar scent of coffee and freshly baked goods, was a comfort. But the uniform I wore now was a reminder of the responsibility I had taken on.

"Good luck out there, Jake," Rosie called out as I headed towards the door.

"Thanks, Rosie. See you around," I replied, pushing the door open.

The cool air slapped my face, clearing the last remnants of sleep. With one last glance at the diner and the town waking up to a new day, I started the short walk to the station.

Shit, this was it. Day one as a Silver Creek police officer. I took a deep breath, feeling the nervous energy and determination. As I neared the station, the past and the hopes for the future filled my mind, but with every step, my resolve strengthened.

Finally, with a determined exhale, I pushed open the station doors.

The police station wasn't the most modern place, but it was functional. The beige walls and dim lighting didn't exactly inspire confidence, but the hum of activity and the determined faces of officers passing by painted a picture of efficiency.

"Rookie!" a voice boomed, pulling me out of my reverie. Officer Mike Danvers, a bulky, middle-aged guy with a bushy mustache, stood before me.

"Yeah, that's me," I replied, extending my hand.

Mike gave it a firm shake, the strength of his grip almost crushing my fingers. "Welcome aboard, kid. Let me show you around."

I followed Mike, taking in the cubicles, the notice boards littered with papers and pins, and the aroma of stale coffee. It all felt so new but in an old, familiar kind of way. This was home now.

Eventually, we reached a corner of the station, relatively quieter than the rest.

"This is gonna be your desk," Mike declared, pointing

to a cluttered workspace. "And let me introduce you to—"

But he didn't get to finish. My breath hitched as my eyes locked onto a familiar figure, her back turned to me, sorting through a pile of files. As she turned around, time seemed to slow. It was Kayla. The same soft, hazel eyes I'd once lost myself in, the same petite frame. But the girl I once knew was replaced by a confident, albeit surprised, woman.

"Kayla," I stammered, almost a whisper.

"Jake?" she replied, a hint of shock in her voice. Her professional demeanor faltered, and for a split second, I could see the raw pain and panic in her eyes. Those eyes used to shine so brightly when she looked at me, but now they held a guarded sadness.

Mike, clearly oblivious to our shared history, clapped his hands together. "Well, isn't this a surprise? You two know each other?"

Kayla cleared her throat, her voice shaky but resolute. "We went to high school together."

It was a gross understatement, and we both knew it. The memories came flooding back: the secret dates, the stolen moments, the laughter, and eventually, the heartbreak. I'd been a damn fool, swayed by the opinions of shallow friends who couldn't see Kayla's worth. And I'd paid the price for it.

"High school sweethearts?" Mike ventured with a knowing smirk, thinking he'd pieced it together.

"You could say that," I muttered, my heart pounding. Every inch of me wanted to reach out and apologize, to explain, but the setting wasn't right.

"Alright," Mike interrupted, seemingly unaware of the tension.

"Jake, Kayla's your new partner. I'm sure you two will catch up in no time."

Kayla took a deep breath, steeling herself. "It's... it's good to see you, Jake." But her eyes told a different story.

"You too," I replied. The guilt was gnawing at me. "I... didn't realize you were on the force. I would have thought with the old chief thing last year..."

"Oh, yeah," she said with a slightly uncomfortable smile. "I was working in the next town over, but there was an opportunity for a promotion here."

The room was stifling, the hum of air conditioning barely making a dent. Papers cluttered Kayla's desk, and I found myself wondering how someone so neat and meticulous back in high school could have such a chaotic workspace. She seemed engrossed in her work, walking me through each case file, her voice steady but distant.

"Here," she began, handing over a folder. "We've got a string of break-ins over by Pine Street. No leads yet. And this,"—she opened another file—"is an ongoing vandalism case at the park. Been happening for a month now. Surveillance hasn't caught anything useful."

I nodded, soaking it all in. But amidst the detailed briefings, what I really wanted was to break through the wall she'd built around herself. The atmosphere between us was tense, every unsaid word like an anchor.

"How have you been, Kayla?" I ventured, hoping to bridge the widening chasm.

She looked up, her guarded hazel eyes meeting mine briefly. "Fine." Her response was curt, quickly shifting back to the paperwork. "Now, about the Harrison case..."

I flinched, feeling a pang of sorrow. There she was, right in front of me, yet so far away. Every evasion, every curt reply was a painful reminder of what I'd lost, what I'd thrown away on the whims of youth. My past pressed down on me, and I could barely concentrate on the cases she was discussing.

At one point, she excused herself, her steps hurried as she made her way out the door. I took a deep breath, trying to steady myself. Every fiber of my being wanted to apologize, to let her know how deeply I regretted the past. But the words got lodged in my throat, choked by shame. What if she rejected my apology? What if she hated me?

When she returned, it was clear she'd been crying. Her eyes, slightly swollen and reddened, darted around the room, refusing to meet mine. She cleared her throat, seemingly eager to get back to business. "Okay, where were we?"

The rest of the shift was agonizing. But every time I mustered the courage to speak, fear held me back. As the clock neared quitting time, I began packing up. "See you tomorrow," I mumbled, hoping my voice didn't betray the whirlwind of emotions inside.

She paused, her hand gripping the edge of the desk, and without making eye contact, she whispered, "I guess so."

And just like that, she was gone, leaving me in the silence of the room, wrestling with my regrets and the palpable tension that still lingered in the air. With a deep sigh, I changed into my street clothes and headed to my truck for dinner with my sister.

The Dalton Ranch stood imposingly on its vast stretch of land, its wooden structure basking in the golden hues of the setting sun. As I pulled into the driveway, a whirlwind of childhood memories came flooding back: running through the fields, nights spent around the fire pit, and countless evenings with Luke, planning our futures. In many ways, the ranch was as much a part of me as it was Luke's.

Stepping inside, I was met with the rich aroma of grilled steak. Luke, wearing his ever-present grin, greeted me with a hearty pat on the back.

"Look who finally showed up! Ready for some real grub?"

I chuckled. "You bet."

But as we moved into the dining room, I noticed Lexi setting the table, her movements methodical, almost robotic. Her usually lively eyes seemed distant. "Hey, sis," I began, hoping to draw her out of whatever thoughts consumed her.

She offered a small smile, her voice lacking its typical warmth. "Hey, Jake. Good to see you."

We settled around the table, and the conversation kicked off with discussions about ranch life and recent happenings in town. But I couldn't shake the nagging feeling that something was off. My gaze kept drifting to Lexi, who seemed to be in another world entirely.

Luke, sensing the change in atmosphere, cleared his throat. "So, how was day one in the blue uniform?"

I sighed, running a hand through my hair. "It was… something. Ran into Kayla."

Luke raised an eyebrow, his expression one of surprise and pity. "Damn. That must've been… rough."

I nodded, rubbing the back of my neck. "Yeah. Didn't expect it to hit me so hard. But seeing her again… Fuck, it was like ripping off a ten-year-old bandage."

"Can't blame her for being frosty," Luke remarked, taking a sip of his drink. "You royally screwed up with her. But give it time. She's tough."

The clink of cutlery against the plate broke the brief silence, drawing our attention to Lexi. Her face was a mask, unreadable. I leaned forward, concern evident in my voice. "Lex, you okay?"

She took a deep breath, her fingers playing with the napkin on her lap. "I'm fine."

But her words, laced with a hint of fragility, belied her

claim. She wasn't okay, and we both knew it.

My gaze met Luke's, the silent exchange speaking volumes. Something was very wrong. As the night wore on, amidst the casual banter and reminiscing, the unease hung thick in the room. A sudden hoot from an owl outside the window made Lexi jump, almost knocking her drink over.

I watched, my gut knotting, as Luke immediately enveloped her in his arms, his voice tinged with concern. "Hey, what's going on, Lex?"

She pulled away slightly, her eyes darting around the room, her breath coming in short puffs. "It's nothing. I'm just... jumpy tonight." The way Luke's fingers tightened on her shoulders told me he wasn't buying it. Neither was I.

"Lex, talk to us," I urged.

Her eyes shimmered with unshed tears, and she hesitated for what felt like hours before slowly reaching into the pocket of her sweater. She pulled out a folded piece of paper, handing it over to Luke with trembling fingers.

Luke's face blanched, his voice cracking slightly as he read aloud. "'I found you, and this time, I won't lose you. You are mine and always will be. Until we are together, my love.'"

"What the fuck?" I muttered, my heart pounding against my ribcage. "Is this some kind of sick joke?"

She shook her head, her voice barely above a whisper. "It's not a joke, Jake. I got letters like this all through college. Some guy was obsessed with me. The police never figured out who it was."

I remembered the few times Lexi had mentioned receiving "weird letters" in college. But this? This was on a whole new level of disturbing. I felt anger and guilt for not being there for her, for brushing it off back then.

Luke's grip on the letter tightened, crumpling it slightly. "Why the hell didn't you tell me about this?"

She sighed, her gaze dropping to the floor. "Once I returned to Silver Creek, things just got... chaotic. And when everything settled down, I hadn't gotten any letters in so long that I thought I was safe."

My fists clenched involuntarily. Whoever this bastard was, he had invaded the sanctuary of our home. Of Silver Creek. And if there was one thing I knew for certain, it was that between Luke and me, we'd make damn sure he wouldn't get near Lexi again. The chilling words in the letter still echoed in my mind, and my pulse quickened with anger.

"Lex," I began, determination seeping through my tone, "I swear, I'll make sure the police force—"

But a sudden loud knock interrupted me. Both Luke and I snapped our attention towards the door, a unified expression of suspicion passing between us. The abrupt nature of the knock felt ominous, given the context, and my heart raced with thoughts of the stalker making a bold move.

Gripping the back of a chair, prepared to wield it as a weapon, Luke and I approached the door. Every muscle in my body was tensed, ready to defend our family. With a swift motion, Luke yanked the door open, revealing a slender woman, her wide eyes filled with surprise. Two large suitcases flanked her.

"Uh... maybe I'm at the wrong place," she stammered, her gaze darting between Luke and me. "Is Lexi Barrows—Dalton, I mean—here?"

Before we could respond, Lexi's voice sounded from behind us. "Mandy?"

The woman's face broke into a smile, bright and relieved. "Lex!" She spread her arms, and Lexi moved past us, wrapping her arms around Mandy in a warm embrace.

"What are you doing here?" my sister asked.

Mandy laughed and took her hands. "Well, I was out of town for a while—book tour for my client—and when I got home, I saw that my baby girl Lexi was getting hitched, but the wedding was a week before I got home. And I didn't have a working phone number for you—"

"Yeah," Lexi said with a sort of sheepish expression. "I got a new one when I got to Silver Creek. I meant to—"

"Seriously, no worries at all," Mandy said with a smile. "But I looked up Mr. Luke Dalton here and found out that he was the owner of this place, and figured I'd drop in and pay you a visit."

For a moment, I felt like an intruder in their reunion, but Lexi soon turned to us, a smile playing on her lips. "Mandy, this is my brother, Jake, and my husband, Luke." She pointed towards us in turn.

Mandy extended a hand, her grin still in place. "It's so good to finally meet you both. I'm Mandy—Lexi's college roommate and partner-in-crime."

Trying to shake off my initial wariness, I took her hand, feeling relief and embarrassment. "Sorry about the, uh, welcome. It's been an intense evening," I said.

Mandy raised an eyebrow, her eyes filled with understanding and mischief. "Guessing that has something to do with the 'ready-to-fight' expressions when you opened the door?"

Luke chuckled, the tension easing out of his shoulders. "You could say that. Let's just say the evening took a turn we weren't expecting."

As the four of us settled into the living room, the earlier tension temporarily forgotten, I felt grateful for Mandy's unexpected arrival. The distraction, the warmth of an old friend, was precisely what Lexi needed.

Still, in the back of my mind, the threat from the letter

lingered, casting a shadow over the evening's newfound brightness.

Chapter Two

MANDY

The living room of the Dalton ranch was comfortably decorated with an amalgamation of old family antiques and new furnishings. It felt cozy and warm, enhanced by the soft orange glow of the table lamps. The clinking of mugs and the faint scent of herbal tea filled the room.

Jake, looking curious and bemused, took a seat opposite me. "Alright, Mandy, spill. What stories do you have on my sister?"

Lexi shot him a warning glance, her cheeks turning a shade of pink. "Don't you dare."

"Oh, I've got plenty," I replied, unable to hide my mischievous grin. "Remember the campus security fiasco, Lex?"

Lexi groaned, covering her face with her hands. "You're really going to bring that up?"

Jake leaned forward, an eager look in his eyes. "Now I definitely need to hear this."

Luke chuckled, sipping his tea, his eyes twinkling with interest. "Same here."

"Well," I began, trying to suppress my laughter, "It was one of those nights, you know, where things were just destined to get out of hand. Lexi may have indulged in a bit too much, erm, liquid courage. Campus security had caught her red-handed with a bottle."

Jake looked at his sister in mock horror. "Drinking underage? Tsk, tsk."

"Oh, it wasn't that bad!" Lexi protested. "And I would've gotten a hefty fine if not for Mandy's, uh, brilliant diversion."

I chuckled, recalling that cold evening. "To save her ass, I decided to strip and go streaking across the quad. Security left Lexi in a flash and chased after me instead."

Luke snorted, almost spitting out his tea. "You're kidding me!"

"Dead serious," I confirmed. "I figured a naked girl running across the campus was a bigger issue than underage drinking."

Jake burst into laughter. "That's wild! Lex, you owe her big time."

"Oh, trust me," Lexi rolled her eyes, "I've repaid that debt plenty of times."

"I can vouch for that," I said, a reminiscent smile on my lips. "Like that karaoke night? The one I absolutely ruined?"

Lexi grinned, "Oh, God. I thought we'd sworn never to mention that again."

"Now you have to share," Jake insisted.

Sighing in mock resignation, I obliged. "It was a dare. I had to sing karaoke, and not just any song – 'Barbie Girl.' And let me be clear, I cannot sing."

Lexi laughed, "It was so bad that people were plugging their ears. But then, I had an idea."

"I see where this is going," Luke murmured, shaking his head.

"My brilliant sister," I pointed at Lexi, "jumped on stage, grabbed another mic, and started singing along. But not just that, she rallied the entire bar. Within minutes, everyone was singing that cringey song at the top of their lungs, turning my most embarrassing moment into one of the best memories of college." Jake leaned back, his eyes wide with surprise.

"Damn, I missed out on some real entertainment."

"You did," Lexi smirked, bumping her mug gently against mine. "To adventures and saving each other's butts."

"To that," I toasted back, my heart swelling with affection for my friend.

The soft clinks of our mugs faded, and the room was filled with a comfortable silence for a moment. Lexi leaned forward, her attention fully on me. "Mandy, you mentioned a book tour when you got here. Tell us about it."

I tucked a stray hair behind my ear and sipped my tea, trying to figure out where to start. "Right out of college, I somehow snagged a job with Davis & Pierce, that major publishing firm? And almost immediately, I signed this monumental client. Guy was up for a Nobel Peace Prize. The whole thing was... I don't even have words."

Luke raised his eyebrows, impressed. "Sounds like a whirlwind."

Jake nodded, his curiosity evident, "A Nobel nominee? That's pretty high stakes."

"It was," I admitted, the memory of the chaos still fresh. "We went everywhere for that book tour."

Lexi's eyes were wide with interest. "Like where?"

"Paris was our first stop. Imagine doing a book signing

by the Seine, with the Eiffel Tower lit up in the backdrop. It felt like something out of a dream."

Luke let out a low whistle. "Never been farther than Denver myself."

I chuckled, "Well, from Paris, we shot off to Tokyo. I've never seen a place with such contrast. Ancient temples, then just streets over you, have the most modern tech and those neon lights. The sushi, though?" I paused for emphasis. "Divine."

Jake laughed, "I bet it's a tad different from what we get here."

"Just a tad," I teased back. "And then there was Cape Town. Ever seen two oceans meet from the top of a mountain? It's breathtaking."

"Sounds like something out of National Geographic," Lexi murmured, clearly picturing it.

"The parties must've been wild," Jake speculated with a smirk.

I grinned, thinking back. "You've no idea. Istanbul? Their rooftop parties are like something out of a movie. The energy, the city lights, dancing without a care? Absolutely surreal."

The group was silent for a moment, taking it all in.

Lexi finally broke the silence, "It's been years, Mand. Why now?"

I looked at her. "The tour was incredible, Lex. But it was also draining. When it ended, I realized there were things, people, I had lost touch with. I wanted to reconnect." The room grew quiet for a moment, and I could feel tension thickening the air. Lexi shifted in her seat, glancing at Luke before clearing her throat.

"Mandy, I'm so glad you're here. Seriously. But the timing's just...we're in the middle of this massive house renovation, and...we don't really have a proper place for you to stay."

I felt a slight pang in my chest. Spending months living out of hotels and airports, I had imagined my return to Silver Creek to be a warm one, staying in a familiar place. But understanding the situation, I just nodded. "Oh, that's okay. The inn in town might have a room available."

There was a brief pause. It was Luke who finally broke the silence. "Jake, man, you've got that guest room, right? Why doesn't Mandy stay with you?"

Jake looked taken aback, almost like he hadn't expected to be pulled into the conversation. His hazel eyes met mine, slightly widened, but then that kind, heartwarming smile spread across his face. "Yeah, sure. I've got plenty of space if you're okay with it."

I gave him a once-over. I mean, I'd heard about Jake from Lexi's stories, but up close? Damn, the man was a sight. Tall, broad-shouldered, with this rugged charm. And that smile? Felt like it was lighting up the entire room.

Without giving away too much of my inner excitement, I smiled back. "Sounds good to me."

Luke chuckled, "Well, that settles it then."

Lexi, seeming relieved, leaned over and hugged me. "Thanks for understanding, Mandy. It's just a mess here right now."

"I get it," I assured her, wrapping my arm around her. "And thank you, Jake. It'll be nice to stay somewhere... homier."

Jake gave a little nod, his gaze lingering on me for a split second longer than necessary, "Not a problem. We can head over whenever you're ready."

The rest of the evening went by with more laughter and stories, and by the time the clock struck midnight, I was ready for bed.

Chapter Three

JAKE

We said our goodbyes, but as Mandy and Lexi chatted a few feet away, sharing a private moment, I pulled Luke aside, eyebrows raised. "What the hell, man? Why'd you volunteer my place without asking?"

Luke just grinned, that ever-present mischief in his eyes. "Consider it payback for that whole fake engagement stunt you pulled with Lexi."

I chuckled, rolling my eyes. "C'mon, that ended up working out perfectly for you two. Without that, you might never have made a move."

Luke leaned in, clapping me on the shoulder. "Exactly. And maybe this will work out for you, too."

I paused, glancing over at Mandy, her laughter echoing as she hugged Lexi. "Look, she seems nice. But after seeing Kayla today? That shit threw me for a loop. I'm not exactly in the mood to dive into anything new right now."

Luke sighed, nodding. "I get it, man. But you know, sometimes life throws curveballs. Just be a good host. If anything, you two might end up good friends."

I shrugged, admitting, "Yeah, I can do that."

As Mandy wrapped up her conversation with Lexi, she walked over, her eyes bright and curious. "Ready to head out?"

"Sure thing," I replied, leading the way.

Climbing into the truck, Mandy took a deep breath, clearly taking in her surroundings. "Silver Creek's smaller than I imagined," she remarked, her eyes roaming over the town's familiar structures.

"Has its charm, though," I replied, shifting the truck into drive. The radio hummed softly in the background as we made our way through town. Every so often, I'd catch her looking out of the window, curiosity evident in her eyes. This was all new for her, and part of me envied that fresh perspective.

As I pulled into the driveway of my modest home, she looked around, her gaze settling on the house. "It's not the massive ranch Lexi and Luke have, but it's got character," I joked, hoping to break the ice a bit more.

She laughed, the sound light and genuine. "It's lovely. Honestly, after months of hotel rooms, any place that feels like a home is a welcome change."

We headed inside, and I gave her a quick tour of the ground floor. Our conversation flowed surprisingly smoothly, considering we'd just met. We shared a bit about our pasts, her life on the road with the book tour, and my experiences in Silver Creek.

The hour grew late, and I could see the weariness in her eyes. "Let me show you to your room," I offered.

She nodded gratefully, following me up the stairs. Stopping in front of the guest room, I reached for the doorknob, the cool metal familiar under my touch. "Here you are," I said, opening the door to reveal the neatly made bed and soft lighting.

"Thank you, Jake," she replied, her voice sincere.

There was an expectant look in Mandy's eyes, something I couldn't quite place. She lingered for a moment, her posture suggesting she was waiting on... something. For all my experiences, reading cues was still a challenge sometimes.

"You're welcome," I finally said, more to break the tension than anything. "Good night, Mandy."

She nodded, a hint of disappointment briefly crossing her face. "Night, Jake."

Closing the door behind her, I took a deep breath and headed for my own room. The day's events pressed on my shoulders. Damn, Luke had planted that seed, hadn't he? The idea of something new with Mandy.

But as I settled into bed, my thoughts drifted, as they often did, to Kayla. It was hard to shake off our past. The feel of her skin, her laughter, the way she would look at me when no words were needed. The memories were both sweet and painful, a contradiction that gnawed at me.

Tossing and turning, I tried to push those thoughts away, focusing on the warmth of the sheets and the soft hum of the fan. But there she was again, in every closed-eye fantasy and half-remembered dream. Shaking the thoughts from my mind, I settled deeper into the sheets, trying to chase away the nagging loneliness with sleep. The new day wasn't far off, and with it came the promise of new challenges. And while Mandy was an unexpected twist, I knew better than to confuse the past with the present.

The next morning came quicker than I'd have liked, the dawn seeping through the blinds, pulling me from the remnants of a restless sleep. The day ahead promised to be long and demanding, yet the previous night's memories clung to me.

The morning light peeked through the blinds as I squinted, my alarm blaring its harsh reminder of reality. Groaning, I shut it off and sat up. Pushing the lingering thoughts of the previous night aside, I geared up for another day at the station.

Upon entering, I immediately noticed Kayla seated at her desk, engrossed in her work. Her profile against the ambient office lights was all too familiar—a reminder of countless days spent working together.

"Hey," I ventured, nodding towards her.

She looked up, her gaze cool. "Good morning, Jake," she replied, her tone all business. Gone was the warmth I once knew. Before I could ponder her distant demeanor, chief Manning strolled over, a grim expression etched on his face.

"Got something for you both," he began, dropping a folder onto my desk. The headline read: "Convenience Store Break-In." I glanced over the details. Simple enough. Probably some teenagers looking for a quick grab. Or maybe someone desperate. Either way, it was our job to figure it out.

"Need you both on this. Seems the owner claims some valuables got swiped. Might not be as cut and dry as it seems." The chief eyed both of us.

I looked at Kayla, trying to gauge her reaction. She looked as eager to be paired with me as I felt about confronting our shared past, which was to say, not at all. Still, we were professionals.

We had a job to do.

"Alright," she sighed, grabbing her jacket. "Let's get this over with."

Rising from my chair, I gathered the case file and followed her. As we walked to the cruiser, I noticed the way she held herself—confident, yet somewhat guarded.

Sliding into the driver's seat, she adjusted the rearview mirror while I took the passenger side. The cruiser's engine roared to life, and we pulled out, heading towards the scene, each lost in our thoughts. The tension in the car was undeniable. But whatever was between us, it was going to have to wait. Duty called.

The convenience store was a rather unremarkable building, sandwiched between a laundromat and a barbershop. The neon 'OPEN' sign flickered sporadically, casting an eerie glow over the glass entrance.

We parked the cruiser by the curb and made our way inside. Kayla, taking the lead, waved me closer. "Stick with me, rookie," she quipped, her tone dripping with sarcasm. The dynamic between us had shifted from last night, and now it felt more like a dance—two professionals tiptoeing around the past while trying to keep their focus on the present.

The bell above the door tinkled as we entered, drawing the attention of the store owner. He was a middle-aged man with weary eyes and a slouched posture. He looked like he'd been through the wringer, and the sight of two officers seemed to add to his stress. "We're here about the break-in," Kayla started, pulling out her badge.

The owner nodded, wringing his hands nervously. "Yeah, they made quite the mess," he muttered, guiding us towards the back. Kayla shot me a look, silently telling me to listen and learn. I nodded, trying to pick up on her cues. We began taking statements, jotting down every detail.

"They took the cash from the register," the owner began, "Not surprising. But then they swiped some antiques and... stationery packs."

I raised an eyebrow. "Antiques?"

He sighed. "Yeah, I have a small section for them. Sort

of a personal collection. A few pieces of jewelry, some knickknacks, and a typewriter."

"A typewriter?" I echoed, unable to hide my surprise. I mean, who steals a typewriter in this day and age?

Kayla shot me a withering look, silencing my train of thought. We weren't here to question the inventory, after all.

The owner nodded, leading us to a shelf that was now in disarray. "It was a vintage one. Had sentimental value. My grandmother used to type on it."

Kayla frowned, noting down the details. She then gestured for me to follow her as we began to examine the area. I watched her, impressed by how she handled the scene. She was methodical, picking up on things I might've missed.

The shattered glass near the entrance, the scuff marks near the counter, and a small, discarded cigarette butt caught her eye. "This might be something," she murmured, bagging it for evidence.

As Kayla meticulously combed over the area, explaining her observations and thoughts, I couldn't shake the nagging feeling in the back of my mind. A typewriter? Stationery packs? The damn connection was staring me right in the face, but the dots were a little too dangerous to connect out loud.

"That was some odd stuff to steal, don't you think?" I remarked, trying to play it casual. "Especially in a digital age."

Kayla snorted, rolling her eyes. "People steal weird shit all the time. I worked a case where someone swiped garden gnomes. Twenty-seven of them."

I chuckled, but the unease didn't leave. "Yeah, but that's just for laughs, right? Or some odd collector. This feels..." I trailed off, not knowing how to express the unease without tipping her off about Lexi.

She shot me a curious look, her eyes scanning my face as if trying to decipher a code. "This feels what?"

"Personal," I blurted out. "Like someone had a reason."

Kayla arched an eyebrow, a smirk playing on her lips. "Damn, Jake. You're full of surprises. Going with your gut, huh?"

I shrugged, feeling embarrassment and frustration. "Just a feeling, okay? Don't give me shit for it."

She laughed, a genuine, deep sound that momentarily reminded me of better times. "Alright, detective. I won't. But let's not jump to conclusions without evidence."

The thing was, I did have a piece of evidence. It just wasn't one I could share without complicating matters. The thought of Lexi's stalker and the eerie typewritten notes was too close for comfort. The timeline, the setting—it all pointed in one dangerous direction. Yet, I kept my mouth shut. This wasn't the time, and this certainly wasn't the place.

Kayla stood up, dusting off her jeans. "I think we've got what we can from here. Let's head back and get started on those statements, yeah?"

I nodded, my secret making me antsy. "Yeah, let's go."

As we headed out of the store, the late afternoon sun cast a golden glow over the streets of Silver Creek. The serene sight did little to soothe my racing heart. The two of us climbed into the cruiser, and for a moment, I hesitated, fingers clutching the steering wheel. Sharing could risk blowing things out of proportion, but keeping silent could put Lexi in danger.

With a deep breath, I started the car, the roar of the engine signaling our departure. The road ahead looked clear, but I knew, in more ways than one, that we were heading into a storm. We barely made it back into the station when Kayla pinned me with a scrutinizing look, her gaze sharp enough to draw blood. "Alright, out with it. What was that weird reaction about the typewriter?"

I sighed. There was no escaping this, and I trusted Kayla. It was time to come clean. Reaching into my back pocket, I pulled out the crumpled letter and handed it to her. "This arrived at Lexi's place," I began, my voice steadier than I expected. "It's from some stalker."

Her eyes widened, the usual teasing gone, replaced with genuine concern. "Shit, Jake! This is serious!" She scanned the letter, her face turning from curiosity to anger. "This is some messed up crap. And you think this might be connected?"

I nodded, swallowing hard. "The typewriter, the stationery. I don't know, Kay. It's all too coincidental."

She took a moment, deep in thought, before finally meeting my eyes again. "Okay, I'm in. If there's even a sliver of a chance this stalker and the break-in are related, we're on it. But we should loop the chief in."

I hesitated, involving the higher-ups dawning on me. But Kayla was right. This was beyond just a personal matter now. "Alright, let's do it."

We quickly made our way to the chief's office, my heart pounding with every step. This was Silver Creek; big crime waves were rare. But with the stalker, the odd theft, and now possibly a connection? We were diving into uncharted territory.

The chief, a gruff but fair man in his early fifties, looked up as we entered. "What's got you two looking so damn serious?"

"Sir," I began, laying out the stalker's letter for him to see. "We believe there might be a connection between this letter Lexi received and the break-in at the convenience store."

He raised an eyebrow, reading the letter quickly. "Well, hell," he muttered, his face darkening. "This is some serious stuff. You think there's a connection?"

Kayla chimed in, "The typewriter theft, sir. It just doesn't sit right."

The chief rubbed his chin, deep in thought. "Alright. We investigate this from all angles. If there's a link, we'll find it. If there's a threat, we neutralize it."

As the heavy door of the chief's office swung closed behind us, the atmosphere between Kayla and me shifted. It wasn't tense, but there was an undeniable thickness. I could feel gratitude pooling inside of me, but there was also another emotion lurking underneath - regret.

I cleared my throat, my fingers flexing against my side. "Kayla, thanks. Seriously."

She gave me a quick glance, her dark eyes softening just a tad. "Of course, Jake. That's what partners do." But there was a shadow in those eyes, hinting at some unresolved sentiment. It was hard to pinpoint, but I knew her well enough to see it.

"Kayla," I began, fumbling a little with my words. I had to tread lightly, especially given our history. "I just wanted to—"

She cut me off, holding up a hand. "Don't, Jake. Whatever you want to say,... save it. It's in the past. We're colleagues now, alright? Let's start from there." Her voice was firm but not cold, and I could detect a trace of pain there.

I took a deep breath, letting it out slowly. The urge to explain, to justify, to plead was so strong it almost consumed me. But she was right. We had to move forward.

"I get it," I said, trying to put as much sincerity into my

voice as I could muster. "I just... I want things to be okay between us."

She looked over, and for a split second, her guard was down. I saw a glimpse of the old Kayla, the one who used to laugh with me, share secrets, and dream about the future.

"Me too," she whispered, her voice almost lost amidst the ambient noise of the station.

I nodded, my throat tight. "We'll get there," I said, more to myself than to her.

She offered a small smile, a silent truce of sorts. "Come on," she said, nodding toward our desks. "We've got work to do."

As we walked side by side, the gulf between us seemed a little smaller. We weren't back to where we used to be, not by a long shot. But at least there was a start. And in that moment, a start was all I needed.

Chapter Four

MANDY

The aroma wafting from the kitchen was tantalizing – a mix of garlic, rosemary, and something rich and meaty. I stood by the stove, stirring the pot and glancing occasionally at the front door. It was a surprise dinner for Jake, and I hoped he'd appreciate the gesture.

When the door finally creaked open, his silhouette filled the entrance. He froze for a second, eyebrows raised. "What's all this?" He looked around, surprise evident on his face.

"Just thought I'd whip up something. Hope you're hungry," I replied, trying to sound casual.

He approached the table, placing his jacket over a chair. "This looks... amazing, Mandy." The hesitance in his voice wasn't lost on me, but his eyes were soft, and his lips pulled into a smile.

"Sit down," I prompted, ladling out the thick stew onto his plate. He obeyed, taking a moment to inhale the aroma before taking a bite. I watched his face closely, trying to gauge his reaction.

"This is really good," he finally said, nodding appreciatively.

"Thanks," I replied, a hint of pride in my voice. "It's from a recipe my mom gave me. She swears by it."

He continued eating, but I could tell his guard was still up a bit. "Tough day?" I asked, attempting to bridge the gap.

Jake sighed, placing his fork down for a moment. "Break-in at the convenience store. Weird mix of stuff taken. Not the usual."

"That sounds... intriguing," I said, leaning in, genuinely curious.

He chuckled. "Not the word I'd use, but it keeps things interesting, I guess."

We continued chatting, the conversation flowing with an unexpected ease. I listened intently, absorbing his tales of Silver Creek, the people, and their quirks. It was all so foreign yet fascinating to me.

As the night wore on, I caught myself stealing glances at him – the way the dim light emphasized the contours of his face, his lips when he spoke, the deep timbre of his voice. There was a palpable tension of gratitude and unspoken attraction.

But when it was time to call it a night, he simply got up, stretching. "Thanks for dinner, Mandy," he murmured, his voice soft. "I'll see you in the morning."

I nodded, disappointment and understanding mingling within me. "Goodnight, Jake."

Watching him disappear down the hall, I headed to my room. As I settled into the soft sheets, my mind wandered, replaying snippets of the evening, lingering on Jake's face, his voice.

My fingers found their way under the fabric of my nightgown, tracing delicate patterns as I let my thoughts roam free. The feel of my own touch, combined with the intimate memories of Jake's presence, created a heady mix. My fingers trailed lower, finding their way to the soft warmth between my thighs. I took my time, savoring each sensation, each pulse of pleasure that spread through me.

The world outside seemed to blur, leaving only the rhythm of my breath and the intimate dance of my fingers. Thoughts of Jake, his lips, his voice, and his touch fueled my imagination. Every stroke, every touch, brought me closer to that edge of ecstasy.

When the climax finally hit, I rode it out, waves of pleasure washing over me, leaving me breathless and sated. Clutching the sheets beneath me, I let out a soft sigh, the evening's emotions and sensations settling deep within me.

Slowly, I drifted into a peaceful sleep, enveloped in the memories of the night and the promise of the days to come.

The following day, I headed over to Lexi's house while it was still early. The morning sun was casting a warm light over Silver Creek, painting the ranch in hues of gold. As I made my way over, I could hear the distant hum of machinery and the occasional shout of contractors, giving life to the tranquil setting.

I found Lexi in one of the upstairs bedrooms, her golden hair tied up in a messy bun, dust smeared on her cheek. She was prying up old carpeting, revealing the wooden floors hidden underneath for years. Every tug she gave was met with a grunt of effort and a spark of excitement in her eyes.

"Hey, you," Lexi said, taking a moment to catch her breath and wipe the sweat from her brow.

"Hey yourself," I replied, my gaze darting around the room, impressed by the progress she had made. "Need a hand?"

Lexi chuckled. "Absolutely. Grab a pry bar from that toolbox over there."

And so, we fell into a rhythm, working side by side, pulling up carpet and tearing out the old padding underneath. There was something therapeutic about the whole process. The work was hard, but with every strip of carpet we removed, the room seemed to breathe a sigh of relief, revealing its true beauty underneath.

After a few hours, Lexi pulled out a bottle of champagne and two flutes from a cooler she'd stashed in the corner. "I think it's mimosa time," she declared, a playful glint in her eyes.

I laughed. "It's not even noon, but sure, why not?"

With mimosas in hand, we continued to work. But as the bubbles tickled our noses and the champagne warmed our veins, our focus started to waver. The work was still getting done, but with a lot more giggles and a bit less precision.

Lexi was yanking at a particularly stubborn piece of carpet when she suddenly hissed, pulling her hand back. Blood welled from a cut on her finger, likely from a hidden staple.

"Shit, Lexi!" I exclaimed, dropping my pry bar and hurrying to her side.

She examined her finger, her expression more annoyed than pained. "Damn staple. I didn't even see it."

Without a word, I rushed to grab the first aid kit conveniently stashed in the hallway. Gently taking her hand in mine, I cleaned the cut before wrapping it neatly with a bandage.

"There," I said, giving her a reassuring smile. "All patched up."

Lexi let out a laugh, her eyes dancing with mischief. "We're such a mess. Maybe we should lay off the mimosas if we're going to be wielding sharp tools."

Chuckling, I raised my glass in agreement. "To not drinking and renovating." That evening, after a particularly tiring day, I was at Jake's place, preparing a hearty meal for the both of us.

"This chicken is amazing, Mand," Jake commented, breaking my reverie.

"Thanks," I replied, "It's just something I threw together."

He smiled appreciatively, "You really have a knack for this. You should cook more often."

"I think I will. You know… you wouldn't believe how fast this week flew by. It's been a whirlwind with Lexi, but every single moment… it's like we're reliving the old days and making new memories. Like the other day, we were yanking out those stubborn kitchen tiles, right? And I kid you not, one of them was so tough that when it finally gave way, I lost my balance and crashed into Lexi. She was holding this jar of paint, and whoosh! We were both drenched in lilac paint."

He laughed, and, encouraged, I joined in.

"You two are a disaster," he teased.

"It was everywhere, Jake, everywhere! And Lexi, oh, she just starts laughing and says, 'You know, Mand, purple has always been your color!' I mean, what could I do? I just wiped the paint off my face and told her, 'Absolutely! And it looks fantastic in your hair, too!' We couldn't stop laughing, covered in paint from head to toe."

"My sister, the graceful swan," he laughed.

"And then there was this other time," I said, thrilled he

was engaging with me so well, "we were taking a break from all the renovation chaos. We headed to the diner for a quick bite, reminiscing about college days over milkshakes. Lexi brought up this hilarious story – remember when I tried to impress that guy with my 'death by chocolate' cake, only to find out he was allergic to chocolate? Yeah, I was mortified! And there's Lexi teasing me, suggesting maybe you'd like that cake. I just brushed it off, you know, trying to play it cool. Anyway, I hope you left room for dessert."

"Sounds amazing," he said, and I rushed to the kitchen to grab it.

Later in the week, after another hearty dinner, Jake and I were lounging on the couch, indulging in some old action movie. At some point, Luke joined us, making himself comfortable between Jake and me.

"Man, Mandy," Luke commented during a particularly dramatic scene, "you've become quite the chef.

Jake's lucky to have you around." Jake chuckled, nodding in agreement, "Definitely, it's been a while since I've eaten this well."

I just smiled, my heart fluttering, but keeping my emotions masked. Throughout the week, whether with Lexi's teasing remarks or Jake's innocent appreciation of my culinary efforts, it became increasingly clear that no one seemed to pick up on the real reason behind my gestures. My feelings for Jake remained my own little secret.

About a week after I arrived, it was oddly cool for a summer morning, which I'd hoped would be filled with labor and sweat, working alongside Lexi. We had made a routine of turning the renovation chaos into some of our best memories, often ending up in laughter more than actual work. I felt a loyalty and bond with Lexi that was hard to put into words. The same way you'd feel for someone who had seen your highs, lows, and everything in between. It was the kind of unspoken understanding that comes from years of friendship.

So, when my phone rang, Lexi's name flashing on the screen, I expected it to be another one of our regular morning chats about the day's renovation plans. Instead, her voice had an apologetic edge.

"Hey, Mands," she began, "I've got some news. The contractors are coming in for the next few days, and they've got a massive crew. It's just gonna be a bit too crowded for us both to be there."

My stomach dropped a little. "Oh," was all I managed to say, trying not to sound as disappointed as I felt.

"I'm really sorry. You know I'd have you there if I could, right?"

"Yeah, of course," I replied, forcing some cheer into my voice. "Just... give me a call when they're done, okay? We'll pick up right where we left off."

She laughed. "Absolutely. Thanks for understanding. And hey, enjoy the time off. You deserve a little R and R."

The house felt quieter after hanging up, so I wandered into the living room, only to find Jake lounging out on the couch, remote in hand. The room echoed with gunfire, fast cars, and the unmistakable sounds of an action movie. The screen displayed a rugged hero evading an explosion, his face smeared with grime and determination.

Jake looked over, his lips curling into a smile. "Care to join? Got a whole lineup of these."

Sitting down beside him, I nodded. "Why not? Looks entertaining."

As the hours rolled by, I found myself getting engrossed in the adrenaline-fueled plots and unexpected twists. Every so often, I'd catch Jake glancing over, laughing at particularly over-the-top scenes, or commenting on the absurdity of a car surviving a ten-story fall. We sat close, but not too close, a gap maintained by Jake's oblivion to my growing feelings.

"Are you hungry?" I asked suddenly as a commercial took over the screen.

"I..." Jake's stomach rumbled. "I didn't think I was until just now. You have something in mind?"

"Nachos sound amazing," I said, my mouth already watering. "I'll make them."

"Let's do it together," he said, standing. "I think you may find I like... unique flavors on my nachos."

Five minutes later, I was looking at his plate in horror.

"Coleslaw and barbecue sauce?" I gasped, looking at my own traditional nachos.

"Don't knock it 'til you try it," he said, holding out a bite.

And I'd be damned if I didn't take it and make every yummy noise I could, even if it was actually really weird.

It was easy to feel a similar loyalty to Jake, like the one I felt for Lexi. Every shared meal, every lazy afternoon—it was all cementing the bond. There was an ease and comfort in our interactions, which, for the time being, was enough for me.

Maybe, in time, that gap on the couch would close, but for now, it was just another afternoon in Silver Creek, wrapped up in the simplicity of good company and cinematic escapades.

Chapter Five

JAKE

The morning started ordinarily enough. Sunlight filtered through the blinds of my bedroom, casting a warm glow across the sheets. I rubbed the sleep from my eyes, the past few weeks resting heavily on my shoulders. My relationship with Kayla, however, had lightened the load considerably. After the conversation in the chief's office, we seemed to be finding our stride again.

I headed into the station, the scent of brewed coffee mingling with the usual background noise of phones ringing and voices conversing. Kayla was already there, pouring over some notes on a desk scattered with papers.

"Morning," I greeted as I approached. She looked up, her face softening into something that resembled a smile.

"Hey," she replied, a hint of warmth in her tone. "Got this car accident report from yesterday evening. No casualties. Just some paperwork to clear."

"Alright," I nodded, moving to stand next to her, "Let's get this done."

We were in the middle of discussing the details when

Officer Warren approached, holding a phone out to me. "Jake, call for you. Seems urgent."

I frowned, taking the phone. "This is Officer Barrows"

"Jake," Luke's voice came through the line, strained with worry. In the background, I could hear the unmistakable sound of Lexi's sobs. Almost nothing got to her like this. Not even when she was kidnapped at gunpoint.

"Luke? What happened?" My heart rate spiked, dread filling my gut.

"It's another fucking letter, Jake," Luke's voice was tight with anger and fear. "From that sick bastard."

I swallowed hard, trying to keep my voice steady. "I'm on my way. Keep Lexi calm, okay?"

Ending the call, I looked to Kayla, who was watching me with a raised eyebrow. "Another letter," I muttered, "Lexi's stalker."

Her expression hardened. "We're on the case, aren't we? So, let's get over there. Scene of the crime."

"Thanks, Kayla," I murmured as we made our way to the cruiser.

She glanced at me as she climbed into the passenger seat. "That's what partners do."

With a nod, I started the engine, heading straight for the Dalton Ranch.

Dust hung in the air as Kayla and I pulled up to the ranch. Its once-pristine appearance was marred by debris and discarded tools, evidence of the ongoing renovations. We stepped out of the cruiser, gravel crunching beneath our boots. Approaching the door, I gave it a few firm knocks.

Luke answered, his face a mixture of relief and worry. "Jake," he nodded, his gaze shifting to Kayla. "Good to see you, Kayla. It's been ages. Not since high school, right?"

"Not unless you count reaching for the same box of

cornflakes at the store that one time I was home visiting my folks," she replied, the edges of her mouth lifting into a small smile.

"Come in," he motioned, stepping aside.

The inside of the house was chaos. Sheets of plastic draped over furniture, paint cans lined up in a row, and tools scattered haphazardly.

"Sent the contractors home after the letter came," Luke explained, leading us deeper into the home.

Lexi was in the living area, curled up on the couch, a blanket wrapped tightly around her, eyes red from crying. A steaming cup of tea sat in her trembling hands. The sight wrenched at my heart. Sitting beside her, I draped an arm around her shoulders, attempting to offer some semblance of comfort.

"Lex, what happened?" I asked softly.

Without a word, Luke handed a folded sheet of paper to Kayla, his face grim. She unfolded it, scanning the contents. As she read, her face drained of color, her eyes widening.

"Shit..." she muttered, handing it over to me with a look of sheer disbelief. The letter read:

Dear Lexi,

I've been watching you. Not from afar, but closer than you think. Each brush of wind you feel, each chill running down your spine? It's me, always near. I've watched you tear apart that old home and witnessed the sweat on your brow as you put your heart into every nail and beam. I know the sound of your laughter, and I've counted the tears you've shed.

You can bring all the deputies in the world, but they can't save you from me. They won't see me, but I see you. Always.

Until we're finally together,

The cold, methodical nature of the words sent shivers down my spine. It was filled with a level of obsession and intimate knowledge that was truly unsettling. The way the stalker described their proximity to Lexi, their observations... It was all designed to invoke terror.

Taking a deep breath, I tried to keep my emotions in check. "We need to find this bastard," I said, determination setting in.

Kayla nodded in agreement. "We'll do everything we can, Lexi. We're here for you. How'd you find the letter? Was it mailed?"

Luke leaned against the wall, the worry in his eyes evident. "It was just in the mailbox," he said. "No stamp, no postmark. Just... there. Left for her."

I exhaled heavily, realizing the implications. "So, you're saying it wasn't mailed? No postman just dropped it?"

"Nope. No postmark or stamp. Just the damn letter."

My blood ran cold at the realization. "That means this asshole was on your property, Lexi."

She let out a soft whimper at my words, and I pulled her close. Her frame was fragile, her fear palpable. I tightened my hold, trying to be the pillar she needed. "We're gonna find this son of a bitch," I promised, my voice laced with anger.

Lexi pulled back slightly, meeting my gaze. "No one has yet," she whispered, voice breaking.

Kayla stepped forward, her professional demeanor battling with the empathy she felt for the woman before her. "Then we can at least keep you safe," she promised, determination in her tone.

I nodded, watching as Kayla took the letter carefully, preserving it for evidence. "I'll bag this and put it in the cruiser," she said, turning to leave the room.

I waited for a moment, the atmosphere heavy with

tension, before turning my attention back to Lexi. "Look, I know it's a long shot, but maybe we should talk to Mandy about this. She was with you in college. Maybe she saw something, heard something that could help."

Lexi looked taken aback. "I... I never told her about it back then. I was too scared, too ashamed. I doubt she knows anything."

"It won't hurt to ask," I pressed gently. "She cares about you, Lex. And she might offer a different perspective."

She hesitated, her gaze flicking around the room as if searching for an answer. "Alright," she finally conceded. "You can talk to her, but I doubt she'll know anything."

My heart clenched at the evident pain in her voice. I nodded, "We're gonna figure this out, Lex."

With that, I headed out, determination fueling my every step. I was resolved to get to the bottom of this, to hunt down the bastard tormenting Lexi. Whatever it took.

The aromatic scent of a homemade dinner wafted through the house as I stepped inside. It was unmistakable – Mandy had cooked again. After a long, distressing day, the gesture was even more touching than usual.

"Hey," she greeted, pulling a casserole dish from the oven. "Thought you could use a warm meal."

"That's... really kind of you, Mandy," I admitted, feeling the tension from the day ease up a fraction.

We settled into the dining area, the clinking of silverware punctuating the silence. I took a deep breath, realizing that if there were ever a time to bring up the issue with Lexi, it was now.

"There's something you should know about Lexi," I began cautiously.

Mandy, looking up in alarm, fork midway to her mouth, asked, "What happened?"

"Today, we found a letter at her place. A really creepy, threatening letter. I guess... well, Lexi has a stalker."

"What?"

"Yeah. This is the second letter this month. And this isn't the first time."

Mandy's face paled, her fork dropping onto the plate with a clatter. "A stalker? Fuck, Jake. Does she know who it is?"

"She doesn't. But here's the thing," I hesitated, unsure of how to phrase it. "This isn't new. Someone stalked her in college, too."

Mandy's eyes widened, shock and confusion playing out on her face. "She never told me anything like that. I mean, we were close in college. Roommates, best friends. We shared everything."

I ran a hand through my hair, feeling every bit of my frustration and worry. "Yeah, it seems she kept it a secret. But I thought... maybe you'd noticed something back then, something off?"

She shook her head slowly. "No. Nothing. I mean, there were the usual college dramas, but nothing like this."

I nodded, absorbing the information. There was a weight in my chest, the kind that builds up when you care deeply about someone's safety. I had that feeling for Lexi, and the realization hit me - I felt the same way for Mandy. Not romantic, but a genuine concern. She had seamlessly woven herself into the fabric of our lives here.

"You know," I began, breaking the silence, "I'm really glad you're here. With everything going on, it's good to have someone else who's just as worried about Lexi as I am. It means a lot."

Mandy managed a small smile. "I'm just here for a

visit, but she's my best friend. Whatever you need, Jake, I'm here."

The soft orange glow from a single table lamp filled the room, casting a gentle light over the remnants of our dinner. The evening had evolved from simple conversation to deeper contemplation, the kind of heart-to-heart that comes from exhaustion and earnestness.

Mandy swirled the remnants of her wine glass, the dark liquid catching the light. "You ever look back and think, 'damn, I wish I could redo that?'"

"All the time," I admitted, taking a sip from my own glass. The bitterness of the wine mirrored the sour notes of my past regrets. "There's a lot in my past I wish I could change."

She tilted her head thoughtfully. "Like what?"

I hesitated, taking a deep breath. "Losing touch with people who mattered. Missing out on chances. Hurting people I cared about..."

She nodded, her eyes distant. "I get that. After college, I kept bouncing around, trying to find where I fit. Thought I'd find love, settle down. None of that happened. Now, I'm just... here."

A small smile played on my lips. "But being 'here' brought you to us."

She laughed lightly, "True. And I'm grateful for that."

The silence settled between us, comfortable yet contemplative. She broke it with a question. "Did you ever love someone, but... you just couldn't make it work?"

"Yeah," I murmured, unable to separate the words from the image of Kayla in my mind. "Sometimes love isn't enough. Timing, circumstances, priorities... everything plays a part."

She sighed, "I thought I found 'the one' a few times. But life's a bitch, and it never panned out."

We exchanged stories, tales of love lost and lessons learned. The conversations were raw, honest. And with each passing tale, my respect for Mandy grew. The image I'd held of her – just Lexi's college roommate – was shifting. She was complex, layered, and resilient.

It was close to midnight when I finally said, "Thanks for this. I don't usually open up."

She stretched, stifling a yawn. "Me neither. But tonight felt... right. Thanks for listening, Jake."

I nodded, memories of the conversation lingering between us. "Anytime, Mandy."

We headed to our respective rooms, the emotional exhaustion from the day and our late-night chat weighing heavy. As I lay in bed, I pondered the unexpected layers I'd discovered in Mandy. My admiration for her resilience and spirit had deepened, but the feelings remained firmly platonic. Still, the bond we'd forged tonight was undeniable, and I was grateful for the unexpected friendship that had blossomed in the most trying of times.

Chapter Six

KAYLA

The clock on the wall ticked the early morning hours away, a soft counterpoint to the hum of the overhead fluorescent lights. I'd come in early, deliberately so. The empty room provided a quiet solitude that allowed my mind to wander. The metal chair was hard against my back, but I barely noticed, lost in thought.

Ten years. A whole damn decade since I last saw him before he was assigned as my partner. I'd managed to avoid him almost completely by moving to the next town, but now there was no escaping contact with him. The memories of Jake in high school still felt so fresh, they might have been yesterday. How he'd made me feel so special, so cherished. Then, just like that, he shattered everything, leaving me broken and vulnerable.

I remember the nights I cried into my pillow, the days when seeing a couple laughing together felt like a dagger to my heart. I'd tried to move on, gone on countless dates, but the walls I'd erected to protect my heart were insurmountable. I could never let anyone get too close, not after Jake. Hell, I hadn't even let anyone touch me in that intimate way. The idea of being vulnerable again, of opening myself up to that kind of pain... it was unbearable.

And now? Fate had thrown him back into my life. Every day. His smile, his voice, the way his eyes crinkled when he laughed– it was all so familiar. Those damn feelings, the ones I'd buried deep, were resurfacing. It was infuriating. I had to constantly remind myself: he broke you once. Remember how that felt?

Lost in my thoughts, the sound of the door creaking open jerked me back to reality. The rush of cool air that accompanied his entrance caused a shiver to run down my spine. I looked up, finding those all-too-familiar eyes.

There he was, Jake, looking every bit the guy I'd fallen so hard for. My heart did that stupid fluttery thing, betraying the strict pep talk I'd just given myself.

He offered a soft smile, the kind that reached his eyes, making them shine just a bit brighter.

"Good morning, Kayla."

"Morning," I replied, trying to sound more casual than I felt. The fluttering in my chest was just a stupid, vestigial response to seeing him. It meant nothing.

Chief Daniels, an older man with a stern face that belied a much gentler nature, stepped out of his office. "Kayla," he started, nodding in acknowledgment as his gaze shifted between Jake and me, "could you take a look at these?" He pushed a thick stack of files across the counter.

"Of course, chief," I said, pulling the first folder towards me. I glanced at Jake, who was watching with a curious expression.

The familiar weight of responsibility settled on my shoulders. Everyone always said I had a knack for spotting connections others missed. Being dubbed the station's "best detective" was both an honor and a curse.

As I leafed through the files, one by one, something started to nag at me. Various reports detailed break-ins at the city hall, specifically targeting files connected to the Barrows family.

Pages were missing from some files, the paper edges left jagged from being torn out in a hurry.

An unexpected detail caught my eye: smudges of ink on the corner of one of the reports. It wasn't ballpoint or printer ink, but the kind you'd find in old typewriters. That detail was odd enough to stand out. Lexi's stalker had sent letters before, and the type of ink used to write them was notable.

A chill crept up my spine. The implications of what I was seeing made the hairs on the back of my neck stand on end. Someone was digging deep, trying to unearth secrets about the Barrows, and it seemed they were doing it with an almost obsessive thoroughness.

"Jake," I said, turning my eyes to meet his. I could see the concern and interest mirrored in his own gaze. "Coffee? I think we need to talk about this."

He nodded, "Sounds good."

We left the files on the counter, promising the chief we'd return shortly. As we headed towards the exit, I felt a renewed sense of determination. Whoever was after Lexi, whoever was trying to dig up the past, they were leaving behind clues. And I was hell-bent on following them to the end.

The diner's soft hum of chatter and clinking dishes served as a familiar backdrop to our intense conversation. It was the kind of place that felt like home, with the smell of bacon and freshly brewed coffee in the air. And for a while, our conversation was all about the case, throwing ideas and theories back and forth.

Jake sipped his black coffee, the heat seemingly not

bothering him. His eyes met mine, and my breath hitched, just as it always had, even after all these years. Time had only honed his features, adding an air of maturity that made him even more striking. His dark hair, once always slightly too long and rebellious, was now neatly trimmed, giving him a more distinguished look. Those piercing green eyes, which I remembered all too well, still had that intense, searching quality, as if he could see right through to your soul.

He had filled out since high school, the lanky frame now replaced by broad shoulders and a physique that spoke of regular visits to the gym, or maybe it was just the demands of his job as a officer. The uniform he wore seemed tailor-made for him, accentuating his athletic build. And there was something in the way he carried himself—a confidence, a certain gravitas—that wasn't there before.

"This whole situation with Lexi is fucked up," he began, his voice laced with concern. "I mean, whoever's stalking her has some serious issues."

I nodded, stirring sugar into my cup. "The break-ins at city hall, the missing pages about the Barrows family, and now that typewriter ink. It's like this person is trying to piece together a puzzle about Lexi or...or maybe even you."

Jake ran a hand through his hair. "Yeah, it's unsettling. But why go through all that trouble just to get info on us? There's got to be a reason."

"We need to find out what they're after," I mused. "The sooner we do, the sooner we can put an end to this madness."

Jake's expression hardened. "We will, Kay. No matter what it takes. I won't let anything happen to Lexi. Or you, for that matter."

The sincerity in his voice sent a shiver down my spine. I knew he meant it. "We've got to be smart about this. The stalker's smart, calculated even. This isn't just a random obsession."

Jake leaned in, eyes fierce. "They made a mistake with that ink, though. It means they're getting sloppy, maybe even desperate. We can use that to our advantage."

I tapped the file on the table. "We need to go over everything with a fine-toothed comb. Every detail matters. And if there's a pattern or a connection we've missed, we need to find it."

His eyes met mine, a silent promise of unwavering support. "We're in this together, Kayla. We'll figure it out."

The thought of Lexi living in constant fear angered me, and the notion of a shadow lurking around Jake was terrifying. We had to get ahead of this, and fast.

Reaching for the creamer at the same time, our fingers brushed against each other. The unexpected jolt that shot through me was intense, catching me completely off guard. My defenses, so carefully erected over the years, began to falter as I met Jake's eyes.

"Kayla," he said softly, his voice pulling me back from the storm of emotions swirling inside. The way my name rolled off his lips caused butterflies to dance wildly in my stomach.

His expression was one of deep regret. "I... I am so sorry for the way I acted when I broke up with you."

I held my breath. Years of pent-up anger, confusion, and pain lingered in the space between us. He'd never apologized before, not sincerely. And I'd never allowed him to, too fearful of reopening old wounds. But working side by side had changed things. I remembered all the good times, the laughter, and the love. His face now was an open book, each line etched with remorse.

"I was an idiot," he continued, his voice cracking slightly. "I let some stupid people get in my head, people I don't even talk to anymore, and because of that, I lost the love of my life."

"The what?" My voice was barely above a whisper. A part of me was scared to hear the answer, scared to believe that the connection we once shared was still there.

"Yeah," he said, swallowing hard. "I never fell in love after you. No one ever measured up."

We sat in silence, his words settling around us. I blinked away the tears threatening to spill. My heart ached as memories of our past rushed back in full force.

"Me neither," I finally admitted, looking straight into his eyes. "No one ever measured up to you either."

The vulnerable moment that followed was filled with so much emotion that it felt almost tangible. It didn't mean that everything was magically fixed, but it felt like a first step towards healing. A step towards understanding and, maybe, a future where past mistakes didn't overshadow the present.

Chapter Seven

JAKE

The moment I stepped into the station, I could tell something was wrong. Kayla was pacing, her face taut with stress. She looked up as I entered, her gaze sharp.

"Jake, we've got a problem."

I felt a jolt of anxiety. "What happened?"

She inhaled deeply. "Someone broke into the city hall again, but that's not the worst of it. They also got into the local hospital.

Every damn file about Lexi has been taken."

My heart plummeted. Images flooded my mind: a shadowy figure rifling through papers, discovering Lexi's deepest secrets, vulnerabilities she might not even be aware of herself. My stomach twisted with unease.

"This is bad, Kay. Real bad."

Her voice was tight. "I know. The fact that they're so hell-bent on digging into Lexi's life is chilling. We're dealing with someone who's methodical, organized, and has resources."

I hesitated. There were things about my sister I didn't

want to know. Things every brother would rather remain ignorant of when it came to their sibling. "Is there... I mean, could there be something in those files that might... I don't know, be incriminating? Or something she'd want to keep private?"

Kayla shot me a look. "Honestly, Jake? It doesn't matter. Even if there is, it's no one's damn business. Our priority is to make sure this asshole doesn't use whatever they've got against her."

I nodded, gripping the edge of a desk. "We have to let Lexi know. She needs to be prepared."

"We'll handle it, Jake. We'll find this son of a bitch."

I stared at her, my resolve hardening. "Together."

She gave a short nod. "Together."

We spent the next few hours gathering whatever information we could from the scenes of the break-ins. Every moment that passed was another moment our stalker could act on the information they had stolen.

The dim light from the desk lamp cast long shadows over the pages as we pored over them, searching for anything that connected Lexi's current stalker notes to the ones from years ago.

The first thing that struck me was the handwriting. It was meticulous, almost unnervingly so, with each letter painstakingly crafted. The way the 't's were crossed, with a slightly heavier stroke at the top, and the 'i's dotted with a small, precise circle – it was identical to the notes we'd filed away years ago. Whoever this stalker was, they were either the same person or someone hell-bent on imitating them to the smallest detail.

Then, there were the phrases used. Chillingly familiar, almost verbatim from what we'd seen before. Phrases like "always watching" and "you can't escape me" were repeated, a haunting echo from the past. The newer notes had evolved slightly, with an added intensity, a desperation that was less pronounced in the older ones. It was as if the stalker's obsession had deepened over the years.

I noticed, too, the paper quality. It was high-grade, not your run-of-the-mill printer paper. This was someone who took pride, almost a sick pleasure, in their craft. The older notes had the same, slightly textured feel to them.

As we sorted through the stacks of paperwork, Kayla suddenly looked up from a document she was reading. She cleared her throat and shot me a concerned glance.

"I think I should head to the ranch and update Lexi about this mess," she began, her tone gentle. "If there's anything in those files you'd rather not know about, I'll handle it. You won't have to be in the middle."

Relief surged through me. "Thanks, Kay. I appreciate it." I let out a shaky breath, realizing just how much this whole situation was gnawing at me.

She gave me a reassuring squeeze on the shoulder. "It's what partners do. I'll let you know once I've spoken to her. Just promise you'll get some rest, okay?"

"I'll try," I replied, the exhaustion from the day's events finally catching up to me.

She gave me a small nod, her eyes filled with concern. "Take care, Jake. We've got a hell of a case to figure out."

I watched as Kayla grabbed her jacket and keys, heading out of the station. The thought of some sick bastard digging through Lexi's life made my blood boil. I needed a moment to breathe, to reset.

With a deep exhale, I decided to head home. The thought of some semblance of normalcy was comforting. And then, of course, there was Mandy. The thought of her waiting, likely with another delicious meal, tugged at the edges of my mind, offering a small respite from the day's chaos.

As I drove, the familiar landscape of our town passed by in a blur. Each turn, each stop sign, was a testament to the life I had built here, but now everything felt tainted, overshadowed by this looming threat.

Pulling into my driveway, the soft glow from the windows of my house offered some warmth. I could smell the delicious aroma of dinner wafting from inside even before I reached the front door.

Pushing open the door, the scent intensified, pulling me in. My stomach grumbled in response, reminding me I hadn't eaten all day. The cozy ambiance of my living room met me — the soft glow of the lamps, the gentle hum of the refrigerator, and Mandy, busy in the kitchen.

"Hey, Mandy," I greeted, my voice weary but grateful.

She turned, flashing me a welcoming smile. "Jake. Perfect timing, dinner's ready."

The scent of roasted chicken and garlic mashed potatoes wafted through the room, making my stomach growl in response.

I hadn't expected to have a houseguest go to so much trouble, but as long as she was willing, I was glad for the homecooked meal each night. As we sat down to eat, I filled her in on the stalker situation and just how deep it seemed to run.

Mandy's face went from shocked to genuinely concerned. "Damn, Jake. Lexi must be losing her mind over this."

"Yeah, it's messed up. I'm hoping Kayla can get through to her, help her understand the gravity of the situation without panicking her," I said, stabbing a piece of chicken.

The doorbell's shrill ring cut our conversation short. Pushing back from the table, I stood and went to answer the door. "Kayla?" I raised an eyebrow, surprised to see her. "Thought you'd be with Lexi longer."

She brushed a strand of hair behind her ear, looking a tad uncomfortable. "I needed to fill you in on how things went. Figured face-to-face was better."

I nodded, stepping aside to let her in. As she entered, her eyes landed on Mandy, who was dabbing her mouth with a napkin. "Oh, I'm sorry," Kayla said, looking slightly taken aback. "I didn't realize you had company. Maybe I should come back later."

I chuckled, dismissing the awkwardness. "No, you're not interrupting anything. Mandy's an old college friend of Lexi's. She's in town, and since Lexi's place is a construction zone right now, she's bunking in my guest room."

Mandy stood up, extending a friendly hand. "Nice to meet you, Kayla."

Kayla shook her hand, offering a polite smile. "Likewise. And sorry to intrude on your evening."

"Trust me, you're not," I assured her, trying to alleviate the tension. "Let's take this to my room. We can talk more privately there."

I could feel Mandy's eyes on me as I said that, her eyebrows drawing together in a slight frown. "Sure," she said, her tone a bit frosty. "I'll clean up here. Don't mind me."

I winced inwardly, picking up on her annoyance. I knew our routine had become a comforting constant in recent days, and my abrupt departure to chat with Kayla was disrupting that.

"Thanks, Mandy. I'll be right back," I said, trying to sound apologetic.

Guiding Kayla down the hall, I couldn't shake the feeling that this evening was becoming more complicated than I had anticipated. Pushing open the door to my room, I gestured for her to step inside.

Kayla's nervous energy was palpable as she scanned the space, her gaze finally settling on a trophy displayed prominently on my bookshelf. It was from our high school days—a proud achievement for most.

"You got the big win," she remarked, her voice distant, fingers tracing the polished gold facade.

I stiffened, old memories pressing down. The cheering crowds, the euphoria of the game, and the stinging realization of what it cost me—all jumbled together. My steps echoed slightly on the hardwood as I approached her, reaching out to reclaim the emblem of my misplaced priorities.

"No, I didn't," I said softly, my voice laden with regret. Without a second thought, I set the trophy face down on my desk and, with a swift movement, knocked it into the garbage bin. The sharp clang it made resonated in the room. "We won the game, but I lost big. I lost you. Every time I looked at that damn trophy, it was a kick in the gut —a reminder of just how much I fucked up."

Kayla's face turned a deep shade of crimson, her eyes darting away, clearly not expecting my admission.

My throat felt tight. "So," I began, trying to redirect the tension, "how did it go with Lexi?"

She offered a non-committal shrug, her voice subdued. "About as well as it could. She's scared shitless, obviously. And Luke? God, he's livid."

I ran a hand through my hair, processing her words. "Then why did you feel the need to tell me all this face-to-face? Could've just texted."

She hesitated, her eyes searching mine with an intensity I hadn't seen in years. "Maybe," she said, her voice a soft whisper, "I just needed an excuse."

My heart rate quickened, each beat echoing loudly in my ears. "An excuse for what?"

Without another word, Kayla closed the distance between us, her fingers lightly grazing the back of my neck, sending electric jolts down my spine. Her gaze was locked onto mine, piercing, challenging. She stood on tiptoes, her breath warm against my face, making my skin tingle with anticipation. I was lost in the moment, every wall I'd built over the years threatening to crumble.

Then, with a sudden surge of boldness, she pressed her lips against mine. A rush of emotions swirled inside me—a mixture of surprise, elation, and regret. The world faded as her lips met mine, and everything else ceased to matter.

I pulled back, a rush of unexpected emotion flooding me. "Are you sure about this?" I questioned, my gaze probing her face for any hint of regret.

She looked away for a second, biting her lip, seemingly in contemplation. "Honestly? No," she admitted, locking eyes with me. "But I've been craving to feel your lips on mine. To see if that spark is still there."

"And?" My voice was hoarse with anticipation, every fiber of my being alert to her reaction.

She gave a faint smirk, her eyes gleaming. "And it's just as intoxicating as it always was."

A rush of warmth surged through me. My fingers traced the side of her face, delicately brushing a strand of hair behind her ear. Closing the gap between us, I gently pressed my lips to hers, trying to convey all the unspoken emotions swirling inside me. I felt her initial hesitation, a slight stiffness, but with every gentle move I made, she relaxed, eventually reciprocating with fervor.

Without even realizing, I'd picked her up, my hands finding the small of her back, pulling her close. I set her gently on the bed, our bodies perfectly aligned, lips never parting. The rush of sensations, memories, and unspent years washed over me.

"God, Kayla, I missed you. No one's ever felt this right," I murmured, pulling back just enough to see her reaction.

She let out a soft whimper, her fingers tangling in my hair.

"Are you okay?" Concern filled me, thinking I might've been too forward.

"Yes," she whispered, catching her breath. "It's just... no one has ever felt like this for me either." She paused, swallowing hard. "Actually, Jake, there hasn't been anyone else."

I blinked, momentarily taken aback. Memories of our younger selves came flooding back, of nights spent under the stars, of whispered secrets. "You mean...?" I hesitated, realizing what she was implying.

She gave a small nod, her cheeks flushing. "Yes, Jake. I never... went all the way with anyone."

A swirl of emotions overcame me—surprise, disbelief, and an overwhelming sense of honor. "Hey," I said gently, cupping her face. "There's no pressure, okay? Whatever you're comfortable with."

She smiled, a blend of vulnerability and determination. "I want to, Jake. Just like we wanted to all those years ago. I trust you."

I smiled, leaning in to kiss her again, feeling a connection that was always meant to be.

As our lips danced in sync, a fire, long dormant, blazed back to life. Kayla's hands found their way to the hem of my shirt, and with a swift motion, it was gone, leaving my chest exposed to her touch. The sensation of her lips on my skin was electrifying. Every brush, every soft bite, sent waves of pleasure that coursed through me.

The Rookie's Second Chance

My hands ventured beneath the fabric of her shirt, feeling the smooth curve of her waist and the warmth of her skin. As I skimmed upwards, my fingers grazed the delicate lace of her bra. The sensation of her soft breasts through the fabric made my heart race. I could feel myself getting harder, my body reacting viscerally to her closeness.

A part of me wanted to go further, to rediscover every inch of her, but the reality of the situation held me back. She'd waited all these years, and our sudden reconciliation didn't give me the right to push boundaries. I wanted her to be comfortable, to be sure. And to be honest, I wasn't sure about myself either. The tumultuous mix of emotions —the passion, the history, and the newfound vulnerability —had me teetering on the edge.

My hands roamed freely, her soft moans spurring me on. But as the line between desire and restraint grew blurrier, a nagging voice in my head kept me grounded. Don't push it. Not now. I realized I was toeing a dangerous line. It wasn't just the physical aspect—it was the emotional connection we were rekindling. I didn't want to mess it up. I didn't want a single mistake to jeopardize whatever this was.

So, before I lost myself completely, I slowly pulled back, ending our fiery reunion. Taking a deep breath, I met her gaze, silently begging her to understand why I'd stopped. Her eyes shimmered with a passion and understanding, a silent acknowledgment of the unspoken bond we shared.

Kayla and I were mere inches apart, our heavy breaths mingling in the stillness. She looked up at me, her eyes searching for something.

"I don't want to rush this, Kay," I finally broke the silence, my voice huskier than I intended. "It's been years, and...fuck, it feels amazing to be close to you again. But I don't want to mess it up by going too fast."

She looked taken aback for a split second, then her features softened. "I get it. I do. It's a lot," she admitted, tucking a stray strand of hair behind her ear. Let's just see what happens without the past or expectations for the future. Just... us."

Feeling a warmth in my chest, I grinned. "So, no rush?"

She smirked, "No rush." Walking her out, we navigated the dimly lit hallway. I felt an odd sense of déjà vu. It was as if we were teenagers again, sneaking around, cautious of who might see. At the porch, I leaned in and captured her lips one last time—quick, but meaningful. Our own little secret.

As I watched her leave, I couldn't shake off the nostalgia and hope churning inside me.

Heading back inside, the aroma of Mandy's cooking filled my nostrils. She sat at the dining table, swirling a glass of wine, seemingly lost in thought.

I took my seat across from her, digging back into my previously abandoned dinner. We chatted about random stuff—movies, books, the city. But Kayla's name never once came up. Mandy, it seemed, had an uncanny ability to sense boundaries, or maybe she just didn't care. I appreciated it either way.

Though there was so much left unsaid between Kayla and me, for now, I was content. The journey had only just begun, and the road ahead looked promising.

Chapter Eight

KAYLA

I closed the door behind me, leaning against it with a heavy sigh. My apartment was dim, with just a lone lamp illuminating the room. The silence felt almost deafening after the whirlwind of emotions at Jake's place.

"Stupid, stupid," I muttered to myself, but there was a smile tugging at the corner of my lips. My heart thudded against my ribcage as memories flooded back—sweet, sour, and everything in between.

Shaking my head, I made my way to the bathroom, turning the tap for a hot shower. The steam filled the small space, and as I stepped under the warm cascade, it felt like the droplets were trying to cleanse away the years of pain and distance. I ran my fingers through my hair, letting the water soak my thoughts.

Jake had been my everything. My first love. My first heartbreak. The fact that I was still a virgin at my age was not something I usually thought about. After Jake, I just... couldn't. There were opportunities, of course, but every time I thought I might be ready, memories of him would surge back. Memories of promises made under hushed whispers, of stolen kisses, of plans that never materialized.

But tonight, there was no escaping the thoughts of Jake—the taste of him, the feel of his hands. It was overwhelming. Why now? Why, after all this time, did it feel like he could just walk back into my life?

I turned off the shower, stepping out and reaching for my towel. As I wrapped it around me, I caught my reflection in the steamy mirror. My cheeks were flushed, not just from the heat of the shower. My eyes looked...hopeful. And that scared the shit out of me. Donning a comfy pair of pajamas, I sat on the edge of my bed, thinking about how things ended between us. We were young, with dreams too big for our small town. He had his path, and I had mine. And somewhere along the way, they stopped intersecting. He moved on, or so it seemed. But me? I built walls. Walls that no one, including myself, could breach. Until tonight.

I reached for the pendant necklace I always wore—a gift from him. It reminded me of him, of us, of what was and what could be. I remembered the exact moment he gave it to me, the promise it held, and the pain of our inevitable parting. "Fuck," I whispered, blinking away tears. It was all too much.

Too soon. Yet, there was a part of me—a big part—that wanted to dive headfirst into whatever this was.

Sighing, I tucked myself into bed. My head was buzzing with a million thoughts, and I knew sleep wouldn't come easy.

The soft hum of the air conditioner was the only sound in the room, but in my mind, it was all noise and chaos. I couldn't shake the memory of Jake—those intoxicating eyes that had always drawn me in, the way his hair always looked effortlessly perfect. His body had matured over the years, leaner, stronger, and undeniably more appealing.

I shifted in bed, feeling a growing warmth between my legs as I replayed our recent encounter. His scent still lingered on my skin, the smell of earthy cologne and the faintest hint of sweat. The taste of his lips, the heat of his mouth on mine... damn, I was wet just thinking about it.

I hesitated for a moment, then let my hand slip beneath the covers, sliding down my body. I bit my lip as I gently touched my swollen clit, thinking about Jake, imagining his mouth trailing down my neck, his hands on my breasts, tweaking my nipples. His body pressed up against mine, feeling his hard cock against my thigh. The pressure built, and I moved my fingers in slow circles, teasing myself, drawing out the pleasure.

My other hand found its way to my breast, squeezing and pinching the sensitive nipple. The combination of my hands, coupled with the images in my mind, was driving me wild. My breath grew ragged, my body writhing beneath the sheets. I thought of that evening, how he'd picked me up and pressed me against the wall, the friction between our bodies electric. What if he'd gone further? What if he'd slipped his hand between my legs, feeling how wet he made me? Or if he'd taken out his cock, letting me feel its weight and hardness in my hand?

I moved my fingers faster, each motion deliberate, each touch echoing with the memory of Jake's hands on me. My mind was a whirl of fantasy, building a narrative that was fueled by the ache between my thighs.

I imagined him standing at the foot of my bed, watching me, his green eyes dark with desire. I pictured him slowly unbuttoning his shirt, revealing that chiseled chest that I had felt just earlier. His hands would glide over his body, mirroring my own movements, showcasing his understanding of the intense pleasure that self-touch could bring.

He would inch closer, and in this fantasy, I spread my legs wider, inviting him to see just how wet he made me. I imagined the look of pure hunger on his face, the bulge in his pants growing larger, harder. He'd kneel on the bed, his mouth mere inches from where my fingers danced. His hot breath would tease me, making me even wetter, heightening my arousal.

"Jake," I'd whisper, urging him on. And like a predator, he'd close the distance, replacing my fingers with his mouth. The sensation of his tongue on my clit would send shockwaves through my body, making me arch my back and moan his name louder.

In my mind, I felt his fingers slipping inside me, curling just right, hitting that spot that always sent me over the edge. My fantasy was so vivid, so intense, that my body was responding as if it were reality. My breath grew erratic, my moans filled the room, and the tension in my belly coiled tighter and tighter.

And then, just as I envisioned Jake looking up at me, his eyes locking onto mine as he sucked on my clit, I shattered. The waves of pleasure consumed me, making me tremble and gasp. The release was exquisite, leaving me floating on a cloud of euphoria.

Once the tremors subsided, I slowly removed my fingers, bringing them up to my lips, tasting myself and wishing it were Jake's taste mixed with my own. My chest heaved, trying to catch the breath that the fantasy had stolen.

I felt both drained and energized, deeply satisfied yet hungry for the real thing. Pulling the sheets tighter around me, I nestled into my pillow, the fantasy of Jake still vivid in my mind, promising myself that the next time, it wouldn't just be a fantasy. Sleep, when it came, was restless, filled with dreams of him.

The morning light streamed through the windows, casting a soft, golden hue on the room. Groaning, I stretched my limbs and slowly came back to consciousness, rubbing the sleep from my eyes. The remnants of the dream, Jake's phantom touches, still lingered on my skin.

Taking a deep breath to center myself, I pushed the thoughts aside and got ready for the day.

As I walked into the station, the absence of Jake's voice, his laughter, the way he'd be teasing one of the guys or sharing some story from the night before felt like a void. I kept reminding myself that I was here for work, not Jake. But I couldn't deny the pang of disappointment that he wasn't there. Get it together, Kayla, I thought, cursing my brain for making everything about him all of a sudden.

With a cup of stale coffee in hand, I headed to my desk, booting up the computer. My main focus was Lexi's stalker. Pulling up the case file, I started piecing together the timeline of events that had occurred while she was in college. Lexi had gone to an out-of-state school, and the details surrounding her stalker remained a mystery to everyone in town.

Sifting through old emails, online comments, and messages Lexi had received, I searched for a pattern. And then, while cross-referencing her old class schedules with the times she'd reported being stalked, it hit me. The stalker always seemed to know exactly where she'd be, even when it wasn't on a regular schedule. This wasn't just someone who was following her; this was someone who knew her routines, her habits, and her entire schedule. "Fuck," I whispered, my heart racing. This wasn't just a random fan or a stranger. This was someone who was close enough to have that kind of information. The implications were unsettling. As I delved deeper, I found an email from an anonymous sender, hinting at events and secrets from Lexi's childhood, details only someone who had known her personally would be privy to. No specifics, but enough to confirm my growing suspicion.

I needed more concrete evidence, but this was a start. Damn it, Jake, why aren't you here? I found myself wishing he was with me so that we could brainstorm together.

Sighing, I continued digging, determined to unearth more clues. Hours slipped by as I pieced together fragments of Lexi's past.

My stomach growled, reminding me that I hadn't had breakfast. Glancing at the clock, I realized it was almost lunchtime. But the pieces were beginning to fit together, and I was too engrossed to stop.

By the end of my shift, my eyes were blurry from staring at the screen, but the picture was clearer. Someone from Lexi's past, possibly someone she considered a friend or trusted confidant, was haunting her. The real question was: why? And more importantly, who?

The reports lay scattered across my desk, their contents burning images into my mind. With a sigh, I rubbed my temples, feeling a dull ache start to form.

Suddenly, a thought resurfaced. Mandy. She had roomed with Lexi in college. If anyone would know about someone potentially obsessed with Lexi to stalker levels, it'd be her. No more putting it off. I needed to talk to Mandy.

Grabbing my coat, I made my way to Jake's house. Every time I approached that house now, memories of our recent encounter rushed back, sending anticipation and anxiety through me.

Reaching his door, I hesitated for a moment, then knocked firmly. The door swung open to reveal Mandy, her

The Rookie's Second Chance

auburn hair falling in waves down her back. She regarded me with those clear blue eyes, cold and assessing.

"Jake's not here," she said curtly, not bothering with niceties. Her gaze lingered on me for a moment, almost challenging.

"I'm not here for Jake," I replied, trying to keep my voice steady, though my palms were sweaty. "I need to ask you something about Lexi. You roomed with her in college, right?"

Mandy leaned against the doorframe, crossing her arms. "Why? What do you want to know?"

"There's something about the stalker... a lead," I said, choosing my words carefully. "I need to know about any unusual people who might've been obsessed with Lexi during college."

She raised an eyebrow, looking genuinely surprised. "You think someone from college is stalking her now? That was years ago."

"It's just a hunch," I admitted. "But I have to explore every lead."

Mandy sighed. "Look, college was a blur. Parties, late-night study sessions, more parties. You know how it is. But I never noticed anyone being overly obsessed with Lexi."

"But surely you must've seen something," I pressed. "Any ex-boyfriend? Or maybe someone from a class or a party who couldn't take their eyes off her?"

She hesitated, chewing her lip. "There was this one guy... Jared, I think? He was always hanging around our dorm. He claimed he was friends with Lexi from a shared class, but he always gave me the creeps."

"Jared?" I echoed, scribbling the name in my notebook. "Do you remember anything else about him?"

Mandy shook her head. "Just that he had this weird tattoo of a crow on his forearm. Why?"

I frowned. "No reason. Just trying to piece things together." The tattoo detail could be significant or a complete dead end, but it was worth noting.

We stood in silence for a moment. I clenched my jaw, wanting to ask what her problem was but deciding it wasn't the right time for that conversation.

"Well... Thanks for the information, Mandy."

She gave a mocking half-smile, "Just doing my part, Detective."

The moment I got back in the cruiser, my fingers immediately began their dance across the keyboard, searching through old reports, college rosters, and anything that would lead me to this 'Jared.'

As the screen flickered with search results, a cold shiver crept down my spine. Mandy's unease was hard to miss. Was it a genuine concern for Lexi, or was she hiding something? Searching, I tried to push away the nagging feeling. Mandy was a new factor in this, but my focus had to remain clear. Still, the way her gaze had shifted, the slight hitch in her voice... It all made me wonder.

Before my mind could spiral further, a name jumped out from the roster. Jared Ravenna. Registered during the same years Lexi attended college. Quickly pulling up his records, my heart raced as I stumbled upon a recent arrest report: Domestic Abuse.

"Shit," I muttered under my breath, my pulse quickening. This Jared could actually be our guy. If he was aggressive enough to get arrested for domestic abuse, who's to say he wasn't twisted enough to be our stalker?

Maybe Mandy's standoffish attitude was just that. Or maybe it was more. But I couldn't dwell on it. Not now. This lead on Jared was too strong.

I started the engine. This could be the break we needed. The short drive back to the station, I could feel the tension in my shoulders, my grip on the steering wheel a little too tight.

Once inside, I made a beeline to my desk, searching databases, trying to piece together everything I could find on Jared Ravenna. I needed to know his connections, his habits, places he frequented. Any detail could be the key.

"Looks like someone's on a mission," a voice interrupted my thoughts. It was Danny, one of the guys from narcotics who was always checking in on the "new detective in town." He peered over, catching a glimpse of the screen.

"Just following up on a lead," I replied, not looking up. I was on a roll.

"Need help?"

I hesitated for a split second, then shook my head. "I've got it. But thanks."

He gave a knowing nod, a smirk playing on his lips. "Just don't forget to come up for air, okay?"

I forced a smile, appreciating the sentiment, but my mind was elsewhere.

As the hours dragged on, I dove deep into Jared's past. Multiple charges, not just for abuse, but for cyber-harassment. This was looking more and more like our guy. But I needed to be sure.

Whatever the connection, whatever the truth, I was going to uncover it. And soon.

Chapter Nine

JAKE

I'd barely settled into my chair the following morning when the blaring of the emergency line jolted me. Fumbling for a moment, I snatched up the receiver, "Silver Creek PD, Officer Barrows."

"It's Lexi!" The unmistakable panic in her voice sent a jolt down my spine. "He was here, Jake. In our home. Luke and I found... just get here, please."

On any other day, her plea might've thrown me off. But today? The urgency in her voice made it clear. The stalker was escalating.

"On our way," I said tersely, slamming the phone back on its cradle. I shot up, snatching my jacket off the chair. "Kayla!" I called out, locking eyes with her across the room. "We need to roll. Now."

She didn't hesitate. Grabbing her coat, she met me at the door, her face a mirror of the concern I felt. "What happened?"

"Stalker hit Lexi's place," I responded tersely as we made our way to the cruiser. "Don't know the full extent yet, but it sounds bad."

The drive was a blur, tires squealing, sirens blaring. We reached Lexi and Luke's place in record time. The morning chill prickled at my skin as I stepped out, but that was nothing compared to the cold dread that settled in my gut. Their front door was ajar, swinging ominously. Kayla drew her weapon, motioning for me to do the same.

We moved methodically, checking each room as we made our way to the living area. The sight that met us there made my stomach turn.

On the pristine white wall was a message scrawled in what looked disturbingly like blood. "YOU CAN'T ESCAPE ME."

"Motherfucker," Kayla hissed under her breath, her knuckles white around her gun.

I scanned the room, my anger mounting. Lexi and Luke were huddled on the couch, Luke's arm protectively around her. Both looked shaken to the core.

"We need to keep you safe," I said, holstering my gun. "This is crossing a line."

"We can keep a patrol on duty nearby," Kayla chimed in, her voice tense. "And in the meantime, we'll get a team to comb this place for evidence."

Lexi looked up, tears pooling in her eyes. "Why is this happening, Jake? Why me?"

I felt a surge of protectiveness. "We're working on it, Lexi," I murmured, squeezing her hand. "We'll get this bastard."

As Kayla coordinated with the arriving officers, I pulled Luke aside, lowering my voice. "Make sure Lexi doesn't stay alone, alright? And keep that location to yourselves. This guy's getting more daring by the day."

Luke nodded, determination etched on his face. "You have my word."

The following hours were a blur. officers combing the

scene, snapping photos, gathering whatever evidence they could. The message on the wall, it turned out, was written in animal blood. A sick game to the stalker, but a clear sign for us – we were dealing with someone deranged.

Back at the station, my mind raced. We were now against an opponent who wasn't just shadowing from a distance but actively moving in. The thought made me feel sick.

"Jake," Kayla said, snapping me out of my thoughts. She handed over a baggie. Inside was a small piece of cloth. "Found this near the window. Doesn't match anything in Lexi's house."

I squinted at it, the wheels turning. "Let's get it to the lab. Maybe it's our first real lead."

With the evidence turned over to the lab, we returned to scouring reports for anything we missed. Lexi's past was the key. I leafed through some printouts of documents from her college, dating profiles, social media posts. An old case, nearly buried in the stack, caught my eye.

"Hey, Kayla," I called, waving her over as I spread out the report. "Look at this. Another stalking case. Same college. Lexi's freshman year."

Her eyes quickly scanned the document. "Shit, this is almost identical. Who was the victim?"

"Doesn't say; all names are redacted for confidentiality. But check out the dates. Matches Lexi's timeline."

Kayla leaned in closer, her brow furrowed in concentration. "You think this could be our guy? He started with someone else and then moved on to Lexi?"

I shrugged, running a hand through my hair. "It's a damn possibility. Especially if he knew her back then."

Her gaze locked onto mine, a hint of realization dawning. "Jared Ravenna. I looked him up earlier. He got out of jail a couple of weeks ago."

My heart skipped a beat. "Are you shitting me?"

She shook her head, handing me another file. "He was in for assault. The timeline fits. He would've been free during Lexi's freshman year."

I stared at the mugshot on the file. Jared Ravenna. A name to a face. This could be the link we needed.

Pulling up the computer, I quickly ran a search on his last known whereabouts. "Fuck, Kayla. He's just a couple hours out from here."

Without wasting a second, she was on her feet. "Let's go. We need to talk to him."

"Let me see what Lexi knows first."

I called her, and she didn't answer, so I shot her a text, but she was probably resting or panicking. I know I would be in her shoes.

It was a stretch, linking an old college case with our current stalker situation. But it was a lead, one of the strongest we'd had so far. We moved with renewed energy, urgency driving us forward.

"Think he'll cooperate?" I asked as we approached the cruiser.

Kayla smirked, buckling in. "Oh, he will. One way or another."

The cruiser hummed as we merged onto the highway. I gripped the steering wheel, trying to focus on the task. But the heaviness of the silence between Kayla and me was hard to ignore. My thoughts were swirling, constantly being dragged back to that unexpected kiss.

Glancing over at her, I searched for the right words. How the hell do you shift a conversation from a potential stalker to...well, us?

Before I could figure it out, the opening notes of a familiar tune floated from the radio. My heart thudded loudly. It was our song. The one we'd dance to at those ridiculous high school parties, the one we'd belt out in the car, the soundtrack to our summer all those years ago.

She turned to me, a ghost of a smile playing on her lips. "Haven't heard this in ages."

"Yeah," I replied, my voice surprisingly steady. "Brings back memories."

A soft sigh escaped her. "That night at the lake... under the stars. Remember?"

"How could I forget?" The memory was vivid—us, young and carefree, tangled up in each other as the waves lapped nearby.

She hesitated before speaking. "That kiss, Jake. Was it just...?"

"I've wanted to do that for a long time," I admitted, glancing at her.

She looked surprised but not displeased. "Even after everything?"

"Especially after everything," I whispered, my gaze locking onto

hers. "I know it was my fault, Kay. I messed up, big time. But I never got over you."

She bit her lip, a sign I knew meant she was thinking deeply. "You weren't the only one. I tried moving on, I really did. But it never felt right. You were always there, in the back of my mind." The rawness of her words hit me hard.

"I'm sorry, Kay."

She nodded, looking straight ahead. "Me too."

We rolled into Jared's neighborhood as the last light of day faded. The houses were all similar, little post-war builds with neatly trimmed lawns and peeling white picket fences. The address led us to a small brick house with blacked-out windows.

Kayla checked her notes. "Last known address is nearby. Let's hope he's there."

But when we reached Jared's place, it was clear he wasn't home. It was dark, and there were no cars in the driveway.

"Looks empty," Kayla observed, squinting as she tried to peer inside.

"Let's see if any of the neighbors know anything," I suggested. We approached the house next door, where an elderly woman was tending to some roses in her garden. She looked up as we approached, wiping her hands on her jeans.

"Evening," she greeted, a guarded expression on her face. "Can I help you?"

"Hey," I started. "We're looking for Jared Ravenna. Do you know when he might be back?"

Her eyes narrowed for a second, assessing us. "You police?"

Kayla nodded, flashing her badge. "Yes, ma'am. Just need to ask him a few questions."

The woman hesitated, then sighed. "Jared works nights. Construction. He won't be back till morning."

Shit. This wasn't going as planned. Out of our jurisdiction meant we had to play by a different set of rules, and barging onto a construction site unannounced wasn't one of them.

"Well, thanks for your help," I said, forcing a smile.

"He does go to that diner out by the highway after his shift, though," the woman said suddenly. Her eyes lingered on Kayla and me. "Jared knocked around my niece, my sister's kid, while they were dating. He's an asshole." She turned back to her rosebush.

We retreated to the cruiser and, after a quick discussion, settled on staying nearby until morning. The town had a small motel that seemed to be our best option.

The place was a bit run down, with peeling paint and neon signs flickering in and out. But it was a bed. We got rooms next to each other.

Standing outside our adjacent doors, the tension from the car ride returned full force. There was a charged energy between us, and I was hyper-aware of her every move.

"You okay?" she asked, breaking the silence, her voice soft.

"Yeah," I replied, rubbing the back of my neck. "Just thinking."

She arched an eyebrow. "About?"

Taking a deep breath, I closed the small gap between us.

"This," I murmured, pressing my lips to hers. The world around us seemed to vanish. I felt her melt against me, her hands curling into my shirt. The kiss was soft but filled with years of unsaid words and pent-up feelings.

Pulling back, I searched her eyes, finding them clouded with desire but also uncertainty. "Kay…"

She placed a finger against my lips. "I know. We should get some rest."

Feeling a familiar heat pooling in my lower abdomen, I nodded, suddenly tongue-tied. "Yeah. Rest."

I unlocked my door, pausing for a moment. "Goodnight, Kayla."

She smiled, her cheeks flushed. "Goodnight, Jake."

Inside my room, I leaned against the closed door, my heart racing. Between the urgent nature of our mission and the sudden rekindling with Kayla, sleep seemed like a distant dream.

Chapter Ten

KAYLA

The door closed behind Jake with a soft click, but the sound resonated loudly in my ears. Alone in my room, I was immediately surrounded by silence, interrupted only by the distant hum of an old AC unit. My pulse, however, was anything but silent. It was racing, each beat punctuated by the sensation of Jake's lips on mine, his touch. A myriad of emotions swirled within me.

Slumping onto the edge of the bed, I buried my face in my hands. Damn it, Jake. He had a knack for upending everything in my world. It was just like back in high school when he'd walked away, leaving me shattered. I could recall nights spent crying into my pillow, wondering why I wasn't enough. Now, here we were, both changed, both scarred in our own ways, but that electricity was undeniable.

I rose and moved to the small mirror above the dresser, examining my reflection. There were a few loose strands of hair and traces of fatigue in my eyes. But they also held a spark I hadn't seen in a while. Beneath the officer's stern facade, a young woman's desires and dreams still existed.

Deciding a shower might clear my head, I gathered the spare set of clothes I always kept in the cruiser. The warm water cascaded over me, but it did little to wash away my racing thoughts. I remembered the feel of Jake's fingers intertwined with mine, how they'd felt against the small of my back. With golden-brown wavy hair and those intense green eyes, Jake was undeniably handsome. But it wasn't just about looks. It was the way he looked at me, the way he made me feel.

Wrapping a towel around myself, I hesitated for a moment. I was still inexperienced, naive in some ways, while Jake… Jake had lived. He'd had relationships, experiences I couldn't begin to fathom. But right now, in this motel room, with our shared history and the urgency of the present, I didn't care about any of that.

There was an undeniable pull between us, one I couldn't ignore anymore. Taking a deep breath, I changed into the spare clothes, a simple white tee and jeans, and left my room. Before I could rethink my decision, I found myself knocking on Jake's door.

Seconds felt like hours as I waited, my heart pounding so loudly I was sure he'd hear it through the door. The thoughts raced: What if he regrets it? What if he turns me away?

But I didn't have to wait long. The door opened, revealing Jake, his hair damp, probably fresh from a shower as well. The way his eyes trailed over me, assessing, wondering, was enough to make my skin tingle.

"Can I come in?" My voice was a little breathy, betraying more emotion than I'd intended.

"Yeah, of course," he replied, stepping aside. There

was a soft hesitancy in his tone, and it made my stomach flutter.

I glanced around the dimly lit room, catching sight of his bed. The image conjured a surge of want, a craving I hadn't allowed myself to indulge in for years.

The room felt warmer, or maybe it was just the rising heat between us. I found a spot on the edge of his bed, and he stood a few feet away, creating a charged distance.

Our eyes met and locked, a silent exchange taking place. Time seemed to slow down, the world outside the room fading. And then, without a word, he closed the gap between us. His lips met mine in a rush of pent-up desire. His hands roamed my back, pulling me closer. Our bodies pressed together, the sensations amplified by every touch, every brush of skin against skin.

His mouth moved to my neck, leaving a blazing trail. My fingers found their way through his wavy hair, gripping it as his teeth grazed my collarbone. I gasped, feeling the growing hardness against my thigh. Everything in me screamed for more; my body was alive, wet, and aching with want.

Our clothes became a barrier, the fabric a frustrating hindrance to the skin-on-skin contact we both craved. As the intensity mounted, our breaths coming faster, I found myself being laid back on the bed, Jake's weight pressing down on me. His lips moved down my body, and I arched against him, eager for more.

Jake cupped my face with his hands, his thumb brushing against my cheek. "I meant what I said before, Kayla. We don't have to do anything you're not ready for. I won't push."

I held his gaze, my voice earnest. "I want to, Jake. With you. I always wanted it to be you."

The depth of emotions mirrored in his eyes was

enough of a reply. We were two souls intertwined by past, present, and an uncertain future.

His touch was deliberate, careful, as if he were handling a precious work of art. I watched his eyes, those deep green orbs, searching mine for any hint of discomfort. Every brush of his fingers, every slide of his hands, was punctuated with a silent question. Was this okay? Do you want more?

His thumb traced circles on my hip, and my breathing became ragged. There was an intensity between us, a deep connection we couldn't deny. Every moment was an exploration, a rediscovery of feelings and sensations long buried.

As Jake's fingers found the hem of my shirt, he hesitated for a beat, looking into my eyes. I nodded, biting my lower lip, urging him to continue. He slowly peeled it off, revealing my bra-covered chest. The cool air of the room hit my skin, and a shiver went down my spine. But it wasn't the cold that made me shiver—it was anticipation.

Jake's fingers brushed against the soft flesh of my breasts, his touch igniting a fire deep within me. My nipples hardened under his gaze, and a low moan escaped my lips when he pinched them gently between his fingers.

"God, Kayla," he whispered, leaning down. His warm mouth enveloped one nipple, sucking and teasing, while his fingers played with the other. The combination of his hands and mouth was intoxicating. My back arched involuntarily, pushing myself further into his embrace.

His other hand trailed down my stomach, making its way inside the waistband of my jeans and into my panties. My heart raced as I felt his fingers find their way to my wetness. His touch was gentle but firm, exploring and teasing, driving me wild.

The heat between my legs intensified, and I craved more. I reached down, fumbling with the button of his pants. My fingers slid inside, finding his hard cock straining against the fabric. Jake groaned, his eyes darkening with desire as I wrapped my fingers around him, feeling his warmth and hardness.

We were lost in a haze of lust and want, our bodies moving in sync, each touch heightening the pleasure of the next. It felt like we were floating, every nerve ending alive and buzzing.

But as our actions started to bear down, reality began to seep in. The line we were toeing was dangerous, and with every inch, we were getting closer to crossing it.

As the last button of his pants was undone, Jake pulled back slightly, his breath ragged. "Are you sure about this?" His voice was raw, filled with a cocktail of desire and concern.

"Yes," I whispered.

His lips continued their downward journey from my breasts, the sensation of his warm breath against my stomach making me squirm with anticipation. The heat in his eyes was undeniable as he looked up at me, silently asking for permission to go further. With a slight nod, I gave him the go-ahead, my voice failing me. His fingers found the button of my jeans, and as he began to undo them, the moment hit me. This was uncharted territory, and yet, with Jake, it felt natural, like coming home.

He pulled my jeans off, leaving me vulnerable and exposed in front of him. My heart pounded loudly, echoing in my ears, as he took a moment to just stare, his eyes darkening with want. Slowly, he leaned in, inhaling deeply, his face buried between my thighs. The sensation of his breath on my wetness sent shivers racing down my spine.

"You smell wonderful," he murmured, the raw desire in his voice making me throb with need. His fingers found their way to my clit, rubbing in soft circles, and I bit back a moan.

Then, without warning, he replaced his fingers with his tongue, swirling it around and teasing me.

It felt like electricity, every stroke of his tongue sending shockwaves of pleasure through my body. I gripped the sheets, my knuckles white, as he continued to taste and explore me. He glanced up, and our eyes met, the intense connection only amplifying the sensations.

His finger pressing against my entrance made me gasp. He paused, looking up, his eyes searching mine. "Okay?" he asked softly.

I nodded, breathing heavily. "Yes," I managed to whisper, eager for him to continue. Slowly, he slid one finger inside me, the unfamiliar sensation making me clench around him. He moved in and out, his pace slow and deliberate, allowing me to adjust. A second finger soon joined the first, stretching and filling me in a way I'd never felt before.

Combined with the sensation of his tongue on my clit, the overwhelming pleasure built rapidly. My breath came in short gasps, and I felt a heat starting to build deep within me. The world blurred, narrowing down to just Jake and the sensations he was evoking.

My body tensed, and I felt the wave crash over me, every muscle clenching in pleasure. Jake continued to coax every last drop of ecstasy from me until I was left breathless and trembling.

He pulled back, his lips glistening, and looked up at me, his eyes filled with wonder and admiration. "You okay?" he asked, his voice gentle, as he moved up to lay beside me.

My mind was racing, struggling to form coherent

thoughts. "That was... intense," I managed to say, my voice shaky.

Jake chuckled softly, brushing a strand of hair away from my face. "We can stop here if you want," he whispered, the warmth of his breath tickling my ear.

I took a moment, considering his words. But my desire for him was undeniable. "I need you, Jake," I admitted, my voice filled with raw honesty. "I'm all in."

Laying there beside him, feeling the heat emanating from his body, the natural progression of where this was heading became clear. There was an unspoken need, a deep yearning to know him more intimately.

"Jake," I began, my voice laced with determination and curiosity, "I want to taste you."

His eyes widened momentarily, surprise evident, but then he nodded, swallowing hard. Shifting his position slightly, he sat up, allowing me access to his pants. My hands trembled slightly as I worked on the button and zipper, exposing him. I could feel the heat of his arousal even before I fully pulled his pants down, revealing his hard cock.

Swallowing nervously, I took a deep breath and leaned forward, my lips brushing against the head. The taste was unfamiliar yet not unpleasant. I glanced up, meeting Jake's gaze, seeking reassurance. His eyes were dark, filled with lust and need, but there was a tenderness there too. I took him into my mouth, the sensation of his length pressing against my tongue and the roof of my mouth sending a shiver down my spine.

I began to stroke him, using my hand in tandem with my mouth. His groans grew louder, urging me on. The taste of him, combined with the sounds he was making, was like nothing I had experienced. I felt powerful and vulnerable all at once.

But soon, he gently grasped my shoulders, pulling me away.

"Kayla, if you continue... I won't be able to hold back," he whispered raggedly.

Seeing him so undone because of me was empowering. It gave me the courage I needed.

"I'm ready, Jake," I whispered, my voice quivering with anticipation and anxiety.

He reached into his wallet sheepishly and pulled out a condom. "You never know when…" He shrugged.

He pulled it on and repositioned himself, settling between my legs, his cock pressing against my entrance. I could feel the heat of him, the desire coiled tightly inside him.

"Are you sure?" he asked again, his voice gentle, his eyes searching mine for any hesitation.

"Yes," I breathed, my heart pounding so loudly I was sure he could hear it.

The pressure of him entering me was unlike anything I'd ever felt. A mixture of pleasure and pain, the unfamiliar stretch causing me to gasp. He was gentle, moving slowly, allowing me time to adjust to the sensation of him inside me.

Every inch of him filled me, the intimate connection deepening as he moved. Emotions swirled within me— trust, love, desire— all mixing into a heady cocktail. My fingers dug into his back, urging him closer.

With each rhythmic movement, the intensity between us grew. The room was filled with the mingling of our breaths and the soft noises of our bodies moving together. Jake's fingers gripped my hips as he pulled out and then pushed in again, deeper, drawing a moan from my lips.

"Fuck, Kayla," he groaned, his voice husky with need. "You feel so damn good."

My back arched, pushing against him, craving more. The connection, the intimacy, the sensation—it was all-consuming. I could feel every inch of him, every pulse and throb. The pleasure was intense, every nerve ending alight with sensation.

"Jake," I panted, the coil in my belly winding tighter and tighter. "I need... I need..."

Suddenly, Jake shifted, changing our positions. Now on top, I had more control, and I rode him, savoring the feeling of him deep inside me. The angle was different, hitting spots I hadn't even known existed. The pleasure was sharper, more pronounced, and I lost myself in the rhythm we created together. His hands roamed my body, one cupping my breast, pinching and teasing the nipple, while the other moved lower, fingers circling my clit. The double assault on my senses made me see stars, my vision blurring with the onslaught of pleasure.

"Oh God, Jake... I'm... I'm gonna come," I moaned, my body shaking with the force of the impending climax.

"Come for me, Kayla," he urged, his own movements becoming more frantic. "Fuck, I'm close too."

The coil snapped. Pleasure washed over me in waves, consuming me, drowning me. "Jake!" I screamed, my voice echoing off the walls.

He thrust up into me one last time, holding me tight against him. "Kayla... fuck," he groaned, our climaxes intermingling, rendering us both breathless.

We clung to each other, the aftershocks of pleasure still vibrating through our entwined bodies. The world outside ceased to exist. All that mattered was the here and now—the overwhelming connection we shared.

Chapter Eleven

JAKE

Kayla's steady breathing filled the room. I lay on my back, her head nestled on my chest, her dark locks spilling across my skin. I brushed a strand behind her ear, feeling the warmth of her against me. My other arm was wrapped securely around her, afraid that if I let go, this moment would shatter.

I allowed my fingers to drift across her back, tracing small patterns. The soft glow from the streetlight outside painted her features in a pale amber hue. She looked so peaceful, so beautiful, and so content. It was hard to believe that just hours ago, we were on a case, and now... this.

Fuck, I thought. How the hell did we end up here?

The memories of our shared intimacy played in my mind, almost like a reel. Her lips on mine, the taste of her skin, the soft moans she tried to stifle as I explored her body. The way she responded to every touch, every kiss. The hesitant, almost shy way she'd touched me, her fingers skimming over my hardness with curiosity and eagerness. The way she'd gasped when I entered her for the first time.

Her nails digging into my back, urging me on, pushing me deeper. It was a dance of passion, of rediscovered intimacy, of two souls that had once been lost to one another finally reconnecting.

I couldn't help the swell of emotions that rose within me. It was a mixture of gratitude, guilt, and a depth of love that had lain dormant for far too long. I'd broken her heart, torn it apart, and she'd let me in again. That trust bore down on me. She'd given me another chance, and the thought of losing that trust again was terrifying.

"Shit," I whispered to myself, guilt gnawing at me. I remembered how I'd walked away from her all those years ago, too young and too stupid to realize what I was leaving behind. It was a choice that had haunted me every day since.

I kissed the top of her head, breathing in the familiar scent of her shampoo. "I won't fuck this up again," I vowed silently.

Drawing her even closer, I let the soft rise and fall of her chest lull me into a fitful sleep, holding onto the hope that the morning wouldn't take this newfound connection away.

The first thing that hit me as I blinked my eyes open was the soft light filtering through the gaps in the curtains, its glow painting the room in muted tones. The second was the sensation of Kayla's skin pressed against mine, her rhythmic breathing indicating she was still fast asleep. I shifted slightly, trying not to disturb her, and caught a glimpse of her face nuzzled into the crook of my neck. It was one of those small, serene moments, the kind you wish you could freeze and keep forever.

"Morning," she murmured, her voice husky from sleep, startling me. She shifted, her blue eyes looking up at me, filled with a warmth that mirrored my own feelings.

"Hey," I replied, my voice barely above a whisper, my fingers brushing a stray strand of hair behind her ear.

A soft smile played on her lips, but before it could fully form, she seemed to remember where we were and why we were here, and her expression shifted. The playful glint in her eyes was replaced by a look of determination. "We need to get moving," she said, pulling herself up and away from our cocoon of warmth.

"Yeah, shit, Jared," I muttered, rubbing my face with my hands, trying to shake off the lingering drowsiness.

She nodded, grabbing her clothes that were scattered around the room. "We need to find him and get answers. The sooner we wrap this up, the sooner we can get back to... well, everything else."

I understood the unsaid words hanging between us – our past, our potential future, and everything in between.

After a quick shower and dressing, we headed out, the chilly morning air waking us up further. The motel's gravel crunched beneath our feet as we walked toward the car.

The local diner was a short drive away. It had that old-school vibe with checkered tiles and neon lights. We spotted Jared almost immediately, seated at the counter with a mug of coffee and a plate of half-eaten pancakes standing behind the counter. He was taller than I expected, large with tattoos up and down his arms and a shaved head.

"Can we join you?" I asked, indicating the empty stools next to him. Jared looked up, surprise evident in his eyes, but he nodded.

"Sure, officers. Was wondering when you'd catch up to me."

Kayla raised an eyebrow but stayed silent as we took our seats. I signaled for two coffees, sensing we'd need it.

"You knew we were looking for you?" I questioned, trying to gauge his reaction.

He smirked, "Word gets around fast in a small town. Neighbor told me when I got home last night."

The waitress set down two mugs in front of us, and the rich aroma filled the air. Taking a sip, I felt the warmth spread through me, readying myself for the conversation ahead.

"Jared," Kayla began, her tone all business, "We have some questions for you."

Jared leaned back, his casual demeanor not matching the gravity of the situation. "Shoot," he said, taking another bite of his pancake.

I felt our responsibility and the urgency of our case pressing down on me. This wasn't just another interrogation; there was so much at stake. And as I looked over at Kayla, I knew she felt it too.

Kayla wasted no time, "Start from the top, Jared. Tell us about your relationship with Lexi."

He smirked, stirring his coffee nonchalantly, "Relationship? We hooked up a few times in college. Nothin' serious."

I felt a tightening in my gut. I hated how casual he was about this, especially considering the severity of the situation. "A few other people seem to think otherwise. Some said it got a bit obsessive."

Jared's eyes flashed with irritation. "Look, people talk shit. College was a blur for me, alright? Parties, booze... I barely remember half of it."

"And the other half?" I pressed.

He shrugged, "Mostly just drunk nights and bad decisions. Lexi had her share of flings. Why pin it all on me?"

Kayla's sharp gaze didn't waver. "Because multiple sources indicated you had an unhealthy fixation on her."

Jared scoffed, "What? 'Cause I liked her photo on Instagram now and then? C'mon. We were friends. If others had issues with her, that's on them."

"So, you're saying there were others?" I asked, trying to get more out of him.

He exhaled slowly, "Look, she had other guys around. College, remember? Parties, drama. But if you're trying to get me to name names, I was too wasted most of the time to keep track."

I could feel the frustration building. "You must remember something. Anything that can help us."

Jared rolled his eyes. "Yeah, there was this one dude – older guy. He seemed pretty hung up on her. But for the life of me, I can't remember his damn name. Only met him once, at some party."

Kayla looked at me, her eyes glinting with hope and exasperation. "Any idea where we can find this guy?"

Jared threw his hands up. "How should I know? It's been years!"

I leaned in, my voice low and steady. "Listen, Jared, a young woman's life might be in danger. If you know something, anything, now's the time."

His cockiness seemed to waver a bit, but he remained defiant. "Already told you all I remember."

Switching tactics, Kayla interjected, "Where were you two nights ago? All night?"

Jared looked almost relieved at the change in topic. "At work. Twelve-hour shift at the mill. Check with my supervisor if you want."

I could feel the walls closing in. Every lead seemed to be hitting a dead end. "Anyone else besides this older guy that might've had an issue with Lexi?"

Jared thought for a moment. "Not that I can remember. Look, I've been straight with you both. Yeah, we had a thing, but I moved on. Haven't talked to her in years."

I took a deep breath, trying to calm my frustration. "If you think of anything else, you let us know. Immediately."

He nodded, clearly eager to end the conversation. "Will do, officer."

As Kayla and I left the diner, I could feel our unanswered questions pressing down on me. The case seemed to be slipping through our fingers, and I wasn't sure where to go next.

Chapter Twelve

KAYLA

As we stepped back into the station, the dated case file on Lexi was my sole concern. I plunked down at my desk, spreading the paperwork in front of me.

Jake settled across, rubbing his temples. "You think Jared was telling the truth?"

I barely glanced up, my attention riveted on a particular page detailing a string of unsettling events from Lexi's college days. "Hard to say. But there's something here. Similarities. Patterns."

He looked up, curious. "What kind of patterns?"

Pulling a pen from my hair, I began underlining relevant sections. "Look, here," I said, pointing to a written account. "It mentions Lexi feeling like she was being watched during her sophomore year. Here again, two years later, notes about someone leaving anonymous notes in her mailbox."

Jake's brow furrowed, "But she never reported these?"

I shook my head, flipping a few pages. "No, it seems she brushed them off as college pranks, or maybe she was too scared. I can't believe she kept all of this a secret for so long."

"I wish she'd told me," Jake's voice had a raw edge of concern and frustration.

We sat in silence for a moment, the past and its ties to the present looming over us. My fingers traced over another list, and a name caught my eye.

"Here's something," I murmured, "a list of acquaintances, friends, maybe even flings from her college days. Any of these names ring a bell?"

Jake scanned the page. "A few, but no one that stands out as suspicious."

I sighed. "We need to dig deeper into these names. See where they are now, if any have connections to Silver Creek."

Jake nodded, his face serious. "Let's do it methodically. One by one."

I agreed, "Absolutely. But not yet. First, we need to see if we're missing any connections between then and now. We're dealing with someone who's held onto this obsession for years. There might be more to this story than we know."

There was a restlessness in Jake's demeanor. His sister's safety weighed heavily on him, especially being his first case on the force.

"We'll find this bastard, Kayla. We have to."

"We will," I affirmed, clenching my fist. The game of cat and mouse was far from over, and I was determined to win. For Lexi. For Jake. For justice.

The room was silent save for the rustling of paper and the distant hum of office chatter. As night began to cloak Silver Creek, the station's dimmed lights cast elongated shadows, creating an ambiance that seemed fitting for our ongoing investigation.

Determined, I dove back into the files, searching for the missing puzzle piece that would lead us closer to the truth.

Jake hovered by the station's exit, his worry evident. "Hey, can I drive you home?"

I hesitated for a beat before nodding. "Sure."

The ride was silent but not uncomfortable. The hum of the engine seemed to blend seamlessly with my thoughts.

As we reached my place, I turned to Jake, my voice soft. "Want to come in for a bit?"

He looked surprised but managed a slight smile. "Yeah, that'd be nice."

Inside, the atmosphere was a strange mix of tension and comfort. Jake's fingers brushed against mine as he took off his jacket, sending a shiver down my spine. I turned to face him, and without thinking, I reached out, pulling him into an embrace. The warmth of his body against mine felt grounding, yet there was a fragility to the moment.

Pulling away slightly, he met my gaze. "God, Kayla, this is all so fucked up. I'm scared for Lexi and can't shake the feeling that I'm failing her."

I cupped his cheek. "You're doing everything you can, Jake. This isn't on you."

His fingers laced with mine. "I know, but the thought of something happening to her… and then there's us. This thing between us. It's... confusing."

I sighed, leaning my forehead against his. "It's complicated, yeah, but it feels right, doesn't it?"

Jake hesitated, then nodded. "It does. And it scares the shit out of me."

A soft laugh escaped me. "Me too. But we'll figure it out. One step at a time."

We stood there for what felt like hours, absorbing the warmth and comfort of one another. When I finally pulled away, Jake's face held a new determination.

"We'll get this bastard, Kayla. For Lexi."

"I know we will," I whispered.

The next morning, the station was buzzing with activity. Leads were coming in, but they all seemed to hit dead ends.

"Damn it!" Jake's outburst caught everyone's attention as he stood up from his computer. "None of the main leads on her social media followers check out."

I moved closer, trying to find the words to calm him, but what could I say? Our relationship had shifted, and there were moments when I found it hard to separate the personal from the professional.

Jake's eyes were dark with anger and anxiety. "I can't stand this, Kayla. I need answers."

I took a deep breath, fighting the urge to pull him into a comforting embrace. "We'll find them, Jake. We just need more time."

He stared at me, the raw emotion in his eyes piercing through me. It was then that I realized the depth of our connection and the responsibility it carried. As the day wore on, I found myself battling my own emotions, trying to maintain a sense of professionalism while watching Jake grapple with his.

The precinct was packed that day. officers and detectives buzzed around, but Jake and I found ourselves at my desk, surrounded by files and notes. Our knees touched occasionally, sending little shocks through me. The close quarters only reminded me of how much closer we'd become emotionally, but the case kept us focused.

"Why the hell can't we get a solid lead?" Jake muttered, flipping through a stack of papers. "It's like chasing a fucking ghost."

I exhaled, rubbing my temples. "We need a break in the case. Something. Anything."

He shot me a sidelong glance. "Remember college? The all-nighters? I think this is gonna be one of those nights."

A soft chuckle slipped from my lips. "You know... I never thought we'd be pulling all-nighters together like this."

Our hands brushed against each other's, and a charge ran up my arm. It was ridiculous how a mere touch could send my senses into a whirlwind.

But just as quickly as the moment started, it ended. The phone on my desk rang, and I picked it up. "Detective Green."

"Kayla," Luke's voice was tight with distress. "Another message. Inside the house."

Heart pounding, I tried to keep my voice calm. "What does it say?"

Luke hesitated. "It says, 'You can't keep her safe.'"

I sucked in a sharp breath. "Lock everything. We're on our way."

I ended the call, meeting Jake's anxious gaze, and repeated what Luke had said.

"How the hell did they get past the patrol?"

"We need to figure that out," I said, grabbing my jacket.

The ride to Luke and Lexi's was tense. Jake's grip on the steering wheel was white-knuckled, and the silence was deafening.

I placed a reassuring hand on his arm. "We'll catch this bastard."

"I can't do this without you," he murmured.

"You won't have to," I whispered back.

The boundary between our personal and professional lives was blurring, but it didn't matter right now. All that mattered was our growing bond and our mutual resolve to bring Lexi's stalker to justice.

The ranch glowed in the setting sun, and despite the moment's tension, I enjoyed the golden fields and bright white of the ranch house. As I pulled up, I saw Luke and Lexi huddled together on the porch, waiting. Before Jake even fully stopped the car, he was out and rushing towards his sister, enveloping her in a tight embrace.

"Are you okay?" he whispered to her. She was trembling, trying to hold back her tears.

"I'm scared, Jake," Lexi managed to say.

Jake responded with a comforting kiss on her forehead, his concern evident. "We'll get through this."

Luke seemed weary, rubbing his neck. "Whoever it is, they've bypassed our security," he observed with a hint of dread.

I scanned the area, trying to assess the situation. "Looks like we have our work cut out for us," I remarked.

We entered the house, searching for any clues the intruder might have left. Aside from the unnerving note, nothing seemed out of place.

After a while, Jake and I found ourselves in the living room, both clearly frustrated. "This is a dead end," I muttered.

Jake ran a hand through his hair, an idea taking shape. "Luke, I think you should leave for a while. Head to my uncle's place by the lake. I doubt they'll follow you there."

Luke looked surprised. "You think it's that bad?"

Jake nodded solemnly. "It's the best option for now, until we catch whoever's behind this."

I considered it. "It might actually be a good move. Change the scene, throw the stalker off."

Lexi bit her lip, clearly conflicted. "I don't want to run, Jake. But if it's for our safety..."

Jake reassured her gently. "It's just for a little while, Lex. Trust me."

She nodded, albeit reluctantly. "Alright."

We put the plan into action immediately. As Luke packed, Jake pulled me aside. "Thanks for being here, Kay," he said earnestly.

I smiled, offering a small gesture of comfort. "That's what partners are for, right?"

Partners.

The term meant so much more now.

As we saw Lexi and Luke off, driving away to safety, the gravity of the situation weighed heavily on me. Jake had to protect his family, catch the perpetrator, and ensure everyone's safety.

"We'll solve this, Jake," I whispered, squeezing his hand for assurance. As I met his gaze, I saw a reflection of my own determination.

"I know we will."

Chapter Thirteen

JAKE

As I unlocked the front door, the muted lights inside cast a soft glow onto the porch. The drive back from Luke's ranch with Kayla had been quiet as we processed this latest development.

Mandy sat on the couch, her posture stiff, dark hair cascading around her face. I wasn't expecting to see her still up; it was far too late for casual visits.

"Hey," I started, slightly off-balance. "I didn't think you'd be awake still at this hour."

She looked up, her eyes searching mine. "I wanted to see you. I haven't in days."

There was a tone in her voice I hadn't heard before. Gone was the cheerful friendliness I'd gotten used to. Instead, it was edged with...was that resentment?

"I've been swamped with the investigation," I replied, unease clawing at my insides. "You know that."

Her lips twisted into a humorless smile. "Of course. And how's Kayla? Must be... intense working so closely with her again." There was a biting edge to her words, an undercurrent I couldn't ignore.

"She's good," I replied, my defenses raising, "It's been intense, sure, but it's a part of the job."

Mandy's gaze lingered on me a moment longer before dropping away. "It just feels like you've been distant. And not just because of work."

This wasn't the Mandy I had been getting to know. She was always so upbeat, supportive even. Now, with this cold demeanor, I wondered if our previous camaraderie had been just a facade.

"Look, I get that you're worried or maybe even pissed. But right now, Lexi's safety is my top priority." I ran a hand through my hair, the day pressing down on me.

Her cold facade momentarily cracked. "I just... missed our time, Jake. But I get it, family first."

"You have no idea what's going on, Mandy." I could feel the frustration bubbling up. "It's not just about spending time or hanging out. Someone's after my sister. It's been tough on all fronts. But I need to crash. We can talk later, okay?"

She nodded, hesitating for a moment before speaking up. "Just... don't forget about the people who are here for you too, okay?"

As I ascended the stairs, I felt guilt and unease. I'd found solace in Mandy's friendship during a difficult time in my life. But tonight's interaction threw me off-kilter. Maybe I didn't know her as well as I'd thought. Shaking off the thoughts, I reached my bedroom, seeking the oblivion of sleep.

The next day, I was looking over files at the precinct when Kayla burst in, her face flushed with urgency. "Jake, I think we have something. Remember that list of Lexi's college acquaintances she gave us? One of them, Derek Kline, lives two towns over. Worth a shot?"

My heart raced as I grabbed my jacket. "Hell yes, it's worth a shot."

Driving to Derek's place felt like the longest drive of my life. Unknown secrets weighed heavy on me. Why didn't Lexi ever mention anyone from college? What was she hiding?

We pulled up to a rundown bungalow. The lawn was wild, betraying signs of neglect. Kayla knocked firmly, and after what felt like an eternity, the door opened to reveal a disheveled-looking man. His eyes widened in recognition at the mention of Lexi's name.

"Lexi Barrows? Haven't heard that name in years. What's she done now?"

Kayla's eyebrow quirked at his tone. "She hasn't done anything. We're investigating a case that involves her. Mind if we ask a few questions?"

He hesitated before stepping aside, allowing us entry. "What do you want to know?"

I tried to control the impatience in my voice. "Did you know Lexi well in college?"

He snorted, rubbing his unshaven chin. "'Know her well'? That's a way to put it. We dated, if you could call it that. It was... complicated."

"Complicated how?" Kayla pressed.

Derek glanced at me, a smirk playing on his lips. "I was her secret. Nobody knew about us. Especially not her family, from what she told me."

The room suddenly felt too tight, the air too thin. My sister's secret relationship? "Why was it a secret?"

He shrugged. "Who knows? Maybe she was embarrassed about dating a townie. Or maybe it was something else. But it doesn't matter. It ended badly. She left without a word."

"And you've had no contact since?"

"Not a word. I tried reaching out, but she blocked me on everything. But then again, Lexi always had her... secrets."

The way he emphasized the word sent shivers down my spine. Kayla, sensing the tension, steered the conversation back on track.

"Derek, do you know anyone who might have had a grudge against her from those days? Someone who might be targeting her now?"

He leaned back, regarding us with a measured gaze. "Well, there was this one guy, Ethan. He was obsessed with her. Even after she and I started whatever it was we had, he wouldn't leave her alone. Sent her tons of messages, some pretty creepy shit. She never took it seriously, thought he was just a harmless nerd."

My fists clenched. "Do you have any idea where this Ethan might be now?"

He shook his head. "No clue. But if anyone had a reason to be pissed at Lexi from back then, it was him."

Kayla and I exchanged glances, a new lead taking shape. As we made our way to the car, a flurry of emotions raged within me. The surprise of Lexi's hidden relationship, and the revelation of a potential stalker from her past, was a lot to process.

Kayla put a hand on my arm, her touch grounding. "Hey, we'll figure this out. We're close, Jake. I can feel it."

I nodded. With Kayla by my side and a new lead to chase, I felt a renewed sense of determination.

I was on the road, parked just around the corner from Derek's place, when I decided to call Lexi. I didn't want to, not really, but it felt like the right thing to do. She needed to know about the past crawling up behind her.

The phone rang once, twice.

"Jake?" Her voice trembled on the other end.

"Lexi, there's something I need to ask you." I took a deep breath. "Do you remember someone named Derek Kline from college?" Silence. A thick, heavy pause.

Then, a whispered, "Yeah."

"You never mentioned him. He claims you two... dated."

"He wasn't wrong," she finally replied. There was a heaviness to her voice that I hadn't heard before. "We did, in secret. God, I never thought I'd have to revisit that part of my life."

"Why'd you keep it from everyone?" I pushed, trying to keep the frustration out of my voice.

There was a sigh. "He was older, Jake. And he wasn't a student. I knew what people would say, how they'd judge."

My grip on the steering wheel tightened. "Did he ever hurt you, Lex?"

"No," she said quickly, almost defensively. "It wasn't like that. It just... it ended poorly, and I wanted to leave that chapter behind."

I swallowed hard, recalling Derek's disheveled appearance and dismissive tone when talking about her. "There's another name, Lex. Ethan? Derek mentioned him. Said he was a bit... obsessive over you."

A sharp intake of breath on the other end. "Ethan? Shit, I hadn't thought about him in years. He was harmless, just a bit... intense. I can't imagine he'd be behind this, but Jake, I don't trust my own judgment anymore."

I could hear the raw vulnerability in her voice, and my heart ached for her. "It's not your fault, Lex. None of this is. We're going to figure it out, I promise."

"I know," she replied, but her voice lacked conviction. "It's just... it's been so long. Why now? Why is all this happening now?"

I didn't have an answer for her, and it killed me. "Just stay safe, okay? Luke's with you, right?"

"Yeah. He's been amazing, Jake. But I hate that he's wrapped up in all this."

A pang of guilt hit me. This was my first case on the force, and it was spiraling fast. "Look, I'm going to dig deeper into this Ethan guy, okay? You just focus on staying safe. I'll handle the rest."

She was quiet for a moment. "Thank you, Jake. For everything."

We said our goodbyes, and as I ended the call, a burning determination settled in. Whoever was behind this, I would find them. I would end this nightmare for Lexi, for all of us.

I looked over at Kayla, who'd been listening in silence. She squeezed my arm, a silent show of support. "We're close," she said, mirroring her words from earlier. "I can feel it."

The weight on my shoulders felt slightly lighter with her by my side. Together, we were a force to be reckoned with. And we were coming for the stalker.

Chapter Fourteen

KAYLA

I leaned back, the glare of the computer screen momentarily blinded me. Hours had passed as I'd delved deeper and deeper into the digital life of Ethan Mitchell, and what I found was unsettling, to say the least.

"Ethan's online footprint is... disturbing," I began, rubbing my temples.

Jake glanced over from the paperwork he'd been sifting through. "What have you got?"

"You ever heard of 'Red Room Forums'?" I asked, my eyes still on the computer.

He frowned. "No. What is it?"

"It's this sick corner of the internet, where people get off on power plays, stalking stories, and... god, it's just a cesspool of toxicity," I spat out. "Guess who's an active member?"

Jake's face darkened. "Ethan."

I nodded. "He goes by 'ShadowStalker' on there. Fitting, right?" Jake leaned over to take a closer look at the screen, his eyes scanning through posts, comments, and a myriad of disturbing content. "Jesus, this shit's real?"

"Unfortunately, yes. And there's more. He's quite vocal about his... let's say, 'disagreements' with women who 'betray' or 'abandon' him. He refers to someone named 'L' multiple times."

A chill ran down my spine, and I knew Jake felt the same. "That's got to be Lexi," he murmured.

I scrolled down, showcasing an endless list of discussions Ethan had participated in. The conversations varied from basic stalking tips to venting about personal grudges. "This guy's a damn ticking time bomb."

Jake ran his fingers through his hair, frustration evident in every line of his face. "We need more. As sick as this all is, it isn't concrete evidence against him."

I sighed. "Yeah, I know. I did find out he's working at some tech firm in the city, though. Might be worth paying a visit."

Jake nodded. "We'll head there first thing tomorrow. God, I can't believe Lexi was caught up with this creep."

"You and me both," I replied, feeling a growing sense of anger. It was one thing to suspect someone, but having it laid out, seeing the depth of their depravity... it hit differently.

I shut down the computer, feeling drained. "I need a break from this."

Jake put a comforting hand on my shoulder, giving it a light squeeze. "We'll figure this out, Kayla. One step at a time."

I looked up into his eyes, finding solace there. "Yeah," I whispered, "We will."

. . .

The evening air was warm, filled with a promise of serenity as Jake pulled up into my driveway. His tall frame emerged, moving with a certain urgency, but his eyes betrayed a vulnerability that tugged at my heartstrings.

My door swung open even before he reached it, and we wasted no time with words. Our eyes locked, and I pulled him inside, pressing him against the door as it slammed shut. The warmth of his lips met mine, his hands finding their way around my waist, pulling me closer.

His scent—woodsy with a hint of spice—surrounded me, and I lost myself in it, letting go of the fears, the frustrations, the unsolved case. For a few stolen moments, it was just us—two souls desperately seeking solace.

I trailed kisses along his jawline, my fingers working at the buttons of his shirt. His response was a soft groan, sending shivers down my spine.

But just as the world began to blur and all that remained was our entwined bodies, the shrill sound of Jake's phone pierced the room.

I pulled away, our heavy breaths syncing as we both cursed under our breaths.

"Don't answer it," I whispered, a teasing lilt to my voice.

He gave me a wry smile, picking up the device from the side table. His expression changed instantly, face hardening as he read the caller ID, "It's the station."

He took the call, and I watched as the color drained from his face.

"What? Are you sure?" he barked into the phone, eyes darting around the room, each word cutting through the previously intimate atmosphere.

"Fuck," he whispered, ending the call. He looked up, the urgency evident in his eyes. "There's been a break-in at my place."

I could feel my heart rate quicken. "What did they say? Is everyone okay?"

He was already moving towards the door, pulling on his jacket. "I don't know. They said to head home, but Mandy's been blowing up my phone, saying she's scared and doesn't know where I am."

I followed, grabbing my keys. "I'm coming with you."

His face showed gratitude and concern. "Kayla, it might not be safe."

"Like hell I'm letting you go alone. We're in this together."

The drive to Jake's house was a blur. Sirens blared as we tore through the streets of Silver Creek, anxiety mounting with every passing second.

As we pulled up, the scene was chaotic. Blue and red lights flashed, casting an eerie glow over the place. officers milled about, and my heart sank seeing the shattered glass of Jake's front door.

We both jumped out of the car, sprinting towards the entrance. An officer approached us, his face grim. "Looks like someone's sending a message, Jake."

Jake barely acknowledged him, pushing through the crowd to find Mandy. She stood there, wrapped in a blanket, mascara smudged, but physically unhurt. The relief was palpable as Jake enveloped her in a hug.

"What the hell happened?" he murmured into her hair.

She sniffled, wiping away tears. "I don't know. I just heard a loud crash, and then... I hid in the bathroom."

I moved closer, feeling an inexplicable pang of jealousy but pushing it aside. Now wasn't the time. "Did you see anyone?" She shook her head.

"No. But they left this." She handed over a crumpled note.

The Rookie's Second Chance

Jake unfolded it, and I caught a glimpse of the hastily scrawled message: "Stay out of it."

Jake's place was eerily quiet, the shattered glass and upturned furniture a stark reminder of the violation that had just occurred. I watched from a distance as Jake gently ushered Mandy into the living room, his protective instincts glaringly evident.

"You okay, Mandy?" he asked, his voice filled with genuine concern.

She nodded weakly, sniffling. "Just... just shaken, y'know? Never thought this shit would happen here."

"I know," Jake whispered, wrapping her in another hug. The intimacy of the gesture, his hand caressing her back soothingly, left a sour taste in my mouth. I took a deep breath, reminding myself of the circumstances. Mandy was scared, vulnerable. It wasn't about Jake and me right now.

Still, watching Jake with her, the way she leaned into him, seeking comfort and solace, stirred feelings I didn't want to acknowledge.

Jake set about making tea, his movements deliberate, a method to bring some semblance of normalcy to the chaos. "You want some, Kay?" he called out.

I shook my head, though the normalcy did sound tempting. "No, thanks. I think we should discuss our next steps."

But before we could delve into the investigation, Jake was back at Mandy's side, handing her the cup. "Drink this. It'll help."

Mandy took a tentative sip, her hands trembling slightly. "Thanks, Jake," she murmured, her voice barely above a whisper. The vulnerability in her eyes was a far cry from the strong, independent Mandy I knew.

After a few moments, she spoke again, her voice stronger. "I think I should head to bed. Need to... to clear my head."

Jake nodded, giving her shoulder a gentle squeeze. "Get some rest. Holler if you need anything."

As Mandy retreated, I watched Jake, noticing the weight on his shoulders. He was hurting, conflicted. This was his home, his sanctuary. And someone had dared to breach it.

"Jake," I began, stepping closer. "Are you—"

He cut me off, the pain evident in his eyes. "I can't believe this shit, Kayla. This was supposed to be safe. Now... now I don't even know who the hell I can trust."

I reached out, placing my hand on his arm. The contact was electric. "Hey," I whispered. "I've got your back. Always."

He looked at me, the raw emotion in his eyes making my heart skip a beat. "Let's go to my room. We need to talk."

His room was untouched. He sat down on the edge of the bed, patting the space next to him. I sat down, our thighs brushing, the intimacy of the gesture sending shivers down my spine.

He sighed deeply, running his fingers through his hair. "I just... I can't wrap my head around this. My home, Kayla. My goddamn home. If they can get here, where the fuck can't they?"

I placed a reassuring hand on his knee. "We'll figure this out, Jake. Together."

He looked up, and for a moment, it was just us—united against a common enemy. The distance between our lips closed rapidly, our kiss deep, desperate—a reassurance, a promise.

Pulling away, I rested my forehead against his, our ragged breaths syncing. "We've got this, Jake."

He nodded, his resolve evident. "Yeah, we do."

Chapter Fifteen

JAKE

The smell of coffee pulled me from my sleep, and as I groggily rolled over, my first thought wasn't of the broken glass or the violation of my home but rather the events of last night. Kayla's touch, our kiss. Pushing those thoughts aside, I slowly got up and headed to the kitchen.

There, I found Mandy moving frantically, a pan sizzling on the stove and a pot of coffee brewing. Her movements were erratic, a clear sign of her distress from last night's events. It struck me then how much she had been thrown by the break-in. She came here to visit Lexi, not to get involved in this mess.

"Morning," I mumbled, rubbing my eyes.

Mandy nearly jumped out of her skin, clutching the spatula like a weapon. "Shit, Jake! You scared me."

I held my hands up in surrender. "Sorry, wasn't my intention."

She took a deep breath, trying to calm her racing heart. "It's okay, just... everything's got me on edge."

I approached her, placing a hand on her shoulder,

feeling the tension under my fingers. "I know, Mandy. I'm so sorry you got dragged into this."

She gave a weak chuckle. "It's not like you planned a break-in for my entertainment."

There was a pause as I studied her, the bags under her eyes and the weariness of her posture. "You know," I began, "you don't have to make breakfast."

She sighed, looking down. "I just... needed to do something. Keep my mind busy."

I moved closer, enveloping her in a hug. She clung to me, her body trembling slightly. I realized, in that moment, how deeply the invasion had impacted her. Mandy had always been this firecracker, bursting with life and energy. Now, she felt vulnerable, lost.

"It's gonna be okay," I murmured, rubbing her back gently. "I won't let anything happen to you."

She pulled back, looking up at me, her blue eyes searching mine. There was an intensity there, a longing. I recognized it because I had seen it before. In Kayla. In others who had looked at me that way. Mandy was seeing me as more than a friend.

And, against my better judgment, I let her. I didn't dissuade her or pull away. Because, in that moment, she needed me. Not as a friend or an investigator, but as a protector. And so, I stayed.

The morning progressed with an unspoken understanding. Mandy continued making breakfast, and I helped where I could. We didn't talk about the break-in or the investigation or the looming threats. Instead, we talked about her trip, her work, and mundane topics that brought a semblance of normalcy.

Yet, throughout our conversation, there was an undercurrent of something more—a deepening connection that neither of us acknowledged. I could feel it, but I pushed it aside. Mandy was just visiting. She'd be gone soon, once this ordeal with Lexi's stalker was over, and everything would go back to normal.

The setting sun outside the station window cast long shadows across the room as Kayla and I sat huddled over my laptop, our fingers rapidly typing and scrolling through various websites.

"Here," she pointed at the screen, her voice dripping with excitement. "Ethan's posts."

I pulled up a forum that seemed to be dedicated to college reunions and stories, but a few posts stood out. These weren't just tales of drunken nights or study sessions. They hinted at something darker, more covert.

"Listen to this," I began, reading aloud, "'Remember the gatherings at The Vault? Those were the days. Not everyone got in. Only those truly worthy. Some secrets remain buried.' What the hell is The Vault?"

Kayla leaned back, rubbing her temples. "Sounds like some secret society bullshit. Exclusive parties, secret handshakes, and God knows what else."

Scouring the thread, I found multiple mentions of The Vault by different users, but Ethan's comments stood out. He seemed not just a participant but a key player. There were implications of silent deals, covert meetings, and cryptic messages that seemed to be shared only among select members.

"Damn," I muttered. "If Lexi was a part of this, she never breathed a word of it. Not a single hint."

Kayla exhaled deeply, her brows furrowed in thought. "It's not entirely surprising. Maybe she wanted to keep her past buried. God, Jake, if she was involved with this crowd, who knows what they did."

I scrolled further, discovering more posts by Ethan, which hinted at his involvement and possibly even a leadership role within this society. "This one's from a couple of months ago," I noted, reading out, "'The Vault lives on. Our influence extends beyond college. For those who know, you understand. Loyalty above all else.'"

Kayla chewed on her lip, concern evident in her eyes. "This is bigger than we thought, Jake. This isn't just some college fling gone wrong. This is... this is some next-level organized shit."

I leaned back, rubbing my neck. "We need to tread carefully. If Lexi was deeply involved, there's no telling who else from this town might be tied to it."

"And if they know we're onto them?" Kayla's voice trembled slightly, a rare hint of fear.

I took a deep breath, locking eyes with her. "Then we're in deeper shit than we ever imagined. But we've got to protect Lexi. And get to the bottom of this."

Kayla nodded, determination steeling her features. "Let's find out more about The Vault. There has to be someone, some trace, that can lead us to what they're about."

We dug deeper, uncovering fragments of information that painted a shadowy picture of The Vault's activities—exclusive parties where only the elite were invited, whispers of backdoor deals, and ominous dealings that were kept strictly hushed.

Our discovery pressed on my mind, but as the hours ticked by, another issue gnawed at me: returning home. Now that I realized the nature of her feelings, the idea of being alone with Mandy tied a knot in my stomach. I didn't want to lead her on, and I didn't want to be cruel, but I also didn't want to be alone with her. God, what a mess.

"Let's order some takeout," I said. "We can have dinner here and investigate this Vault some more."

Kayla smiled. "That sounds great!"

Chapter Sixteen

JAKE

The crunch of gravel under my boots sounded like an alarm as I walked up to my front door. It was late; I had hoped Mandy would be asleep. The flicker of light through the window and the silhouette of her sitting at the kitchen table punched a quiet sigh out of me. I had not planned for this, for the quiet one-on-one that seemed laden with things unsaid.

Pushing the door open, I found her there, staring at two plates of spaghetti that had long gone cold. A glass of water sat by my plate, beads of condensation racing down its side, mirroring my own desire to escape.

"Hey," I greeted, my voice sounding worn.

She looked up. Her smile was hopeful but tinged with something else, something like loneliness. "Hey! You're home. Are you hungry?"

I ran a hand through my hair, the other finding its way to my back pocket. "No, not really. I grabbed a bite with Kayla. Work stuff, you know?"

Her smile flickered, but she recovered quickly. "That's okay. Sit with me for a bit?"

The knot in my stomach tightened, but I nodded and pulled out the chair. "Sure."

She resumed eating, a quiet symphony of fork against plate filling the space between us.

"You don't have to stay here on account of me," I said after a moment, watching her push spaghetti around her plate.

Mandy looked up, her eyes holding a glimmer of something raw. "After the break-in, I don't know… I just feel safer with someone around."

"Shit, Mandy, I'm sorry," I murmured, the guilt coiling tighter. "I should've been here."

She shook her head, reaching out to touch my hand briefly. I wanted to pull away, but didn't want her to feel alone. "You can't glue yourself to the house, Jake. You have a life and a job. I get it."

We fell into a kind of rhythm, small talk that danced around the edges of the deeper, murkier waters we were avoiding—namely, the way she was barely hiding her interest, which I was doing my best to keep in a platonic territory. I told her about some harmless work antics, keeping it light, while she talked about a book she'd been reading.

As the minutes ticked by, I could see the tension easing out of her shoulders, her laugh more genuine, and the shadows under her eyes less pronounced.

I let her talk, let her fill the space with words that didn't probe too deep. Every once in a while, I'd answer with a nod or a chuckle, but my mind was on the case, on Lexi, and on the plate of food in front of me that I didn't eat.

Her fork finally rested beside her nearly empty plate. "Thanks for sitting with me, Jake."

"Yeah, of course," I replied, pushing my untouched food away, anxious to get to my room and have some time alone. "I'm gonna hit the sack. Big day tomorrow."

She nodded, though the longing in her eyes was clear. "Good night, Jake."

"Night, Mandy."

I flicked off the kitchen light, leaving only the soft glow of the living room lamp to guide her way to bed later. As I closed my bedroom door behind me, the muffled sound of her fork scraping the last bits of her meal was like a whisper, reminding me of the responsibilities I had, the ones I didn't ask for but felt all the same.

My bedroom felt like a refuge as I kicked off my boots and flopped onto the bed. The text icon on my phone blinked with a message from Kayla, and a grin tugged at my lips despite the evening's awkwardness.

"Just got home," I texted back. "Tonight was fun, even with the creepy Vault discovery."

The three dots that signaled her reply seemed to take an eternity. "It felt like old times. No, scratch that. It felt better than any old time."

Her message warmed something inside me, a contrast to the chill of the sheets against my skin. I stared at the ceiling, the glow from my phone casting shadows around the room.

"But hey, I gotta admit something," I typed, my thumbs hesitating over the keys.

"What's up?" she replied almost instantly.

"It's Mandy... she's getting this look in her eyes. I think she's taking a liking to me, and I don't wanna lead her on or hurt her."

The three dots appeared and vanished, once, twice, before her message came through. "Shit, that's a tight spot. But you're a good guy, Jake. She's lucky to have someone to feel safe around."

"Yeah, but it's not just that. I feel protective of her, with the stalker shit going on. It's all tangled up."

"You can be protective without it meaning more. Just be straight with her, and with me, okay?"

I let out a breath I didn't know I'd been holding. "Always, Kayla. I'm with you on this. You know that, right?"

"I do. We'll figure it out. Together."

I smiled in the dark, comforted by her words, by the feeling of being a team. It felt like a weight had been lifted, like I could breathe a bit easier.

"Goodnight, Kayla," I sent after a moment, my eyelids heavy.

"Sweet dreams, Jake."

I set the phone down, the screen's light fading to black. The silence of the house settled around me, Mandy's presence a silent sentinel in the room next door. I felt the pull of sleep dragging me under, but my mind played over Kayla's words, a mantra to keep the complications at bay.

We'll figure it out. Together.

With that thought cradling my worries, I surrendered to sleep, hoping the dreams would be sweet indeed.

Chapter Seventeen

MANDY

Chopping the carrots felt therapeutic, the knife hitting the cutting board in a steady rhythm. I'd chosen spaghetti Bolognese because who the hell doesn't like a good pasta dish? I could do with comfort food and figured Jake could, too, with all this crap going on. The sauce was already bubbling on the stove, filling the kitchen with a rich, herby smell.

I paused, glancing around the empty kitchen. It was just me, which, let's be honest, was both a relief and a knot of disappointment. The house was too quiet, too big for just one person. I shook off the feeling and went back to my task. Focus on the now, Mandy. Make it perfect.

As I stirred the sauce, I let myself daydream a little. It wasn't wrong to want something, right? I knew Jake wasn't mine to want, but shit, the heart wants what it wants, and my stupid heart was practically beating out of my chest for the guy.

I caught myself pressing my lips together, a weird flutter in my stomach as I remembered the way Jake's eyes would linger on Kayla. I had no fucking clue what was going on between them, but I wasn't blind. They had... something.

"A spark," I muttered to the steaming sauce, my hand tightening on the wooden spoon. "But sparks can fizzle out, right?"

I added a pinch of salt, more out of restlessness than necessity. I knew I was playing with fire, staying here, cooking in his kitchen, pretending like I had a place in his life. But wasn't that the whole point? To make a place for myself?

I laughed, a short, sharp sound. It wasn't like I was planning to bunny-boil him into loving me. I just needed to... I don't know, shine a bit brighter when he was around.

I glanced at the clock. Where was he anyway? Probably with her. The thought left a sour taste in my mouth that no amount of culinary success could mask.

"Fuck it," I whispered to the empty room. "I'm not leaving. Not yet." I wasn't a quitter. I'd stick around because the Mandy I knew didn't back down from a challenge. Jake needed to see what he was missing, needed to realize I was right here, and I was fucking awesome.

I took a breath, letting the scent of the sauce calm me. Okay, maybe I was a bit obsessed. But I was here for Lexi, too, right? Right. I could multitask. Protect my friend and maybe, just maybe, turn Jake's head.

I plated the pasta, garnishing it with fresh basil leaves I'd torn with my own hands, making it look as inviting as possible. For a moment, I allowed myself the fantasy of him walking through the door, his eyes lighting up at the sight of the meal, the way they'd light up for her. I'd be cool, casual. I'd say something witty, and he'd laugh, and it'd be like all those stupid rom-coms where the guy suddenly realizes he's in love with the quirky girl next door.

I was elbow-deep in suds, scrubbing the saucepan,

when I thought back to college. Freshman year, when Lexi and I were still getting our bearings as roommates and figuring out whether we would be friends or just cohabitants. God, there was this one party…

It was one of those college parties where the music was too loud and the beer too warm, a blur of faces and laughter in a cramped dorm room. I remember feeling out of place, clutching a red plastic cup like a lifeline as Garrett caught my eye.

I'd watched him from across the room, his arm slung casually around Lexi. He had that easy smile, that confident lean-against-the-wall stance that drew people to him. The kind of guy that never seemed to look my way, always laughing with the pretty girls, the ones who didn't try too hard, whose laughs were light and easy. Not like mine, which always sounded like I was trying to prove something.

He and Lexi started seeing each other within days of the semester beginning, and he was always in our room. I couldn't stop myself from looking over at them, wrapped in each other's arms, every damn night, wishing those arms were around me instead. Wishing that I could be wanted like that.

I leaned against the counter, letting the warm water run over my hands as the memory played out. I was jealous back then, green to the core, feeling like I was always on the outside looking in. It wasn't about any specific person, not really. It was about wanting to be seen, to be chosen. I wanted to matter.

There was a twinge in my chest, a tightness that echoed that old feeling. I turned off the faucet, watching the water swirl down the drain. It was that same old yearning, twisting up inside me now for Jake. I couldn't help but draw parallels, how history seemed keen on repeating itself.

I sighed, drying my hands on a dish towel, trying to

shake off the past. "Get a grip, Mandy," I scolded myself softly. It's not the same. I'm not that insecure freshman anymore.

But the knot remained, stubborn and unyielding, as I remembered the end of that party. How I'd laughed too loud, drank too much, trying to make someone notice me. The details of the evening were hazy, the faces and conversations melting into a smear of insignificance.

I never wanted to feel that way again, like a secondary character in someone else's story. I wanted to be the lead, the one who caught the eye, held the interest. And so I fought against that old narrative, pushed it down where it belonged—in the past.

I went back to my meal prep, cutting the bread and laying out the dishes with more care than necessary. It was almost like setting a stage, each item deliberately placed. I'd make sure this evening would be different. I'd be different.

The kitchen was my domain—a fact that became clear as I navigated it with ease, a dance I'd perfected over the last few weeks. The sizzle of garlic hitting the pan was the score to my thoughts, as they often were when I allowed myself to slip into the past.

College—those years were a mixtape of highs and lows, and Garrett was a track that had been played too often in Lexi's room, our room. I remembered the way she had crumbled when he left, as if he'd taken pieces of her with him. And I, always the reliable one, had picked them up, one by one. It was during those tear-streaked nights and the coffee-fueled mornings that followed I had become her rock, her steadfast.

I shook my head, stirring the sauce with more vigor than necessary. "Not this time," I muttered. The sauce splattered, a droplet landing on my hand, the sting grounding me back to the present. The pain was fleeting, a spark then gone, much like the memory of Garrett.

My bond with Lexi was a tapestry of those moments—each thread a heartbreak, a celebration, a late-night secret shared between only us. It was intimate, exclusive, and damn, it was empowering. I had thrived in that closeness, had basked in the role of the one who was needed, who was essential.

I took a big scoop of the sauce with my ladle, pouring it artfully over the pasta, my mind whirling with a new determination. I wasn't just a consolation prize, a second choice, or a shoulder to cry on. No, I was a fucking prize, and it was high time Jake saw that too.

"I was there for her, always," I said to my reflection on the chrome fridge. "And I can be that for you, Jake. I'll be your goddamn haven."

My heart raced with a cocktail of excitement and nerves. I didn't just want to be present in his life; I wanted to be his confidant, his peace after the storm, the one he'd come home to—not because I was the only one there, but because he wanted me, needed me.

The table was set, the lights dimmed to the right ambiance. I brushed a stray lock of hair behind my ear, my stomach fluttering. It wasn't just dinner; it was a testament to my resolve.

Tonight, I wouldn't be the girl from the party, overlooked and forgotten. I'd be the woman in his kitchen, impossible to ignore, someone whose presence was a comfort, a warmth he wouldn't want to shake off.

The moment I heard the door swing open, my heart raced. He was back—Jake was home. And despite the tinge of disappointment that he wasn't looking at me the way I wanted him to, I couldn't help the rush of excitement.

"Hey," I said, trying to make my voice as warm and welcoming as possible. "How was your day?"

He shrugged, his face etched with exhaustion. "Long. The case... it's a lot of work. I'm lucky I've got Kayla on my team."

As the words spilled from his lips, I couldn't help the pang of jealousy that surged through me. Kayla—always Kayla. It was like a broken record, one that wouldn't stop playing, no matter how many times I tried to tune it out.

I plastered a smile on my face, fighting back the urge to beg him to be with me. "That's great, Jake. You two make a great team."

He nodded, not really looking at me. It was as if I were part of the furniture, an object in the room that didn't require his full attention.

Dinner was served, the food untouched, the conversation limited to a few sentences here and there. The more I tried to engage him, the more I felt the distance between us grow. He was a planet, and I was just a satellite orbiting in his periphery.

The dishes clinked and clattered as I cleared the table, my thoughts swirling in a chaotic storm. I had to find a way to win him over, to make him see that I was the one who could be there for him. It wouldn't be easy, but I was determined. I couldn't be just a consolation prize.

As he retreated to bed, I watched him, longing and frustration swirling inside me. He was right there, so close yet so far away. I wanted to be the one to ease his worries, to be the person he leaned on.

Once the kitchen was spotless, I retreated to my temporary room, my mind whirring with plans and possibilities. I wasn't going to give up. I was going to find a way into his heart, to make him see me for who I was, not just as a friend but as something more.

I let out a breath I didn't know I was holding and smiled to myself. It was just a matter of time. Jake would see me, really see me, and I'd be there like I was for Lexi, steadfast and true.

And until then, I'd wait with the patience of a saint and the subtle maneuvering of a chess master. Because I knew how to play this game—I'd been playing it all my life.

Chapter Eighteen

JAKE

I slipped through the door of the precinct, the familiar buzz of radios and ringing phones greeting me like an old, persistent friend. I looked over at Kayla as I shrugged off my jacket; she was hunched over her desk, papers fanned out like a deck of cards laid out for a fortune telling.

"Morning," I said, aiming for casual. But there was a warmth there, a private sunshine that I hoped reached her across the room.

She glanced up, a ghost of a smile flickering across her face, gone as quickly as it appeared. But it was enough. It was our little secret handshake.

I settled at my desk, trying not to look too eager as I booted up my computer. "What've you got?" I asked, leaning back to watch her, tired but gorgeous, the pretense of checking emails just a cover. I tried not to be obvious as I looked at her, the way, even in our standard issue police uniforms, she managed to look like a bombshell, all legs and curves, accented by the perfect placement of her belt on her waist.

She slightly adjusted the angle at which she sat, giving me the slightest peek down the "v" made by her top buttons. It could have been an accident if not for the slight curling of her lips at the sides to let me know she caught me looking.

She leaned back, rubbing her temples. "I kept digging into the society. And I..." She trailed off, meeting my gaze with a steady one of her own. "I think Lexi might've been involved with it."

"Christ," I muttered, rubbing a hand over my face. "If my little sister was mixed up in some Eyes Wide Shut bullshit, I—"

Kayla let out a soft laugh, a genuine one this time. "We don't know anything for sure yet. But, Jake, this is deep. And dark."

A leaden feeling settled in my gut. "Just how deep does this rabbit hole go?"

"We're just on the edge of it. But I have a feeling..." She paused, eyes narrowing as she scanned the documents again. "I have a feeling we're about to find out."

I nodded, my jaw setting firm. This was what we did – followed the leads, uncovered the dark. But it was personal now, and that made the darkness seem all the denser.

I rubbed the back of my neck, the world feeling like it rested squarely on my shoulders. Kayla caught the gesture, the corners of her mouth tipping downward for a split second before she squared her own shoulders.

"I'll handle the society stuff," she said, and I could hear the determination steeling her voice. "You don't need to dive into that shit, especially if it's about Lexi."

I nodded, grateful, but a nasty feeling curled in my gut, like I was shirking my duties as a brother. I was about to protest, to claim that I could handle it, when her phone rang, cutting through the tension.

Kayla answered, her tone professional but tight. "Ethan, we need to talk about your college days."

I watched her, reading the conversation in the play of her expressions. Her brows drew together; her lips pressed into a thin line. Whatever Ethan was spitting back, it wasn't making her happy.

"Yeah? Well, that's not gonna cut it," she shot back, irritation spiking her words. There was a pause, a moment where her gaze flicked to mine, and I knew Ethan was giving her the runaround. "In person? Seriously?"

She hung up with a click, her eyes flashing. "He's being a dodgy asshole. Says he'll only talk if we do it face to face."

"And he's on the East Coast?" I asked, the pieces falling into place like a fucked-up puzzle.

"Yep, where all this shit started." She looked at me, and I could see the 'what now?' hanging unspoken between us.

"We're running out of damn leads, Kayla." I stood up and started pacing. "We might need to make the trip. We can keep poking around here, but Silver Creek's only giving up so much."

Her chair squeaked as she stood, mirroring my restlessness. "I know. And the trip could give us what we need to really crack this thing wide open."

I stopped and faced her, feeling the pull of that damn sense of duty. "Let's plan for it. But first, let's squeeze Silver Creek till it bleeds dry of information. The stalker is or was here. There has to be some trace of him."

A sharp nod from Kayla, and we were back in it, heads together, planning our next move. But I couldn't shake the feeling that we were stepping into a storm that we could only hope to survive.

The door to the evidence room closed with a click that

seemed too loud in the silence that enveloped us. Kayla shot me a look full of determination and that raw edge that came with hunting for something personal. I felt it, too, like a thrum under my skin, the need for answers about Lexi's stalker pushing me on.

"Alright, let's dig through this crap from the break-in again. Maybe we missed something," I muttered, scanning the shelves lined with bagged items and tagged evidence.

Kayla nodded, her hand brushing mine as she reached for a box. "Yeah, sometimes it takes a fresh—"

Her words cut off when my hand found hers, gripping it firmly. She looked up, her eyes locking with mine, and for a moment, there was nothing in the world but us. No stalker, no unsolved cases, just Kayla and the way my heart seemed to beat in time with hers.

Before I could second-guess it, I leaned in, and our lips met in a kiss that was half desperation, half reassurance. It was a moment of something good amidst all the shit we were wading through.

A sound from the door had us springing apart like guilty teenagers. I glanced at the entrance, half-expecting to see our boss or another detective. But it was nothing, just the echo of the station, the creaks and groans of the building settling.

We stared at each other, and then the absurdity of it hit. The tension broke, and we both laughed, low and quiet. "Fuck, that was close," I whispered, the adrenaline from the near miss mixing with the rush from her lips.

Kayla's laugh was a hushed sound, but it filled the room with something light, something needed. "Yeah, we're definitely not teenagers anymore," she said, her eyes bright with mischief and something else, something deeper.

I shook my head, still chuckling, and turned back to the task at hand. But that shared moment of humor lingered, hanging between us like a promise that no matter how dark things got, we had this—us—to come back to. It was a sliver of normal in the chaos, and I'd take it, every damn time.

Chapter Nineteen

KAYLA

That night, the station was quiet. I stayed behind after Jake left, knowing there was more work to be done. I dug deeper into the research, determined to uncover any hidden secrets about this secretive society.

As I scoured the internet for any mention of this clandestine organization, my thoughts often drifted to Jake. I knew that if there was a sexual component to this society, it would be uncomfortable for him to learn about his sister's involvement. I couldn't imagine what it would feel like to discover such a thing about a loved one, and I was determined to spare him from that pain.

Hours passed, and I found myself reaching a frustrating dead end. There was barely any information available about the secret society, let alone any details that would hint at a sexual nature. It was maddening, but I couldn't give up. I had to find a way to get to the truth.

I tapped out an email to the chief, requesting approval for a trip out east to meet with Ethan, the elusive link to this enigmatic society. I explained our need for more information and the urgency of the situation, hoping he would grant us permission.

The chief's response came sooner than I expected, and my heart soared with relief as I read the approval. We were a go. I quickly called Jake, my excitement barely contained.

"Hey," I said when he answered, "We have a flight in the morning. We're going to meet Ethan."

He didn't hesitate. "Okay. I guess I should get some sleep then, huh? Unless... you wanted to come over?"

I paused, considering his invitation. A part of me longed to be with him, to share the same space, even if we couldn't reveal our relationship at the station. But I knew there would be days together without the need for secrecy soon.

"I would, but I have to pack," I replied. "Besides, we'll have days together without having to sneak around."

There was a hint of disappointment in his voice as he responded, "Yeah, you're right. I'll, uh... see you bright and early. Sleep well."

I smiled even though he couldn't see it. "You too, Jake. I'll see you in the morning."

We boarded the morning flight to Miami, the city where Lexi had attended college, a place that might hold the key to unraveling the mysteries surrounding her past. The journey was long, and silence filled the air between Jake and me. There was anticipation and anxiety as we neared our destination.

Upon our arrival, we quickly got checked into the hotel. We paid for two rooms, as the station would be covering the expenses, but it was an unspoken agreement that we would share one. As we entered Jake's room, he flopped down onto the bed, exhaustion evident in his demeanor.

I hesitated for a moment before breaking the silence.

"We really should go try to find Ethan," I said, an underlying urgency in my tone.

"Yeah, probably," Jake replied, his voice heavy with fatigue. "Why would I make any choices that would lead to me getting back out of this bed? If I stay, I can lay here and stare at you looking all sexy."

My cheeks flushed crimson, and I turned to face him, aiming to be seductive. However, it was clear that I was still navigating the territory of such encounters, my inexperience shining through. A hint of amusement flickered in Jake's eyes as he seemed to recognize my newfound efforts.

Unperturbed, he rose from the bed and closed the distance between us. His lips met mine in a hungry kiss, and my body melted against his, longing and desire coursing through me. Our tongues danced together, a passionate tangle of lust, and my fingers instinctively found their way to his shirt, pulling it from his pants with a wanton, unchaste eagerness. The kiss was a fervent promise, a declaration of our yearning and the electricity that crackled between us.

We stayed locked in that searing kiss, lost in each other, the rest of the world fading into insignificance. The room was filled with the heady scent of desire, and the heat of our bodies pressed against one another was undeniable. Jake's hands found my waist, his touch setting my skin ablaze, and the fierce desire between us refused to be tamed.

As the kiss deepened, I let out a soft moan of pleasure, my body quivering with the intensity of our connection. The boundaries of our professional relationship had been crossed, and there was no turning back.

The taste of Jake's lips was an intoxicating addiction, and I surrendered to it, our tongues dancing with a newfound urgency.

His hands were firm but gentle as they traced the contours of my body, a soft dominance that sent shivers down my spine. He pulled me closer, and the heat of his body pressed against mine ignited a need within me. My fingers slipped under the fabric of his shirt, craving the feel of his warm skin.

Jake's lips left mine, tracing a path down my jaw and neck, igniting a burning fire within me. His breath against my skin sent delicious tremors throughout my body, and I yearned for more.

"Kayla," he whispered, his voice a sultry caress, "you're so damn sexy."

His words were like a bolt of electricity, jolting through me with a fierce thrill. My fingers tangled in his hair, holding him close as he guided me with his gentle strength. His mouth found my collarbone, and his soft kisses left a trail of longing in their wake.

I could feel his hardness pressed against my hip. My body arched, seeking more of him, more of that delicious friction.

He cupped my cheek, his thumb tracing my bottom lip. "You drive me fucking wild will never forgive myself for ever letting you go, Kayla."

His words fueled my desire, and I tugged at his shirt, desperate to feel his bare skin against mine. As the fabric fell to the floor, his naked chest pressed against me, his heartbeat echoing my own frenzied pulse.

With each kiss, each caress, I surrendered to the passionate frenzy that enveloped us. Jake's touch left me wanting more, and I knew that I was already his.

Our lips remained locked in a desperate kiss as Jake's hands, steady and sure, began the slow journey down my body. He undressed me with a tantalizing patience that sent shivers of anticipation racing through my veins.

Our kisses were fierce and consuming, but his touch was gentle, almost reverent. His fingers traced the curve of my shoulder, the softness of my skin, leaving a trail of fire wherever they roamed. With every caress, my desire for him intensified.

Jake's mouth left mine, and he peppered kisses down my neck, his lips trailing a path of heat that left me breathless. The warmth of his breath against my skin was a sweet torment.

As he unbuttoned my shirt, the thrill of exposure surged through me. I let out a sigh of anticipation, vulnerability, and aching need. My chest heaved as he slid the fabric off my shoulders, revealing the contours of my breasts to his intense gaze.

"Fuck, Kayla," he murmured, his voice laced with hunger. "You're so damn beautiful."

His words were like a caress, adding to the mounting intensity of the moment. The knowledge that he desired me with such fervor made my heart race. His thumb brushed over my hardened nipple, sending a jolt of pleasure through me. I arched my back, silently begging for more.

His fingers traced the gentle curves of my breasts, and the sensation was electrifying. I moaned as he leaned in, his lips capturing my hardened nipple, and he suckled gently, sending ripples of pleasure through me. My fingers found their way into his hair, holding him close as I surrendered to the pleasure he evoked.

Jake's hands continued their sensual exploration, tracing every contour of my body with an intimacy that left me trembling. As he unzipped my pants and tugged them down, the cool air against my exposed skin sent a thrill down my spine.

His lips found mine once more, and the fiery kiss was a

testament to our shared desire. My hands moved to his belt, eager to return the favor, and I began to undress him in kind.

"Kayla," he whispered, his voice filled with a sweet urgency, "I need to touch you everywhere."

The raw desire in his words sent shivers of anticipation racing down my spine. With a sultry smile, I nodded, granting him the permission he sought.

Jake gently guided me toward the bed, his hands never leaving my body. The moment I lay down, he covered me with his powerful frame, his lips trailing kisses down my throat, over my collarbone, and lower, igniting my skin with each caress. I gasped and writhed beneath him, overwhelmed by the heady mix of pleasure and longing.

My body thrummed with hunger as Jake continued his passionate exploration. He kissed his way down my torso, leaving a trail of scorching fire, and his lips traced the contours of my abdomen with a teasing tenderness that made me writhe with desire. I couldn't tear my eyes away from his heated gaze, a silent plea for more dancing between us.

His mouth traveled lower, down my thigh, and the wet heat of his breath sent shivers coursing through me. I gasped as he moved between my legs, his lips parting the soft, sensitive flesh that ached for his touch. The sensation was electrifying, and I let out a soft, needy moan.

"God, Kayla," he whispered, his voice heavy with desire. "I need to taste you."

I could only manage a fervent nod in response. With a delicious slowness, Jake lowered his head, his tongue trailing a path along my inner thigh. The anticipation was exquisite torture, and I trembled as I waited for his mouth to reach my throbbing center.

When his tongue finally met my most sensitive spot, I

cried out, my body convulsing with pleasure. The wet, velvety warmth of his mouth sent waves of bliss crashing over me, and I clutched the sheets, desperate for more.

Jake's mouth and tongue moved with a relentless determination, his fingers gripping my thighs with a firm, possessive touch. He was in control, guiding me to the brink of ecstasy, and I surrendered to the overwhelming pleasure he bestowed upon me.

"Jake, please," I whimpered, my voice thick with desire. "Don't stop."

He responded by increasing the intensity of his ministrations, his tongue expertly dancing over my swollen clit. I arched my back and moaned as I reached the precipice of climax, the intensity building with each electrifying touch.

With a final, skilled flick of his tongue, Jake pushed me over the edge, and I screamed his name as pleasure crashed over me in a tidal wave of ecstasy. My body convulsed with the force of it, and I clung to him, my heart racing and my breath ragged.

As I slowly came back down from the dizzying heights of pleasure, Jake crawled up my body, capturing my lips in a searing kiss. I could taste the intoxicating mix of us on his tongue, and the intensity of our connection left me breathless.

I clung to him, my fingers tracing the contours of his back, feeling the play of taut muscles beneath my touch.

"Jake," I whispered, my voice laden with need. "I want to taste you too."

He locked eyes with me, his desire mirroring my own, and without a word, he shifted to give me better access. His arousal stood proud and eager, the sight of him leaving me breathless with anticipation.

I took him into my hand, feeling the heat and hardness of his cock against my palm. With a delicate touch, I traced my fingers along his length, eliciting a guttural moan from Jake. His breath quickened as I continued to explore him, my fingers dancing with a gentle but firm grip.

"Fuck, Kayla," he groaned, his voice thick with desire. "You feel so good."

I leaned in, capturing the tip of his cock with my lips, and he gasped in pleasure. The sensation was electrifying, and I reveled in the feeling of him hardening further within my mouth. I couldn't imagine having given this moment, this first, to anyone else. I closed my lips around him, moving with a sensual rhythm that left us both craving more.

Chapter Twenty

JAKE

Her mouth enveloped me, and I moaned. I straddled her chest, my heart pounding with desire and love. The connection we shared was unlike anything I had ever experienced. I knew I loved her, had known it all along, even when we were supposed to keep things professional. But it was too soon to say it out loud. I just hoped she could see it in my eyes.

She looked up at me, her gaze filled with desire, and I couldn't think of anything more beautiful. Our eyes locked, and in that moment, it was just us, lost in the intensity of our connection. It was more than physical; it was emotional and profound.

I gasped as she continued, her mouth working wonders, her lips and tongue driving me to the brink of ecstasy. The feeling was so overwhelming, and all I could think about was her and how much she meant to me.

My fingers found their way into her hair, gently guiding her, and I whispered her name, my voice laced with need. "God, you're incredible."

She increased her pace, her movements deliberate and

passionate. It was like she knew exactly what I needed, and it was driving me insane with pleasure. I watched her, captivated by the sight of her taking me in, her eyes locked on mine.

I could feel the tension building within me, and I knew I was getting close. My hips moved in rhythm with her, and I could hardly contain myself. I wanted to give her all of me, to let her know how much she meant to me, but I also didn't want this incredible moment to end.

I pulled away, my desire for her evident in my eyes, but I needed something more. "Baby," I panted, "I don't want to finish that way."

She nodded, understanding my need to be closer, to be more connected, and straddled my hip. Slowly, she guided me inside her.

We moved together, slowly, passionately, and I kissed her with all the love I couldn't put into words. Our movements were deliberate, as if time stood still, allowing us to savor every moment.

The feeling of being inside her was incredible, and I groaned with pleasure. It was more than just physical; it was emotional, a connection beyond the act itself. I wanted to show her how much she meant to me, how I felt without saying the words. We weren't there yet, but I hoped she could feel it in every touch, every kiss, and every glance.

"Yes... god, yes..." she moaned, her voice filled with longing.

I kissed her again, and we continued to move together, our bodies in perfect harmony. I could feel the tension building within me, and I knew she was getting close, too.

"Kayla... baby..." I groaned, my movements becoming more urgent. "You're amazing."

She nodded, her eyes locked on mine, and I could see the same desire in her gaze that I felt in my heart.

"Jake," she whispered, her voice husky with need. "Don't stop."

I couldn't have even if I wanted to. I was lost in the sensation of her, in the pleasure that was consuming both of us. I could feel her tightening around me, and I knew she was on the edge.

"Shit," I breathed, unable to hold back any longer. "I'm close, baby."

She moved with me, her hips grinding against mine, and I could hardly contain myself. We were both so close, and I wanted to be with her every step of the way.

"Come with me, then," she moaned, her voice filled with ecstasy.

It was too much, and I felt the waves of pleasure crashing over me. I cried out her name as I came, my body shuddering with the intensity of my release. She followed, her climax echoing mine, and it was like we were two halves of the same whole.

We stayed connected, our hearts racing, our breaths coming in short gasps. I looked into her eyes, and it was as if the world had disappeared, leaving only the two of us. It was more than just physical; it was emotional, and I hoped she felt the same way I did.

I kissed her softly, and we held each other close, our bodies still trembling with the aftermath of our passion. There were no words to express what we felt, but in that moment, they weren't necessary.

The morning sunlight filtered through the curtains, casting a warm glow across the room. As I stirred awake, I smiled as I found myself wrapped in Kayla's embrace. The memories of last night's passionate reunion filled me with a sense of contentment, an overwhelming feeling I hadn't experienced in years.

We lay together, our bodies entwined, basking in the intimate aftermath of our physical connection. The tender touches and lingering kisses spoke of a deeper connection, a love that had never truly waned, just laid dormant beneath the surface.

As the day began to pull us from the cocoon of our shared warmth, Kayla moved slightly, her eyes fluttering open. The first thing she did was to reach up and brush a strand of hair from my face. It was a simple gesture, but it carried with it all the love and desire we'd hidden for so long.

"Morning," I said, my voice still husky with sleep.

Her smile lit up the room as she replied, "Good morning. I could get used to waking up like this."

I agreed. The idea of being with Kayla every day was a dream I'd thought was unattainable until now. We shared a sweet morning cuddle, savoring the moments we'd missed out on all these years.

But reality came knocking when Kayla, ever the practical one, got out of bed to check Ethan's address. The urgency to find him and uncover the truth behind Lexi's torment had driven us to this point. With a few taps on her phone, her face shifted from anticipation to concern.

She showed me the message from Ethan.

You came so far… only to miss the very thing you sought right back where you were.

His vagueness sent shivers down my spine, and I knew that something wasn't right.

"He's not in Miami," Kayla said, her brow furrowed.

I sat up, alert. "What do you mean?"

"His message," she explained. "It's almost like he's

taunting us, telling us he's not here. I think he's been in Silver Creek this whole time."

The realization hit me like a punch to the gut. If Ethan had been in Silver Creek, it meant he was the one behind Lexi's torment, the break-ins, and the threatening messages. Our suspicions were finally validated.

We needed to get back to Silver Creek immediately, track down Ethan, and put an end to this nightmare. There was no time to lose.

Kayla and I quickly dressed, packed our things, and left the hotel. Our minds were racing with plans and fears as we made our way to the airport. The flight back to Silver Creek couldn't come soon enough.

This wasn't just about uncovering the truth anymore; it was about ending the reign of terror that had plagued Lexi, disrupted our lives, and had now taken us down a path of rekindled love and shared secrets.

The return flight to Silver Creek felt like a blur. There was an air of anticipation, and neither Kayla nor I could find much comfort in the confined space of the airplane. We had put out an APB on Ethan before our departure, hoping for any lead, any sign of his whereabouts.

It was the middle of the night when we landed back in our hometown. The streets were quiet, shrouded in an eerie silence that matched the uncertainty gripping our lives for so long. We knew this wasn't the time to hunt for Ethan, but we felt our mission pressing on us.

Kayla had picked me up before our flight, and as she pulled up in front of my house, I noticed the darkness within. Mandy had gone to bed, most likely worn out by her concern for Lexi and the uncertainty of her safety.

I looked at Kayla, our eyes locking in silent communication. Our bond had deepened since our reunion, and the magnetic pull that had brought us together again was undeniable. I leaned over and kissed her, feeling her lips respond eagerly to mine. The taste of her, the feel of her, ignited a fire within me that had long been dormant.

She whimpered when I pulled away, and I saw the hesitation in her eyes. But before she could say anything, I whispered, "Do you want to come in?"

Her response was a subtle nod, and without further words, I got out of the car and walked around to her side. Our bodies brushed against each other as we climbed the stairs to my house. The key slipped easily into the lock, and the door creaked open, granting us entry.

We made our way to my room in silence. As the door closed behind us, we were no longer the same individuals who had separated all those years ago. We were two people who had experienced life's ups and downs and finally found their way back to each other.

The act of making love this time was different. It wasn't just about rekindling lost passion; it was about exploring the depths of our desires, about embracing the undeniable connection that had brought us together once more. Our movements were filled with urgency and longing, each touch, each kiss, stoking the flames of our shared desire.

We lost ourselves in each other, relishing the pleasure that only the familiarity of an old love could provide. The emotional connection we'd always had was now infused with an intense physical desire, each touch and whisper carrying years of yearning.

As we reached our climax, we held onto each other, savoring the moment, recognizing that this was a second chance at love. The sensations were overwhelming, and as we lay in each other's arms, I thought about the twists and turns our lives had taken to bring us here.

We were two souls who had experienced the complexities of life but had finally found their way back to one another. The darkness outside was mirrored by the profound connection we had rekindled, and it was in each other's arms that we found solace, comfort, and the hope of brighter days to come.

In the aftermath, as fatigue began to set in, we nestled closer to each other, our fingers intertwined. It was a moment of quiet contentment, a brief respite from the storm surrounding us. As the night deepened, we fell asleep, holding onto one another as if to reassure ourselves that no matter what challenges lay ahead, we would face them together.

Chapter Twenty-One

KAYLA

I walked into the station with Jake, our steps echoing in the quiet hallway. The atmosphere was tense, everyone on edge due to the ongoing case, and the pressure had been mounting.

As we entered, the receptionist immediately approached Jake, who informed him about a call they'd received. Lexi and Luke were on the line, no doubt anxious to know if there were any updates on the case. Jake wasted no time and headed for the phone, leaving me standing near the chief's desk.

While Jake was absorbed in his conversation with Lexi, the chief motioned for me to approach his desk. He leaned in, his voice low and urgent.

"There's been a possible hit on someone in town who shouldn't be here," he said, the lines on his face etched with concern.

My heart skipped a beat. "Ethan Mitchell?" I asked, my voice betraying the urgency I felt.

The chief shrugged, but that was good enough for me to want to check it out. The man we'd been searching for, the one who had been leaving those menacing messages and had possibly broken into Lexi's home, was seemingly back in Silver Creek. It was a crucial lead, one we couldn't afford to miss.

I contemplated the situation. Every instinct in me screamed to wait for Jake, to ensure we were on the same page. But I could also see that he was deeply engrossed in his conversation with Lexi, trying to offer her some reassurance and updates on the case.

I knew I had to act swiftly. Time was of the essence, and if Ethan was indeed in town, we couldn't afford to let him slip through our fingers. Without a word, I turned and headed out of the station.

My steps quickened as I approached one of the cruisers parked outside. I could feel the adrenaline surging through me, the anticipation of a potential confrontation with the man responsible for Lexi's torment.

As I settled into the driver's seat, I glanced back at the station, hesitating for a second before I revved the engine, the low growl of the cruiser matching the intensity of the moment. My hands tightened around the steering wheel, a sense of determination and resolve washing over me. We were one step closer to unmasking the person behind these threats and putting an end to Lexi's ordeal.

I parked the cruiser a good distance from the general store, the van in question just within sight. It was one of those nondescript white ones, the kind that screamed 'nothing to see here,' which meant there was definitely something worth seeing in our line of work. I cut the engine and settled back, watching. The silver sunscreens were a smart touch; couldn't see shit through those.

I hadn't been sitting long when my phone vibrated against my thigh. Glancing at the caller ID, I saw Jake's name and answered immediately. "Yeah?"

"Kayla, where the hell are you?" Jake's voice was terse, edged with worry.

"At the store. There's a van," I said, keeping my eyes on the unmoving vehicle.

"The store? Jesus, Kayla, I told you to wait—"

"I am waiting," I lied, feeling the familiar itch of impatience under my skin.

"Good. Stay put. I'm on my way. Don't do anything—"

"Ethan might bolt. I'm just sitting here, Jake," I cut in, assuring him but feeling the lie twist in my gut.

"Promise me, Kay," he pressed. A quiet desperation in his voice had me squeezing the phone tighter.

"Promise," I whispered, the word tasting like ash. We both knew I was full of shit.

The line went dead, and I let out a breath I didn't realize I was holding. My gaze flickered back to the van. Something about it felt off, and I couldn't shake the feeling that we were running out of time. Minutes crawled by, but my patience was wearing thinner with each passing second.

"Fuck it," I muttered under my breath. I stepped out of the cruiser, keeping low, and approached the van. The silence of the morning was a blanket over the world, the soft crunch of gravel under my boots seeming loud as hell. I told myself whoever was inside couldn't see out any better than I could see in.

A rookie mistake, assuming.

I reached the back of the van and crouched down, trying to make sense of any sound that might come from inside. That's when the world turned upside down. The engine roared to life, a sound so unexpected it sent a jolt through me, and before I knew it, the van was backing up fast.

Instinct had me diving out of the way, but not fast enough. The van clipped me hard, sending me sprawling to the dirt. Pain exploded in my head, bright lights dancing in my vision. I tried to call out, to move, but everything was sluggish; sounds were muffled, and my body wouldn't cooperate.

Footsteps approached, heavy and deliberate. Through the swimming dots of light and shadow, a figure knelt beside me. I tried to focus, tried to make out a face, any identifying feature, but it was like trying to see through a fog.

A hand touched my shoulder, and I wanted to recoil and fight, but I was trapped in my failing senses. A voice said something, but it was like I was underwater, the words distorted and distant. The figure leaned closer, and I could feel their breath against my face. Panic flared in my chest, a scream building there but never making it past my lips.

Then, the world went black, and I knew no more.

Chapter Twenty-Two

JAKE

My car's tires screeched as I took the corner faster than I should have, my heart pounding against my ribs like it was trying to escape. My mind was stuck on the last thing I said to Kayla, that goddamn promise she made. I shouldn't have hung up; I shouldn't have left her alone.

As I skidded into the lot of the general store, the sight that greeted me punched the air out of my lungs. There was Kayla on the ground, a figure in a black hoodie towering over her, crowbar raised high. "No, no, no!" I shouted, though I knew she couldn't hear me.

I laid on the horn, a desperate, blaring sound that shattered the morning silence as I jumped out, my gun already in hand.

"Police! Drop the fucking weapon!"

My voice was lost in the roar as the figure, spooked by the sound or maybe the sight of a gun, darted back into the van. The engine revved, and the van peeled out, dirt and gravel spitting up from its tires.

For a second, I was torn. My instincts screamed to

chase the assailant, to bring them down. But Kayla was on the ground, so damn still.

"Fuck!" I cursed, holstering my gun and pulling out my cell with shaking hands. "Dispatch, this is Officer Jake Barrows. I need units tracking a white van heading north from the general store on Fifth, suspect involved in a felony assault."

I rattled off the details as I dropped to my knees beside Kayla. "And get me a goddamn ambulance! We have an office down!"

I tossed the phone aside, my attention entirely on Kayla. "Kay, come on, open your eyes." I tapped her cheek lightly, my hands trembling. Her eyes fluttered, a groan escaping her lips, and relief washed over me in an icy wave. She wasn't dead. Thank God she wasn't dead.

"Stay with me, Kay. Help's coming." I could hear the fear in my voice, the anger at myself for not being there sooner, for ever leaving her side.

Her eyes finally opened, glassy and unfocused. "Jake?"

"Yeah, it's me. Just hang in there, okay?" Her eyes closed again. I was vaguely aware of the sounds of sirens approaching, but it felt like they were miles away.

The EMTs arrived in what must have been minutes, but it felt like hours had passed as I watched them load Kayla onto a stretcher. Her hand found mine, her grip weak but there, and I clung to it until they pried her from me to get her into the ambulance.

"I'm coming with you," I said, moving to climb in after her.

"Sir, you can't—"

"The hell I can't. She's my partner."

"Jake," one of the EMTs started, the same one who always responded when we were on duty. "We'll take care of her. Follow in your car."

I was about to argue, but the look in his eye stopped me. That look said he needed the space to work to keep Kayla safe. So I let them go, my hands balling into fists as I followed the wail of the siren to the hospital.

The sterile smell of the emergency room was a slap in the face. I gave Kayla's name to the nurse at the desk, my voice hoarse, my badge held out like a shield.

"I'm sorry, only family can go in right now," the nurse said, not unkindly.

I wanted to scream, to demand they let me back there, to see with my own eyes that Kayla was alive and going to stay that way. Instead, I slumped into the hard plastic chair, the fight draining out of me. I was a cop; I knew the procedure, but that did nothing to quell the fear eating at me.

The van, the hoodie, the crowbar — they blurred in my mind, but what remained sharp, what cut at me, was the sight of Kayla on the ground. And the thought that kept circling back around: what if I lose her again? I couldn't fucking bear it.

I buried my face in my hands, waiting for news, any news. Because until I saw her, heard her voice, I was holding out hope. And in this sterile place of white walls and too-bright lights, hope was all I was clinging to.

I paced the length of the waiting room like a caged animal, each step a drumbeat in the otherwise hushed space. Goddamn hours ticked by, marked only by the shuffle of nurses' shoes and the distant beeping of machines. I felt like I was stuck in some cruel limbo, waiting for any sign that Kayla would be okay.

Finally, a doctor in blue scrubs approached, the look on his face reading neutral. My heart lodged in my throat.

"Officer Barrows?" he asked.

"Yeah, that's me. How's Kayla? Is she—"

The Rookie's Second Chance

"She's stable for now. But the head injury is... it's serious. We're monitoring her closely."

Stable. That word should've brought relief, but it hung there, incomplete. "What the hell does 'serious' mean? What are you waiting for?"

His sigh told me he'd had this talk too many times. "We're checking for any signs of bleeding in the brain. It could be hours before we know the full extent and whether she'll require surgery."

"And the 'or'?" My voice was a low growl; I couldn't help it.

He paused, weighing his words. "Let's just wait for the results, officer."

I gave him a sharp nod that said, 'I'm holding you to that,' and rattled off my cell number. "Her folks are gone, and there's no siblings. I'm her partner. And her... friend." I choked a little on the last word, a fear and unspoken truths lodging there.

He jotted the number down and nodded. "We'll call with any updates, officer."

As soon as I stepped out of the hospital, the night air hit me, sobering my spiraling thoughts. The fucker who did this was still out there. And I'd be damned if I was going to sit around playing the waiting game.

Back at the station, I kicked open the door to the evidence room and started yanking files. Ethan's name popped up in too many of them. Kayla had been digging deep, and now she was lying in a hospital bed because of it.

I spread out everything on the table. My eyes flicked over the documents, searching for anything that would lead me to him. I didn't care about what dirt I might dig up on my sister anymore. Kayla was in the crosshairs. Even Mandy had been dragged into this mess.

I ran my hands over my face, feeling the stubble and

exhaustion. But I shoved it down. Sleep was a luxury I couldn't afford — not while Kayla was fighting for her life, not while that son of a bitch was out there, thinking he got the upper hand.

Kayla wouldn't quit — she never did. And I sure as hell wasn't about to start now.

Dawn was breaking when I finally leaned back in my chair, the first rays of sunlight creeping through the blinds, casting bars of light across my desk. I hadn't found the smoking gun yet, but I was piecing it together, bit by bit. Somewhere amidst the sea of information, a path that would lead me straight to him.

I closed my eyes for a moment, envisioning Kayla's face, the fire in her eyes when she was on to something. That same fire was kindling inside me now, a blaze that wouldn't be extinguished until I brought this fucker to justice.

And I would. For Kayla. For all of us.

Kayla had left her research easy for me to access—message boards, emails, social media location stamps. The first thing that struck me was a series of emails between Ethan and someone from The Vault. They were laced with references to events and people that weren't explicitly named but implied a deeper, darker layer to their college days. It was like reading code, and I could tell that Ethan was deeply involved yet trying to distance himself at the same time.

In another series of emails and forum transcripts, his tone shifted to defensive, a hint of fear underlying his words when the topic veered too close to some guy named Garrett's disappearance. I looked him up but found only a single picture of him with Lexi, looking intimate, at a party early in their freshman year.

More photos showed Ethan at various campus events,

always on the periphery, watching and observing. In some, he was with Garrett, the two of them looking like typical college students, but the tension in Ethan's posture suggested something more.

Bank statements and phone records hinted at an erratic lifestyle post-college, with unexplained large deposits and calls to unknown numbers in the dead of night. It was as if Ethan was trying to erase his tracks, staying one step ahead of something - or someone.

But the most telling piece was a picture of a handwritten note I found buried at the bottom of the pile deep in his online posts on Tumblr. In it, Ethan spoke about 'regrets' and 'secrets too heavy to carry.' It was vague, but the desperation in the scrawl was clear. This note, more than anything, made me wonder what Ethan had gotten himself into and what he knew about the darkness that seemed to shroud The Vault and everything connected to it.

My keystrokes echoed in the dim room, a ticking clock reminding me of the precious minutes slipping away. Kayla was fighting for her life, and the bastard responsible was still out there, lurking in the shadows. My anger fueled my determination. I would make him pay for Kayla and for everything he'd put us through.

I logged into the account Kayla had been using to trace Ethan's posts. My heart raced as I sent a direct message, not holding back on the words.

"I know what you did to Kayla. You hurt her, and you're gonna pay, you son of a bitch. You're lucky I'm a cop, or I'd show you a world of hurt."

Seconds felt like hours as I watched the screen, my fury simmering beneath the surface. Then, a notification popped up. Ethan was online.

His response came in, swift and panicked, a chink in

his armor. "I didn't do anything. I'm not even in Silver Creek. I was trying to throw you off. You don't get it — The Vault's former members are watching. Powerful people. They'll do whatever it takes to keep their secrets hidden."

"The Vault? What secrets are you talking about?" I typed, my fingers clenched, demanding answers.

Ethan's reply was a terse one. "I can't talk about them online. It's not safe. Not with... the incident."

My blood ran cold. What the hell did he mean by "the incident"? Questions buzzed in my head, but I couldn't let him slip away now, not when we were finally close to the truth.

The station phone rang, and I snatched it up without a second thought. It had to be Ethan, and he was going to talk. He had to.

"Hello," I said, my voice hard and unwavering.

The voice on the other end was unmistakably Ethan's. "You want answers? We can't talk here. It's not safe. I'll come to Silver Creek, and we can discuss everything face to face."

A lump formed in my throat. "Fine, but if I get even a whiff of you doing something to anyone in my town—"

Ethan chuckled, a sinister edge to it. "Understood... officer."

I hung up, my mind racing with dread and anticipation. Ethan was coming to Silver Creek. I had no idea what would happen when he arrived, but one thing was clear — we were closer to the truth than ever before.

The hospital room was too damn quiet, the beeping of the heart monitor filling the space like some cruel metronome counting down. As I approached Kayla's bedside, seeing her lying there, so fucking vulnerable, hit me like a punch to the gut. This wasn't the Kayla I knew, the one who could take down a perp twice her size without breaking a sweat.

"I talked to Ethan," I murmured to her, unsure if she could hear me. "He's coming to town. I'm gonna meet with him tomorrow."

Her face was peaceful, a stark contrast to the chaos that landed her here. I wanted to press my lips to her forehead, to somehow transfer strength to her, but the damn bandages made me opt for a gentle kiss on the cheek instead.

"You just hang in there, Kayla. We've got a bastard to catch, and I need you with me."

Back at my place, Mandy was sprawled on the couch, her attention glued to the TV until she noticed me.

"You're home early," she commented, that look of concern etched deep into her features.

I grunted in response, tossing my keys onto the counter. "Been a long day," I said, it all settling on my shoulders.

"Is there anything I can do?" Mandy's voice was soft, almost hesitant.

I was tired, every part of me screaming for a break from the chaos. "Just need to crash. Not think for a while."

She offered up a distraction. "It's still early. Movie? Pizza? My treat?"

I hesitated, keenly aware of the lines I didn't want to cross. Mandy was great, but the last thing I needed was more complications. But shit, I was so damn tired of being alone with my thoughts. With Luke and Lexi tucked away, and Kayla... I couldn't face the night solo.

I sank into the armchair, feeling the day's adrenaline crash leaving me bone tired. "Sure," I finally said. Mandy's small smile was a slice of normalcy, something I desperately craved.

She got up, her movements easy as she grabbed a beer

for me. The cold bottle felt good in my hand, a temporary balm.

"Thanks," I muttered, tilting the bottle back and feeling the bitter liquid slide down my throat.

The movie started, some action flick that would normally have me all in, but the images just blurred together. My mind was on tomorrow, on Ethan, on the information he claimed to have. On Kayla, lying in that hospital bed.

I could feel Mandy's eyes on me every now and then, probably trying to read me or offer comfort without getting too close. It was a dance we both seemed to have learned the steps to, even if the rhythm was all off.

The pizza arrived, and we ate in an odd silence, the movie's explosions a distant backdrop. I knew she wanted to ask and dive into what happened, but she held back, and I was grateful for that.

"Good pizza," I said eventually, because I had to say something to acknowledge her effort.

"Yeah, it is," she replied, and I caught the hint of relief in her voice.

As the movie played on, my phone buzzed with updates from the hospital. Stable. No change. The words were meant to be reassuring, but they felt like a fucking mockery when all I wanted was to hear that Kayla was awake, that she was going to be okay.

I excused myself early, claiming exhaustion, which wasn't a lie. Mandy understood, or at least she didn't push. In my room, I tossed and turned, every scenario with Ethan playing out in my head. When I finally slipped into a restless sleep, it was filled with blaring sirens and Kayla's voice, urging me to find the truth.

The greasy scent of overcooked bacon and stale coffee was thick in the air of the diner. I'd picked a booth in the back corner with a clear view of the door, my gut twisting with anticipation and dread. I'd gotten there early, way too early, drumming my fingers on the cool tabletop, glancing at my watch every other minute.

Ethan was punctual, arriving just when he said he would, despite what felt like a goddamn year of waiting. He slid into the booth across from me, an envelope thick with papers in his hand.

"So," I started, no niceties, no bullshit. "What's so damn important that it couldn't be said over the phone? And why the hell should I trust a word that comes out of your mouth? You know what happened to Kayla. You know about Lexi's stalker."

Ethan's eyes were darting around, his voice low and strained. "I swear, I had nothing to do with it. I just—I can't get involved."

"Can't or won't?" I pressed, the anger a hot coil in my chest.

"Can't!" He hissed, pushing the envelope towards me. "This, this is why. It's all in there. My life's on the fucking line, man. It's a secret that needs to stay buried."

I eyed the envelope like it might bite. "What kind of secret?"

He leaned in, dropping his voice to a whisper. "A cover-up from my college days. Big names, big fucking consequences. And Lexi... she's at the center of it all."

I grabbed the envelope. It felt like holding a grenade, ready to explode and turn my world upside down. I could feel Ethan's eyes on me, waiting.

With a deep breath, I broke the seal and pulled out the files. Documents, transcripts, dates, names... It was a rabbit hole, one that promised no easy climb back out.

"Jesus Christ," I muttered under my breath, the first page already sending shock waves through me. Ethan's leg bounced nervously, his glance still flickering to the door, to the windows, to any potential threat.

"You see? You see why I couldn't talk about this over a traceable line?" Ethan's words were a rush, a floodgate opened.

Ethan's fingers tapped a staccato rhythm on the tabletop as he watched me thumb through the documents. The diner buzzed around us, but we were in a soundproof bubble, just him, the files, and me.

"The first document," Ethan started, his voice hushed, "is the university's quiet way of saying this guy, Garrett, no longer existed to them. See how it's worded? 'Abandoned his responsibilities.' Like he chose to disappear."

Garrett. The guy who supposedly ghosted my sister back in college, but, looking at what Ethan was showing me... maybe he didn't.

I scanned the text, noting the cold, administrative tone. "And this," I flipped to the missing person's report, "is from his parents?"

"Yeah," Ethan nodded. "They kept looking for him, even after the university washed their hands of the whole thing."

The report was detailed. Garrett's full name, description, the last time he was seen. His parents' desperation shone through the formal wording of the document. I couldn't imagine what they had gone through, still probably were.

I moved to the third paper, the one about the body. The report was sparse on details, but the implications were heavy. "They find this body, burnt to shit, and someone says, 'Hey, that might be Garrett because of the clothes?' That's it?"

The Rookie's Second Chance

"That's it," Ethan confirmed, swallowing hard. "No dental records match, no DNA test. Just... closed case."

"So, what's the connection to The Vault, to Lexi?" I prodded, feeling the plot thicken.

Ethan leaned in closer. "Garrett was Lexi's boyfriend," he whispered like he was divulging state secrets. "And when he vanished, it was The Vault's rule – no talking about Garrett, no asking questions, like he never fucking existed."

My head was starting to pound, and I felt a clench of something dark in my gut. "And you're telling me Lexi just went along with that? What about his family?"

Ethan's laugh was a bitter sound. "Lexi didn't have a choice, man. You don't say no to The Vault. As for his family..." He shrugged. "Who were they to these people? Nobody. Just collateral damage."

The dots were starting to connect, forming an ugly picture. "And what about you, Ethan? Where do you fit into all of this?"

"I was an initiate, like I said. With Garrett and Lexi."

I eyed him skeptically. "You expect me to believe you were just totally innocent in all this?"

Ethan's eyes were hard, his voice edged with steel. "Believe what you want. But I didn't sign up to be part of a goddamn cover-up, and you won't find anyone else who took the time to gather all the evidence."

There was an honesty in his tone that was hard to dispute. He slid the documents toward me, a silent offering of proof.

"You can keep those," he said, standing up abruptly. "Just... don't say you got them from me. And Jake, be careful. This shit... it's bigger than us."

I gathered the papers, my mind racing. Garrett, a student who vanished into thin air. Lexi, bound by the secretive rules of The Vault. A body, unclaimed and unidentified, except for a set of clothes. The silence of an institution. And now Kayla, lying in a hospital bed, connected to all this by a thread I was just starting to see.

As Ethan started to walk away, I found my voice, raw from the churn of information. "Hold on. Why the hell would anyone cover this up? What's the point?"

Ethan stopped, half-turned toward me, his face shadowed. "That, Officer Barrows, is a damn good question," he said, voice low. "But it's not one you heard from me. Okay? You didn't hear any of this from me." There was an earnest plea in his eyes, a silent bid for anonymity.

I grunted, frustrated. "And what do you get out of this, Ethan? Why spill now?"

He glanced back with a hollow laugh. "Get out of it?" He shook his head. "Nothing. I don't get shit out of this except maybe a clear conscience." His gaze held mine. "And for the record, I might've held a torch for Lexi once, but it was never what people thought. I fell hard for someone else. Lexi... she was just a friend who tried to help."

A pang of something—sympathy, maybe—twisted in my chest. "You're really not our guy?" I didn't expect him to say yes—who would?—but I still felt compelled to ask.

Ethan's nod was solemn. "I'm many things, but not a stalker, not a threat. I just hope you find who is. I hope Lexi's okay." And with that, he turned, walking away with his past lingering in the air between us.

I sat there for a long moment, the files in front of me. Garrett, Lexi, The Vault—it was all a web of secrets and silence. I was a officer, used to chasing down leads and shaking out the truth, but this? This was a different kind of darkness.

Shoving the papers into my bag, I pushed out of the

booth, the vinyl seat squeaking in protest. The diner continued its hustle and bustle around me, oblivious to the conspiracies being unearthed at a corner table. Outside, the air was cooling as the evening started to creep in, a reminder that the day was ending, but my work was just getting started.

I drove back to the station, my mind on Ethan's words, on Kayla's still form in that hospital bed, on Lexi, who was caught up in something far bigger than any of us realized. Anger bubbled up, fierce and protective, and a newfound determination set in. I'd find this stalker, dig into The Vault's secrets, and I'd be damned if I let anyone else get hurt.

Back at my desk, I spread out the files, the pieces of Garrett's life and disappearance laid out before me. I needed to make sense of it, find the thread that connected it all to the here and now—to Lexi, to Kayla. I pored over every word, every date and signature, looking for something, anything, that could be a lead.

The station clock ticked, marking time in a steady rhythm. I'd look up at it every now and then, the night wearing on, the second hand ticking away moments I felt slipping through my fingers. There were more questions than answers, but I was used to that. Answers were earned, and I was ready to put in the work.

As the clock neared midnight, I needed rest, a clear head, but the thought of sleep seemed like a distant luxury. Instead, I turned back to the documents, to Garrett's faded smile in a picture clipped from a school newspaper, to the cold, bureaucratic language that tried to erase him. It was personal now. It was about justice.

Chapter Twenty-Three

KAYLA

The sound was the first thing that came back, a sort of distant, watery echo. Then, the light—a harsh, bleary fluorescence that made my eyelids flutter in protest. Pain throbbed at the base of my skull, a pulsing drumbeat that surged with every beat of my heart.

Voices murmured around me, their words indistinct and muffled, as if I were underwater. I tried to lift my head, but it was like trying to move through molasses, heavy and resistant. My eyes cracked open, a slit of vision that blurred white coats and clipboards into ghostly shapes before my gaze.

"Ms. Green? Can you hear me?" The voice was closer now, a beacon through the fog. I managed a groan, my throat raw, as if I'd swallowed a handful of sand.

A figure leaned over, a mask and cap obscuring their face. "You're in the hospital," they explained, their voice clinical but not unkind. "You've been in and out. Try not to speak."

I obeyed, not that I had much choice. My body felt like it was encased in lead, heavy and unresponsive. The pain ebbed and flowed, a tide that pulled at my consciousness, dragging me back down into darkness.

Each time I woke, it was like breaking through ice. My brain would kick on, muddled and slow, only to shut down as the pain spiked and sleep reclaimed me.

Once, I caught a snippet of conversation—doctors discussing medication and concussions. Another time, the rhythmic beep of a heart monitor played a steady, unyielding soundtrack to my disjointed thoughts.

The cycles of wakefulness were exhausting, each a little battle I fought and lost, until the moment I opened my eyes to a different presence.

"Kayla?" The voice was thick with an emotion I couldn't place. My eyes dragged open, and this time, they focused on a familiar face.

Jake.

He looked like hell—dark circles under his eyes and a day's growth of beard. There was a tension in his jaw, the lines of his face etched with worry.

I wanted to speak, to reassure him, but when I tried, it was like someone had taken a cheese grater to my throat. I winced, the sound that escaped me more animal than human.

"Don't try to talk," Jake said quickly, his hand finding mine. His grip was warm, a lifeline in the cold sterility of the hospital room. His thumb brushed over my knuckles in a silent message of comfort. His relief at seeing my eyes open was clear.

I mustered the smallest of nods, the action sending a fresh jolt of pain through my skull, but it was worth it to see the way his shoulders dropped slightly, the tension easing.

"Shit, Kayla," he breathed out, and I could see the

sheen of unshed tears in his eyes. "I'm so fucking glad you're awake."

The urge to respond was overwhelming, to tell him I was okay, to ask about the case, about Lexi, about everything my brain was trying to connect. But all I could do was squeeze his hand back, the smallest gesture of 'I'm here.'

He understood, his other hand coming up to lay gently on my arm, careful not to jostle. "You scared the crap out of me," he admitted, and there was a tremble in his voice that told me just how close to the edge he was.

I closed my eyes, not to sleep, but to concentrate on staying present, to anchor myself to his voice, to the warmth of his hand. It was a silent promise I made to myself—to him—that I wasn't going anywhere.

"Rest," he said softly, almost a whisper. "We'll talk when you're up to it. I've got news, but it can wait. Just... get better, Kayla."

I felt the brush of his lips against my hand, a touch so tender it seemed at odds with the rough-edged detective officer I knew. Then I was slipping again, but this time, it wasn't the dark pulling me under; it was sleep, natural and healing.

When consciousness crept back in, it was with less of a vengeance. I was sore, but my mind felt clearer, the fog of medication and pain starting to lift. I could feel the stiffness of the hospital sheets and hear the low murmur of the TV on the wall. My tongue felt swollen in my mouth, dry and unpleasant, but I worked up the saliva to swallow, to speak.

Jake was slumped in the chair beside my bed, his head resting awkwardly against the wall, eyes closed. He looked like he'd been through hell, but he was still there, steadfast.

"Jake," I rasped, my voice a rough whisper.

His eyes snapped open, immediately alert. "Kayla?"

"I need water," I managed to choke out.

He was quick to help, guiding a straw to my lips. The cold water was a minor miracle, soothing the rawness just enough. I took a moment, savoring the relief, before I pushed myself up slightly. Pain protested the movement, but it was bearable.

"Jake," I started again, my voice gaining a little strength, "rest my ass. That son of a bitch tried to kill me."

He looked taken aback, a soft chuckle escaping him despite the situation. "You're unbelievable, you know that?"

I felt a smile tug at my lips, wry and painful. "I've been called worse. But seriously, I want in."

He leaned forward, elbows on his knees, his eyes searching mine. "Kayla, you nearly died. You need to—"

"I know what I need," I cut him off, the determination making my voice steadier. "And I need to see this through. More now than ever."

Jake's face softened, and he took my hand again. "Fuck, you're incredible," he said, and then his lips were on mine, a gentle pressure that was somehow both a comfort and a spark of something more.

In that kiss, I felt all the things we hadn't had the chance to say, the depth of emotion that had been building between us, unspoken but not unfelt.

He pulled back, resting his forehead against mine. "I love you, Kayla," he murmured, so quietly I might have thought I imagined it if not for the intensity in his eyes. "I was scared shitless at the thought of losing you. I don't ever want you to leave my sight without knowing how I feel."

The words wrapped around me, a balm for more than just the physical wounds. The fear that it was too soon to feel this way evaporated, replaced by a certainty that was as deep as the ache in my bones.

"I love you, too, Jake," I said, the words clear and true. "Even if your timing sucks."

A grin broke across his face, the first real smile I'd seen from him in what felt like forever. It reached his eyes, crinkling the corners and lighting them up.

"We're a pair, aren't we?" he said, his thumb stroking over the back of my hand.

"The best kind," I replied, squeezing his hand back. "So, what'd you find out?" My voice felt stronger now, not just a whisper but a force.

Jake hesitated for a moment, the crease in his brow deepening. "Ethan gave me these files," he finally said, pulling out a thick envelope from his jacket. "He was cagey, but he swore he had nothing to do with what happened to you or with Lexi's stalker."

"Let me see them," I insisted, extending my hand with more energy than I felt.

He looked like he was going to argue but must have seen something in my eyes that told him it would be futile. He handed me the envelope. I leafed through the pages. It was like glimpsing into a story halfway through, trying to piece together the plot from scattered pages.

"There," I pointed, my finger trembling slightly from the effort. "A connection. This guy, Officer Kilkenny, he was on the missing person case…" I flipped through the pages. "… And he was the lead on the case where the body was found later."

Jake leaned over, his eyes scanning the document where my finger rested. "Shit, I didn't catch that."

"That's why I'm the detective, officer," I teased, a smirk tugging at the corner of my mouth despite the ache that followed.

A shadow of a smile crossed his face. "Yeah, yeah, don't rub it in."

"Not to outdo myself, there's more. Look here in this interview from the missing person's case. He said he's personally invested. And why? Right here." I pointed to a quote on the page. "Officer Kilkenny mentioned his kid went to school with Garrett, and he didn't want any students to feel unsafe. But then a week later, he said it was a runaway case, no foul play. That's not a coincidence. That's a lead."

Jake nodded, the situation sinking in. "We need to contact Miami PD, see what Kilkenny knows. If he's willing to talk."

I handed the files back to him. "As soon as I'm out of here, we get to work."

"We?" Jake arched an eyebrow, his protective side on full display.

"We," I confirmed firmly. "I'm not sitting this one out. Not after what's happened."

He studied me for a long moment, searching my face for signs of strain. I must have passed the test because he finally nodded.

"Alright, Kayla. As soon as you're out, we'll dive into this mess together. We'll find this bastard."

The satisfaction of that promise washed over me, and I settled back into the pillows, conserving my strength for the battles ahead. There was a quiet determination in the room now, a shared purpose that made the sterile hospital room feel like a war room. I felt the thrill of the hunt rekindling inside me.

I closed my eyes, not to sleep, but to imagine walking through the doors of the precinct, files in hand, ready to chase down leads. The thought of action, of justice, was a far better medicine than anything that dripped from the IV bags beside me.

Jake's presence was a silent vow, an anchor in the

tumultuous sea of the unknown. As he sat beside me, his features set in resolute lines, I knew we were stepping into the fray together. And with that, I let the anticipation lull me into a restful state, preparing for the day I'd step out of the hospital and back into the chase.

Chapter Twenty-Four

MANDY

When Jake stumbled through the door that night, I was ready—beer in one hand, the other tossing the remote onto the couch. I'd figured out that the way to his heart wasn't through elaborate dinners; it was just being there, being easy to be with.

"What's wrong?" I asked as the evening progressed, trying to keep my voice light as I handed him another beer. He looked like he'd gone ten rounds with life and lost every single one.

He took the beer, a silent thanks in the nod he gave me. "I'm just worried about Kayla," he said, sinking into the armchair like it was a life raft.

"I can imagine," I managed, pouring a bit of sympathy into my words, even though deep down, a tiny voice was chanting 'opportunity.' I shoved it down fast. I wasn't that person, was I?

Jake didn't say much after that, just stared at the TV, not really watching the game. I knew he and Kayla were close—partners or whatever—but he never said much about it. I had my suspicions, but nothing solid.

I sat down on the couch, leaving space between us, a casual gap that said, 'I'm here but not pushing.'

"You want pizza again? I ordered your favorite," I said, hoping the familiar comfort food might bring him back to me.

He finally looked away from the screen, meeting my eyes for a second. "Yeah, pizza sounds good, Mandy. Thanks."

As I set up the pizza and grabbed him a slice, I watched him out of the corner of my eye. He was so damn closed off sometimes. It was like he had this wall, and every time I thought I was making progress, something would send him retreating behind it again.

I handed him a plate, and our fingers brushed. There was a charge there, I swear. But he pulled back too quick for me to be sure. "You gotta take care of yourself, Jake," I said, half-teasing, half-serious. "You're no good to anyone if you run yourself into the ground."

He grunted something that might've been agreement, took a bite of pizza, and for a moment, he just looked like a regular guy, not a officer with the world on his shoulders. "I know, Mandy," he said after swallowing. "Just been a long day."

"You can talk to me, you know," I offered, keeping my tone neutral. "I might not be a detective, but I'm not bad at listening."

He gave me a half-smile that didn't quite reach his eyes. "I appreciate it, Mandy. Really."

We settled into silence, the noise from the TV filling the room. Part of me wanted to press, to ask more about Kayla, about him, about us—whatever the hell 'us' might be. But I held back.

This was a game of patience, and I was playing the long game. I'd be the friend, the support, the easy company. And maybe, just maybe, when he was ready to look around, to really see who was there for him, he'd realize what he'd been missing.

But as I watched him sitting there, his mind clearly a million miles away, part of me wondered if I was fooling myself. If maybe, no matter what I did, I'd always be second to the ghost of a woman who wasn't even in the room.

I shook the thought away, focusing on the game, on the moment. This was my chance to show Jake I was here for him, in whatever capacity he needed. If it was just friendship he wanted, then that's what I'd give him. And if the cards played out right, maybe one day it would be more.

"Mandy, did you know a guy in college named Garrett?"

I froze, pizza slice halfway to my mouth, and lowered it slowly. Garrett. Of all the things for Jake to bring up now. It felt like the universe was playing some sick joke, echoing my thoughts back at me through him. I stalled, playing for time. "Garrett? Why do you ask?"

Jake was frowning, running a hand through his hair in that way he did when he was working something out. "There were some... incidents... with Garrett a few years back."

My mind was racing. Incidents. What the hell did he know? I had to tread carefully. "Oh, Garrett?" I said, feigning a casual tone. "Yeah, he dated Lexi for a bit. Then one day, poof, ghosted her completely. Just up and left."

Jake's eyes narrowed, a detective through and through. "What did you think of him?"

I took a sip of beer, buying a second to gather my thoughts. "He was cute, you know? Great smile, great hair." I shrugged. "But I realized pretty fast he wasn't good enough for Lexi. Not by a long shot."

Jake was studying me now, and I could almost see the gears turning behind those eyes. "How so?" he pressed.

I sighed, setting my beer down. This was it, my chance to show Jake I was on his side, that I got it. "Honestly, Jake, no one at that school was good enough for her. Not really. No wonder she came back here to find someone."

He paused, and I could tell he was digesting what I'd said. There was something more he wanted, I could feel it. But he didn't push further, just nodded slowly, a silent acknowledgment that he'd heard me. And in that moment, I felt a rush of victory, however small.

I watched him, this man I was so damn drawn to, and I couldn't help the flicker of hope that flared in my chest. Maybe, just maybe, I could be the one he turned to, the one who helped him through all this shit.

I leaned back, watching Jake's furrowed brow as he grappled with whatever emotions the name Garrett dredged up. "Do you think Garrett could be Lexi's stalker?" I tossed the question into the room like a live grenade, watching it land in the space between us.

Jake's posture tensed, his eyes going distant. "That would be tough," he finally said, the words heavy with something unspoken.

"Why's that?" My curiosity was a wild thing, clawing at the edges of my restraint.

He hesitated, and I could almost see the internal debate. "Well," Jake started, "no one's heard from him in so long. He's like a ghost."

I nodded slowly, digesting this. No leads there, then. "I don't have any other ideas," I admitted, "but I'll answer any questions you have."

Jake eyed me for a moment before throwing his next card on the table. "Does The Vault mean anything to you?" His voice was steady, but I could tell he was fishing in dark waters.

I froze. The Vault. Those secret meetings that were part of a college experience I'd tried to leave behind. I didn't say anything, just let the silence stretch a beat too long, memories of whispered conversations and Lexi's excited face as we joined that ridiculous club together flooding back. I played it cool, though, and kept my voice even.

"Why are you asking?"

"It might help me find Lexi's stalker," he said, his voice like gravel, all detective and no play.

I considered how much to reveal. The Vault had been a bit of a joke to me, a way to pad the resume with some extracurriculars. But for some, it was no laughing matter. "It was an academic club that treated itself like a secret society," I explained, choosing my words carefully. "And yeah, a handful of people took it way too seriously."

As I watched him stand up, stretching his tall frame, I felt a surge of protectiveness. He was out there alone, trying to untangle this mess. And here I was, sitting on information that could help. I bit my lip, contemplating.

"Jake," I said, and he turned back to me, a question in his eyes. "If there's anything I remember that might help, you'll be the first to know."

He nodded, a ghost of a smile touching his lips. "Thanks, Mandy. I appreciate it."

The next day, I found myself pacing the length of my room, phone in hand, debating the kind of flowers that screamed 'I care' without crossing into 'I'm desperate.' It was a fine line, and hell, I was treading it like a tightrope walker. With a decisive tap, I chose a bright assortment of blooms, nothing romantic but cheerful enough to maybe, just maybe, lift Kayla's spirits and catch Jake's eye.

It wasn't like I was glad about what happened to Kayla, but I couldn't ignore the gnawing thought in the back of my mind – this was my chance. If I played my cards right, Jake might see me in a new light and might realize that I was more than just a good time and a cold beer at the end of a long day.

I scribbled a message to go with the flowers, keeping it short and sweet. "Thinking of you and wishing you a speedy recovery! - Mandy." Nothing over the top, just the right touch of concern.

I sent the order through, my heart doing a nervous dance. It was a small gesture, but it felt like a step in a plan I was making up as I went along. The thing was, I knew I was good for Jake, better than Kayla with her detective badge and her dark, haunted eyes. I could be the light to his shadow if only he'd let me.

As the day dragged on, I busied myself with chores, each sweep of the broom or wipe of the counter a way to pass the time and work off the anxious energy bubbling inside me. I imagined Jake walking into Kayla's hospital room, flowers in hand, reading the card, and the look of surprise on his face. Maybe he'd think, 'Wow, Mandy really is thoughtful.'

The image of him smiling, that rare, full-wattage grin that transformed his face, was enough to make me pause in my tracks. I wanted that smile to be for me, because of me.

When evening rolled around, I found myself back on the couch, remote in hand, but the TV screen a blur before my eyes. The waiting was the worst part – waiting for Jake to come home, for some acknowledgment of my gesture, for some sign that I was making headway.

The sound of the door finally opening had me sitting up straighter, a rehearsed casualness in place. "Hey," I called out as Jake trudged in, once more looking exhausted. "How's Kayla?"

He dropped his keys on the counter and shrugged out of his jacket. "She's better, which is good. Doctors say she's gonna be okay." His voice was flat, giving nothing away.

I nodded, biting back the surge of... was it disappointment? Relief? I wasn't even sure anymore. "That's great news," I managed, keeping my tone light. "I sent her some flowers."

Jake paused, turned to look at me, and there it was – a flicker of something warm in his eyes. "That was really nice of you, Mandy. Thanks."

The way he said my name, with a hint of something I couldn't quite name, sent a thrill through me. "Of course," I said with a smile. "Just wanted to do something nice."

We lapsed into silence, the air between us filled with unspoken words and tangled emotions. I watched him sink into the armchair, the lines of exhaustion etched deeper than ever.

I wanted to reach out, to offer comfort, but I held back. Timing was everything, and I needed to be patient, to wait for the perfect moment to step in and show Jake that I was the one he could lean on. Until then, I'd be the friend he needed, the steady presence in his life. And when the time was right, I'd be ready to show him just how much more I could be.

Chapter Twenty-Five

JAKE

The station was a tomb when I walked in, just me and the echo of my footsteps. I chucked my jacket on the chair and fired up my desktop, the glow of the screen the only light in the place. Kayla was still laid up in the hospital, and there I was, stuck in a holding pattern, waiting for her to get back on her feet to chase down the shadows of The Vault.

I'd been combing through forums, chat logs, anything that reeked of college secret societies. That's when I found him – a username that kept popping up in the right places, using the same cryptic language. I shot him a message.

OFFICER-B: I have some questions about The Vault.

ALL4ALL: You and a thousand others.

OFFICER-B: It's important. Police matter.

ALL4ALL: Even less reason for me to tell.

OFFICER-B: It's about Garrett and Lexi.

There was a long pause.

ALL4ALL: How much do you know?

OFFICER-B: Enough to know that Garrett didn't just

walk out of school. Something happened. And now Lexi is in danger.

Another long pause.

ALL4ALL: Fine. I'll meet. But you come alone, or I walk out immediately.

"You're kidding me," I muttered to the screen. The guy was paranoid as hell, but I wasn't about to meet some shadowy figure without backup. I typed back a lie. "Fine. But I won't be alone."

We set the time and place—a dive bar four hours away. I'd have to leave soon if I was going to make it. But first, I had someone to see.

Before I could second-guess myself, I was standing in Kayla's hospital room, the steady beep of her heart monitor a constant reminder of why I was pushing so hard.

She looked up, those fierce eyes of hers telling me she was pissed to still be in that bed. "What're you doing here?" she croaked. "Thought you'd be out there kicking ass by now."

I couldn't help a half-grin. "Just making sure you're not playing hooky. I've got a lead on The Vault."

Her eyes lit up like a Christmas tree. "Well, what are you waiting for? Go get the bastard."

"I plan to," I said, leaning down to press a quick, hard kiss to her forehead. "You just keep getting better, alright?"

She grabbed my hand, her grip strong, all things considered. "Be careful, Jake. I can't do this without you."

I squeezed back, that knot of worry in my gut pulling tighter. "I always am."

I left her with a promise to call and update her, but the truth was, my mind was racing, playing out every possible scenario. The drive would give me plenty of time to plan, or to drive myself crazy with 'what ifs.'

I hit the road, the cruiser eating up the miles. The engine's hum and the blur of the passing scenery were a dull backdrop to the noise in my head. Every now and then, my phone would buzz with a text from Mandy, each one a variation of 'How's Kayla?' or 'Be safe.'

It was nice, I guess. Mandy trying to show she cared, but my head was in the game, not on her well-wishes.

As the miles ticked by, I found my grip on the steering wheel getting tighter, my jaw set hard. The closer I got to the meet, the more I felt it – that itch between my shoulder blades, the one that says you're either onto something big or you're about to step in a pile of shit.

The sun was dipping low when I pulled into the bar's parking lot, a shack of a place that looked like it was held together with spit and prayers. I checked the piece at my side. It was both a comfort and a reminder of what was at stake.

I fired off a quick text to Kayla, letting her know I was there and that I'd call her as soon as I was done. I didn't mention Mandy. I didn't want Kayla thinking about anything but getting better.

The engine cut, the car's silence was a contrast to the riot in my head. I took a deep breath, letting it out slowly, trying to ease the tension in my muscles.

As I stepped out of the cruiser, the gravel crunched under my boots. I locked the car and pocketed the keys, my senses on high alert. The bar's neon sign buzzed in the growing dusk, a beacon calling me to whatever waited inside. I squared my shoulders, ready for whatever was coming.

The bar smelled like spilled stale beer and broken dreams. I grabbed a stool at the far end, where I could keep my back to the wall and an eye on the door. A waitress with a tired smile came over, slid a menu towards me, and popped her gum expectantly.

"Just a beer, thanks," I said, not even looking at the menu. I wasn't here to eat.

She nodded and sauntered off, hips swaying to some silent tune. I scanned the faces in the bar. No one stood out. No one screamed, 'I've got dirt on The Vault.' Every tick of the clock had me wound tighter. Was this a setup? Was Kayla's stalker trying to flush me out?

The beer arrived, beads of condensation trickling down the glass like sweat. I took a sip, the cold hitting the back of my throat but not easing the heat in my gut.

I waited. One beer turned into two. The crowd thinned out, leaving just the die-hard drinkers and a couple so wrapped up in each other they might as well have been alone.

"Shit," I muttered, slamming the empty glass down a little harder than I meant to. The bartender shot me a look, and I raised a hand, part apology, part signal I was done.

I stood up, feeling my gun against my side, and made my way to the door, the feeling of being watched crawling up my spine like a line of ants.

The night air hit me, a slap of cold that had me shrugging my jacket tighter around me. I scanned the parking lot; my cruiser was just a lonely island in a sea of asphalt.

That's when they came at me. Three shadows, moving fast.

"Fuck!" I managed before a hand clamped over my mouth and an arm locked around my throat.

I tried for my gun, but one of them pinned my arms while another kicked behind my knees, bringing me down hard on the gravel. The sharp stones bit into my skin, and I could taste blood in my mouth.

"Go on then," I spat, the words muffled against the hand still clamped on my face. "Do it like you did Kayla."

The one in front of me, the leader, I guessed, let out a dry, humorless laugh. "We didn't touch your detective."

"Bullshit," I hissed, my heart pounding a rhythm of pure, uncut fear. "Then who the hell did?"

"Don't know," he said, and a note of sincerity in his voice gave me pause. "But it wasn't one of us."

I struggled, trying to see the faces behind the masks, but it was no use. "Ethan said The Vault's dangerous," I grunted, calling on every shred of defiance I had left.

Another laugh, this one tinged with something that sounded almost like respect. "That's what we tell the freshmen. Keeps them quiet. All the stories, the 'disappearances'..." He trailed off.

"Yeah? Well, what about Garrett? He did disappear. You gonna tell me that was just a fucking fairy tale too?"

The leader's stance shifted, the first crack in his composure. His laugh was gone, replaced by something that looked a lot like unease. He glanced at his buddies, a silent conversation passing between them.

I held his gaze, my own fear mixing with a grim satisfaction that I'd hit a nerve. I waited for him to speak, to fill in the blanks, to give me something, anything, that could lead me to Kayla's would-be killer. The silence stretched between us.

The leader's eyes held mine, a flicker of something like regret passing through them. "Garrett's disappearance? That wasn't The Vault's doing," he said, and I could hear the truth in his voice. "And we don't know who it was." He was my friend. We had our suspicions, sure, but nothing was ever confirmed."

They let me go then, their grip loosening. I scrambled to my feet, my body aching from the fall and my hands itching for the gun I couldn't reach. "What suspicions?" I demanded, my voice hoarse.

The guy who'd spoken just shook his head, his mask still hiding any expression. "The story didn't sit right with any of us, especially when Garrett's parents started reaching out online, asking if anyone had seen him, if he was okay."

"And?" I prompted, my hands clenched into fists at my sides.

"Supposedly, Garrett left a note saying he needed time to figure shit out. But the only person who ever saw it, outside of the cops, was a guy named Jude Paulsson."

"Jude Paulsson? Who the fuck is Jude Paulsson?"

The masked figures exchanged glances, and the leader shrugged, a gesture that seemed out of place in the tense atmosphere. "Jude was... he's a scary kind of guy. Violent. Got a temper that could turn on a dime. But he was smart, too. Never got caught doing anything concrete, so he's still out there."

I took a step forward, my cop instincts kicking in despite the situation. "You got any info on this Jude? Something I can use?"

The leader hesitated, then nodded slowly. "I'll email you everything I have. Just... don't drag me into this. I've got enough shit to deal with."

I memorized his stance, his build, anything I could use to identify him later if it came to that. "I need that info. And I need it now."

"It'll be in your inbox by morning," he said, and there was a finality in his tone that suggested the conversation was over.

I stared the guy down, trying to read any hint of deceit in his stance, in the tilt of his head, even though I couldn't see his face. "Lexi Barrows," I said, the name like a bullet. "What do you know about her?"

The guy shifted, his surprise evident even behind the mask. "Why do you ask?"

"She's my sister, and she's got a stalker who was after her in college, too," I said, the words tasting like acid on my tongue.

"Funny you should mention it," the guy said, and there was an edge of what? Humor? Irony? "Jude was who she dated after Garrett."

My heart lurched, a cold splash of dread hitting me. "Jude dated Lexi?" I hadn't seen that one coming. My sister had never mentioned a Jude, but then, there was a lot she hadn't mentioned.

"Yeah," he confirmed, his voice taking on a lower note. "After Garrett vanished, Jude swooped in. Always thought it was fucking convenient."

I took a step closer. "And you're telling me this now? What else are you keeping from me?"

The guy held up his hands, a placating gesture. "Look, man, I'm telling you everything I know. Jude was bad news. Always had an angle, always playing some long game. We all thought he had something to do with Garrett, but no one could prove it."

"And my sister?" I pressed, my voice a growl.

He shook his head. "After Jude, she kinda distanced herself from The Vault, from all of us. Can't say I blame her."

I backed off a step, my mind racing. Lexi and this Jude character, a new lead, a new angle. "If you're bullshitting me—"

"I'm not," he interrupted, his voice sharp. "I swear. Check your email tomorrow. You'll have what I've got on Jude."

I gave him a long, hard look. "If you're playing me—"

"I'm not," he said again. "Just... be careful, alright? Jude's not the kind of guy you want to take on without some backup."

I nodded once, tersely. "Thanks for the heads-up."

He nodded back and then disappeared into the shadows, leaving me standing there in the quiet night. I turned and headed back to my cruiser, my mind a mess of thoughts.

As I drove back, the darkness seemed to close in around me, everything I'd learned pressing down hard. Lexi had never mentioned a Jude, but then, there was a lot she hadn't said, a lot she'd kept hidden. And now, with her life potentially in danger, those secrets could be the key to everything.

The drive was long and silent, the hum of the cruiser's engine the only sound in the quiet night. I kept turning it over in my mind – Jude, Garrett, The Vault.

I pulled into the hospital parking lot, the fluorescent lights stark against the night. I needed to see Kayla, to tell her what I'd found out. But when I got to her room, she was sleeping, the rise and fall of her chest a steady rhythm that I watched for a long moment.

"Kayla," I whispered, even though she couldn't hear me. "I'm getting closer. I promise."

I didn't stay long, just long enough to reassure myself she was still fighting. Then I was back in the cruiser, the night stretching out before me, endless and dark. As I hit the road, the lines on the asphalt seemed to blur together, a monotonous rhythm that matched the turmoil in my head.

I had a name, a new lead, but it felt like a drop in the ocean. I needed more, and I needed it fast. As the miles ticked by, I made a silent vow – I'd find this Jude, and I'd find out the truth. For Lexi, for Kayla, for all of us.

The next day was a deep dive into Jude's world, one that felt like swimming through a swamp, murky and full of unseen dangers. His rap sheet was a laundry list of almosts—almost caught, almost convicted. Every damn arrest, from assault to breaking and entering, happened in Miami, a string of run-ins with the law that never stuck. He was slippery, like a damn eel, and I hated him without ever laying eyes on the guy.

First arrest, during his college days—I snapped to attention as I recognized the name of the booking officer. It was the same guy who'd been in charge of the investigation when Garrett disappeared and again when they found that body. "What the fuck..." I muttered, the pieces clicking into place like a loaded gun. A dirty cop—had to be.

I was neck-deep in arrest reports when my cell rang. Lexi's name flashed on the screen, and the knot in my gut pulled tighter.

"Jake?" Her voice was a blade of panic cutting through the line.

"Lexi, what's wrong? Did the stalker find the safe house?" I was already moving, grabbing my keys and my gun.

"No, I... I needed to come home for a bit, but he was here, Jake." Her voice broke, and I felt my control fraying at the edges. "He left me a note on the wall."

"Wait right there. Don't touch anything. I'm on my way." I was out the door before she could say another word.

The drive was a blur, every red light a curse, every slow driver an obstacle to barrel through. My sister's house loomed in the darkness, a beacon of dread as I slammed the cruiser to a stop and ran inside.

The Rookie's Second Chance

The sight that greeted me was a gut punch. "Welcome home" was scrawled across the wall in what looked like blood, a grotesque greeting. Beneath it lay one of the ranch's chickens, its neck twisted, dead eyes staring at nothing.

"Motherfucker," I spat, my hands clenching into fists. "Lexi, you upstairs?"

"Yeah," she called down, her voice shaky.

I took the stairs two at a time, finding her in her room, huddled on the bed, a fortress of pillows around her. "I'm so sorry, Lexi," I said, my voice rough around the edges. "This is all fucked up."

She looked up at me, her eyes wide and haunted. "I just wanted to get some of my things. I didn't think..."

I sat next to her, my arm around her shoulders. "You didn't do anything wrong. This asshole is playing games, but I swear, Lex, we're gonna catch him."

Her head dropped onto my shoulder, her body trembling. "I'm so scared, Jake."

I held her tighter. "I know, sis. But you're not alone. We're going to get through this."

The house felt tainted now, every shadow a hiding place, every noise a threat. I stood up, my resolve winding through me. "Stay here. I'm gonna call it in, get a unit over here to watch the place."

She nodded, and I stepped out of the room, my cell already pressed to my ear. The dispatcher's voice was a calm in the storm, and I rattled off the situation.

"Keep your doors locked, Lexi," I called to her. "I'll be right outside."

I waited on the porch, the night air cold. The cruiser's headlights cut through the darkness as it pulled up, and I briefed the officer, a solid guy named Martinez.

"We'll keep an eye on the place," he assured me.

"Thanks. I owe you one."

I watched them settle in before I got back into my cruiser. The dashboard's glow was a dim comfort as I started the engine and pulled away, my mind a whirlwind of fury and fear.

The road stretched out before me, the night clinging to the edges. But inside, there was a fire burning, a fire that wouldn't be put out until I caught the bastard who dared to terrorize my sister.

Chapter Twenty-Six

KAYLA

I was barely through the hospital doors, the discharge papers still warm in my hand, when the itch to get back to the case settled in. The doc had been clear—rest, no stress, and definitely no work for a few days. But hell, that wasn't happening, not with the bastard who put me here still out there and my mind racing faster than my heart on a treadmill.

I'd barely made it through my front door when my cell buzzed. Jake. I hesitated for a second, knowing what I'd hear in his voice—worry, frustration, that protective edge that had him treating me like I was made of glass.

"Hey," I answered, keeping my voice steady, almost cheerful. "Just got my walking papers."

"Kayla, tell me you're heading straight home to rest," he said, and I could almost see him running a hand through his hair like he did when he was stressed.

"Of course," I lied smoothly. "Already there. Couch-bound for the foreseeable future."

There was a pause, and I knew he didn't quite buy it.

"Good," he finally said. "Because I met with some guys from The Vault last night, and—"

"The Vault?" I interrupted, my brain kicking into high gear. "You find something?"

"Maybe," he said, and I could hear the caution in his voice. "They mentioned a guy—Jude. You ever heard of him?"

The name was new to me. "Nope, first I'm hearing of it. Who is he?"

There was a shuffling sound like Jake was moving papers. "Bad news, from what I can tell. Lots of arrests but no convictions. He could be in Silver Creek; timelines match up."

My pulse quickened. "Jake, I can help—"

"No, Kayla," he cut me off, his voice firm. "You need to recover. I'll handle this."

I bit back a retort, frustration simmering. "Fine," I said, but I was pulling out my laptop as soon as we ended the call. Time to see what the internet knew about Jude.

His last arrest popped up a few months back, and the trail went cold after that. No more run-ins, no current address. He was a ghost, and that made him dangerous. But if he was in Silver Creek, then so was I, and I wasn't about to sit back and wait.

I started digging, tapping into databases and public records, looking for any thread to pull. Hours slipped by, the taxi ride long forgotten as I hunched over my screen. By the time I realized it, the sun was dipping low, casting long shadows across my living room.

A knock at the door startled me, and I closed my laptop with a snap. I wasn't expecting anyone, and every visitor felt like a potential threat.

Peeking through the peephole, I saw it was just the delivery guy with dinner. I'd forgotten I'd ordered food.

The Rookie's Second Chance

With a sigh, I opened the door, exchanging a few bills for the bag of greasy sustenance.

Back to my research, I ate without tasting, my focus narrowing. Jude's name kept popping up, a specter in the background of several incidents, always slipping away before he could be pinned down.

The realization hit me—Jude was careful, meticulous. He didn't get caught because he didn't make mistakes. And if he was the one who'd come after me, who was stalking Lexi, then we were dealing with someone who knew how to play the game.

I leaned back, rubbing my temples. The pain was a dull roar now, my head full of information and possibilities, each one more unsettling than the last.

I glanced at my phone, contemplating calling Jake back, telling him I wasn't just sitting around. But I knew that conversation wouldn't go well. He'd be pissed, and rightly so.

Instead, I got up, pacing the room. Resting wasn't in the cards—not with Jude out there, not with Lexi's safety hanging in the balance. I needed to be in this, even if I had to do it from the shadows.

The evening wore on as I continued my search. I was a detective, dammit, injured or not, and I wouldn't be sidelined. Not by Jake, not by the doctor, and certainly not by some asshole like Jude.

I clicked through the digital maze of reports and records, my finger hovering over the mouse with an urgency that was becoming all too familiar. I shouldn't have been doing this, not with the stitches still fresh on my scalp and the doctor's warnings echoing like an annoying bell. But shit, when did I ever do the should-dos?

And then I saw it—a concealed police report, buried under layers of bureaucracy and, dare I say, intentional misfiling. The name on the report sent a cold shiver down my spine: Officer Kilkenny. That name again, cropping up like a bad penny.

"Son of a bitch," I muttered, zooming in on the screen, my eyes scanning the text as fast as they could while still making sense of the legalese.

The report was a labyrinth of insinuations and half-mentions, but it was clear as day to anyone who knew how to look. This was about Lexi's stalker case, and Kilkenny, that damned cop from Miami, had his fingers all over it.

I leaned back, feeling the pull of the stitches on my skin, a reminder of the fragility of my situation. But it wasn't the time to dwell on personal aches. I grabbed my cell, punching in Jake's number with a fervor.

He picked up on the second ring, "Kayla? What's up? You should be resting."

I could almost hear the eye roll in his voice, but this was too big to wait. "Jake, you're not going to believe this. I found a report, a concealed one. And guess whose name is on it?"

There was a beat of silence, and I knew I had his full attention. "Who?"

"Kilkenny," I said. "And it's tied to Lexi's case. It looks like he misfiled it, maybe on purpose. This is huge, Jake."

I could hear the rustling sound of him moving, probably reaching for something to write with. "Are you sure? How'd you find it?"

I smirked despite the situation. "Would you believe me if I said dumb luck? Because it sure as hell wasn't by following the rules."

A chuckle, tired and strained, came through the line. "You're unbelievable, you know that? Hold tight, I'm coming over. We need to go through this together."

We ended the call, and I got to work, forwarding the

files to Jake's encrypted email. As I did, I thought about Lexi, everything she had been through, and how all these threads—Lexi, Garrett, Jude, Kilkenny—were intertwining into a knot that we were about to untie.

I pushed away from the desk, feeling the room tilt a little. I needed to keep a level head. With a deep breath, I steadied myself. This was no time to falter. I was on the edge of something big, and I knew it.

Jake arrived, and the day passed in a blur of coffee and hushed phone calls as we pieced together what we could from the report. Officer Kilkenny, the man who should have been the protector, the law enforcer, was our prime suspect. The irony wasn't lost on me, nor was the danger.

The room was silent except for our breathing and the soft click of my laptop keys. The screen's glow cast shadows across his face, highlighting the dark circles under his eyes.

"Have you slept at all?" I asked, not looking away from the screen.

"I'll sleep when this is over," he muttered, rubbing his eyes. His dedication was as fierce as it was foolhardy.

"Come on, Jake. You're no good to Lexi or me if you collapse."

He shook his head, a stubborn set to his jaw. "There's no time, Kayla."

I stood up and stretched, feeling the pull of my own aches. "Bullshit. You're going to bed, even if I have to drag you there."

A ghost of a smile flickered on his face. "You wouldn't dare."

"Try me," I challenged, closing my laptop with a snap.

He stood, towering over me, but the exhaustion was clear in the way his shoulders slumped. "Fine. But only a couple of hours."

I led him to my bedroom, watching as he sat on the edge of the bed, looking like he was about to argue again. Instead, he lay down, his body sprawled across the covers.

"Get in," he said, eyes already closing.

I hesitated only a moment before sliding in beside him, pulling him into an embrace. His body was tense at first, but gradually, he relaxed against me, his breathing deepening. I held him, feeling the rise and fall of his chest until his weight settled against me in the deep, even rhythm of sleep.

I watched him, the steady beat of his heart under my hand a comfort. I should have felt the same pull of sleep, but I was preoccupied with the case and the fear of what might happen if we didn't solve this fast.

Eventually, the tension of the day caught up with me, and I drifted off, the warmth of Jake beside me anchoring me to the present.

It was still dark out when Jake's phone buzzed incessantly on the nightstand, waking me. I reached out to silence it, but he was already stirring, the sound jolting him awake.

"Shit," he said, grabbing the phone. His expression darkened as he scrolled through the notifications—missed calls from Lexi, from Mandy.

He was out of bed in an instant, the phone pressed to his ear as he tried to return the calls. I sat up, rubbing my eyes, the peace of the night shattered. I checked my own phone and saw it was three in the morning.

When he got no answer, he turned to me, frustrated. "This is exactly why I can't afford to sleep. If something's happened—"

"Jake, you needed the rest. You were dead on your feet," I protested, my worry rising.

He shook his head, pacing the length of the room. "And what if Lexi needed me? What if Mandy—"

"You couldn't have done anything in the state you were in," I cut in, standing to face him. "You needed to be sharp, for Lexi, for the case. For me."

But he wasn't having it. "I should've been there. I shouldn't have listened to you."

I reached out, trying to offer some comfort, some reassurance, but he shrugged me off, the warmth of last night a distant memory.

"I have to go," he said, grabbing his jacket.

"Jake, let me help—"

"No," he snapped, his voice cold. "I can't do this right now. I can't."

And then he was gone, the door slamming behind him with a finality that left me standing alone, a hollow feeling in the pit of my stomach.

I should have been used to this—the ups and downs of our work, the constant tension. But this felt different, personal. I wrapped my arms around myself, hugging the storm of emotions that raged within me.

I'd pushed him to rest and take care of himself, and now he was alone, thinking I'd held him back. The guilt was a sharp pang in my chest. I needed to make this right, but first, I needed to know what had happened.

I went to my laptop, my hands trembling slightly as I opened it. Whatever was waiting for us out there, I had a feeling it would only get worse.

I couldn't just sit and wallow in hurt feelings. There was work to be done, even if Jake didn't want my help right now. So, I turned to the task at hand, diving back into the mystery of Officer Kilkenny.

My fingers flew over the keyboard, chasing down leads, pulling on the digital threads that might unravel this case.

The dull ache in my head, a leftover from the attack, was a constant reminder of the stakes we were playing for. Then, something clicked—a series of photos hidden deep in the bowels of social media, including one from a school function where families were invited. There he was, Kilkenny, all smiles next to a younger man who bore a striking resemblance to him.

"Jude," I muttered, zooming in on the younger man's face. Different last name, but the resemblance was uncanny. Could it be? Could Jude be Kilkenny's son? It was a long shot, but in this case, long shots seemed the only kind we had.

I tried to access family records to find a birth certificate, a marriage license, or anything that would confirm the connection. But Kilkenny's records were sealed tight, locked behind bureaucratic red tape that would require a formal request to cut through. A request that would take time we didn't have.

"Damn it," I cursed under my breath, the frustration boiling over. I needed access now, not weeks from now. But there was no way around it, so I filled out the request forms, each keystroke a begrudging acceptance of the waiting game I'd been forced to play.

Submitting the request felt like dropping a message in a bottle into a digital ocean. It was out of my hands now. I could only wait and hope it would wash up on the right virtual shore in time to make a difference.

The room's silence closed in on me, and I pushed back from the desk, my eyes burning from hours of staring at the screen. Jake's absence was like a cold draft, chilling the space where warmth used to be. I wrapped my arms around myself, the trust I'd placed in him feeling like a gift that had been carelessly dropped and cracked.

Once, I'd believed we had something that could last,

but that had been before he'd broken my heart, before I'd built walls to protect myself from just this kind of pain. And now, I was tearing those walls down for him, for Lexi, for a case proving to be more personal than I ever imagined.

When six rolled around, I stood up, restless energy coursing through me. I couldn't just sit here, not when there was a predator out there, one that had slipped through our fingers more than once. My gaze fell on my badge and gun, resting on the small table by the door. It was a silent call to action, and I found myself striding toward it, the badge in my hand grounding me.

I clipped the badge to my belt, the familiar weight a reminder of who I was, of the oath I'd taken. I wouldn't let fear or bureaucracy stop me from protecting those I cared about. I wouldn't let Jake face this darkness alone, even if he thought that's what he wanted.

With my gun secured at my side, I headed out the door, a plan forming in my mind. I might not have access to Kilkenny's sealed records, but there were other ways to get information. It was time to shake the tree and see what fell out.

The drive to the station was automatic, the route so familiar I could have navigated it blindfolded. But solitude pressed down on me as I parked the car and stepped out. This was usually something I did with Jake, not in spite of him.

I pushed through the doors, my resolve hardening with each step. I would find the truth, with or without Jake's blessing. Because this was about more than just a case now; it was about justice, about keeping the promise I'd made to myself and those who counted on me, and about upholding the sanctity of law enforcement by bringing a dirty cop to justice.

Chapter Twenty-Seven

JAKE

Pounding the steering wheel, I gunned the engine, cursing under my breath. Kayla's place was fading in the rearview, and my phone was buzzing like a goddamn beehive. Lexi's voice, usually so composed, was tinged with a tension that cut through me like a knife.

"Jake, where are you? I keep hearing noises outside. Luke said he's coming to get me, but he could be a while and I don't want someone breaking in with me in the house alone."

Her words were a splash of cold water, snapping me back to reality. I should've been there, not caught up in a tiff with Kayla. I hit the call button for Mandy's number, but her voicemail cut through before it could ring.

"Jake, Lexi called me saying there's someone outside the ranch, and she's not the only one spooked. There's someone prowling around your house. I can hear them from my window."

Shit. The situation was spiraling faster than I could handle. I felt responsibility like a noose tightening around my neck. I had to get to Mandy and make sure she was safe. The rest of the messages from Lexi and Mandy were a blur, her fear and my concern merging into a symphony of panic.

Then Luke's voice, steady and calm, cut through the chaos. "I've got Lexi, Jake. We're heading back to the safe house. She's safe, man. But get your ass back and check on Mandy, will you?"

His message was a life raft in the storm. Lexi was safe, but Mandy... I had to get back. My mind was racing, trying to piece together this mess. Jude, the stalker, or some other son of a bitch could be at my doorstep, and I wasn't there.

The cruiser ate up the miles back to town, the engine's growl a match for the storm brewing inside me. The night was pressing in, a suffocating blanket of darkness that seemed to echo my dread.

I pulled up to my place, scanning the dark, quiet street. No signs of life, no lurking shadows. I stepped out of the cruiser, my hand instinctively resting on my holster.

"Mandy!" I called out as I approached, my voice low but urgent. "You there?"

The door swung open, and she was there, her face pale in the porch light. "Jake! I'm okay. I didn't know what to do. I heard someone out back."

I rushed past her, checking the perimeter, but there was nothing—no signs of forced entry, no footprints, just the stillness of an empty backyard.

"Fuck, Mandy. You sure you heard something?" My voice was harsh, the adrenaline and fear sharpening my words.

"Yes, I swear. It was like someone was right outside the window," she insisted, wrapping her arms around herself.

I glanced back at the house, the silence mocking me. "Stay inside, lock the doors. I'm gonna check the rest of the place."

Room by room, I cleared the house, but it was empty. No intruder, no sign anyone had been there. It was like chasing ghosts, and my frustration was boiling over.

"Nothing. There's no one here," I reported, holstering my gun as I walked back into the living room where Mandy was waiting.

She looked up at me, her eyes wide and scared. "So, what now?"

"Now," I said, the words gritty with determination, "we wait for daylight, then we go after this bastard. He's made this personal, and I'm going to make sure he regrets it."

I watched Mandy try to steady her trembling hands, her attempt at bravery about as solid as smoke.

Shit.

"You good?" I asked, knowing full well she wasn't.

She gave me a nod, but her eyes were telling a different story. "I was so scared, Jake. I just... I don't know what I'd do if—"

I cut her off with a firm hug, the kind you give someone when words just won't cut it. She melted into it, her body still shaking. "You're safe now. That's all that matters."

She pulled away slightly, enough to look up at me. "Did you really not find anything?"

"Nothing," I confirmed, racking my brain for any missed details. "Did you catch any sounds that stood out? Anything at all that might give us a lead?"

She shook her head, her brow furrowed in frustration. "It was just... noises. Like someone was right outside. But no voices, no nothing."

I sighed, running a hand down my face. "Alright. You should try and get some rest. You'll feel better."

Her eyes darted away from mine and then back. "I don't think I can sleep. Not after all that. Not alone..."

The Rookie's Second Chance

The unspoken request hung in the air between us, and I didn't hesitate. "I'll stick around. I can sit in your room and keep watch if it makes you feel safe."

The relief in her smile hit me harder than I expected. "Thanks, Jake. I'd like that."

So I followed her to her room, a simple space that she'd managed to transform from a plain guest room into her own personal haven in just the short time she'd been staying with me. She'd been working from this room as a mobile office so she could be there for Lexi when this all blew over. She crawled under the covers while I found a chair in the corner, my body angled so I could see both her and the door.

The room was quiet. I watched Mandy's eyes flutter closed, her breathing eventually evening out as sleep took her.

My own thoughts were a whirlwind. Everyone was safe —for now. Luke had Lexi, Mandy was here, and Kayla... well, I was going to have to apologize for the way I acted. She didn't do anything wrong.

But all this was just the calm before the storm. If I didn't piece this puzzle together soon, someone would be in the crosshairs again. And God help me, I didn't know who it would be.

The chair was uncomfortable, a constant reminder that I wasn't here to relax. I kept replaying the voicemails, the fear in Lexi's voice, the worry in Mandy's, the steadiness in Luke's. It was a fucked-up symphony that I was sick of hearing.

My eyelids grew heavy with the effort of the past forty-eight hours. But sleep was a luxury I couldn't afford, not when every passing moment was a chance for this faceless threat to step out of the shadows.

So I sat there, in the dim light of dawn creeping

through the curtains, a silent guardian against the danger I knew was still lurking out there. My hand rested near my gun, a cold comfort against the uncertainty.

And as Mandy slept, I let the quiet rage build inside me, a promise to the darkness that I would tear it apart to keep them safe. My friends, my sister, my town. They were counting on me, and I wouldn't let them down. Not now, not ever.

Mandy's eyes fluttered open as the first light of day filtered through the blinds, and I pushed up from the chair, muscles stiff from the long night. "Morning," I said, a bit more gruffly than intended.

She offered me a weak smile, the shadows of last night's fear still visible in the corners of her eyes. "Did you stay all night?"

"Promised, didn't I?" I replied, scratching at the stubble on my chin. "You hungry?"

She nodded, and I headed to the kitchen to rustle up something that passed for breakfast. Eggs, bread, and a couple of slices of ham found their way onto the skillet. The sizzle and pop of the food cooking was a welcome distraction from the knot of tension sitting heavy in my stomach.

We sat at the kitchen table, the meal between us acting as a temporary buffer against the outside world. I watched Mandy poke at her eggs before looking up. "You okay?"

She hesitated, then said, "You know, with everything going on... I'm not sure anymore."

I wanted to reassure her, tell her everything would be fine, but the words would've been as empty as the coffee pot I now set about refilling. Instead, I asked, "Mandy, do you know a guy named Jude?"

Her fork clattered to the plate, and she went pale. "Jude? Why?"

I leaned back, arms crossed. "Just came up in the investigation."

Her lips pressed into a thin line. "Yeah, I know him. He... he dated Lexi in college. Charming at first glance but a real piece of work underneath. I had to help Lexi get rid of him."

The news hit like a punch to the gut. "Why the hell didn't Lexi tell me about him?"

Mandy shrugged. "She was probably scared. Ashamed, even. You know how she is, tries to handle things on her own."

That sounded like Lexi, alright, always playing the lone wolf. "Do you think he could be the stalker?"

Mandy's gaze dropped. "I don't know, Jake, but... he made Lexi afraid. Really afraid."

I stretched and swung my arms in circles, the need to move, to do something with this information, itching under my skin. "I gotta get to the station."

Mandy reached out, her hand brushing mine. "Be careful, Jake."

I nodded, the case settling on me once again. "Always am."

Stepping out into the crisp morning air, I couldn't shake the feeling that we were getting closer to something dark.

The drive to the station was a blur, my thoughts consumed with the task ahead. Lexi's fear, Mandy's concern, the tight feeling in my chest—it was all part of the storm that was brewing.

I walked into the station, the buzz of the morning shift already humming through the air. I was back in my element, back where I could make a difference. And I'd start with Jude.

Kayla was hunched over her desk, squinting at the

computer screen like it held the secrets of the universe. Even from a distance, I could tell she'd been here for hours, digging, searching.

"Kayla," I called out, a little louder than necessary over the din of ringing phones and chattering officers. She looked up, and for a moment, her eyes were unreadable pools of midnight.

"Can we talk? Privately?" I asked, the previous night heavy on my tongue.

She studied me, then nodded, her movements measured as she rose from the chair. We found an empty interrogation room, the silence a relief from the noise outside.

I took a deep breath, letting it out slowly. "About last night, I was an ass. I'm sorry."

She leaned against the table, arms folded. "You were stressed, Jake. It's okay. I get it."

I shook my head. "No, it's not okay. I love you, Kayla. I should've been there for you, for us, not just the case."

She exhaled, a small smile touching her lips. "I love you too, but Jake, I think I found something."

That perked me up. "A lead?"

"Yeah." She motioned for us to head back to her desk.

Once there, she pulled up a photo on her screen—Officer Kilkenny and Jude, standing side by side like father and son.

I felt a chill snake down my spine. "Shit. Jude might as well have a 'get out of jail free' card if that's his old man."

Kayla's eyes narrowed as she pieced it together. "You think Kilkenny's been pulling strings?"

"It's more than strings. It's like he's been weaving a damn safety net," I said, anger simmering in my veins. "What if he's covering up more than just Jude's petty crimes? What if he's covering up... everything?"

Her gasp was sharp, her hand flying to her mouth. "You mean, like stalking Lexi?"

"Exactly," I said, leaning in. "And what if it's even darker than that? Kilkenny was the lead on both Garrett's disappearance and the John Doe case. What if he made sure Jude was never a suspect?"

The color drained from Kayla's face. "That would mean... he could've killed Garrett. To get to Lexi."

I nodded, the pieces clicking into place. "We've got to dig into Kilkenny's past. See if we can't find any more connections."

Kayla nodded. "I'll pull up everything we have on him. There's got to be something we missed."

"Look at this," Kayla said a few minutes later, pointing at the screen. "Every time Jude's been picked up, Kilkenny's been on duty, even if it wasn't his case."

I leaned back. "It's more than just a father covering for his son. It's corruption, deep and dirty."

Kayla's hand found mine, squeezing tight. "We can expose him, Jake. We can bring him down."

I turned to her, the determination in her eyes reflecting my own. "We will. For Lexi. For Garrett. For us."

Kilkenny and Jude, father and son, were at the heart of it all. We just needed to prove it. And we would, no matter what it took.

Chapter Twenty-Eight

KAYLA

At the station, Jake grabbed his keys with a sense of urgency. "I'm heading to check on Lexi and Luke. You going to be okay here?"

"Yeah, I'll hold down the fort," I replied, offering a tight-lipped smile.

Once he left, a nagging thought urged me to do something... normal. Maybe it was the exhaustion talking, or the need to connect with someone who wasn't tied up in all this mess. I remembered the flowers from Mandy and figured a thank you was overdue.

Driving to Jake's house felt strange, like stepping into a parallel world where life was mundane, and the biggest worry was whether you'd need a second cup of coffee. I shook off the unease as I parked and walked up to the front door, knocking softly.

Mandy opened the door, surprise flickering over her features. "Kayla, what are you doing here?"

"I wanted to thank you for the flowers," I said, stepping inside when she gestured.

"Of course. Coffee? Tea?" she asked, leading me into the kitchen.

"Coffee, please," I said, settling at the kitchen table.

Mandy moved around the kitchen, her back to me as the coffee brewed. The silence stretched out.

Finally, I spoke. " Mandy, the flowers were beautiful. Thank you."

She turned, a practiced smile on her face. "It was the least I could do. We're all so worried about you." Her eyes searched mine, looking for... what? I wasn't sure, but I felt a sudden unease, my detective experience taking hold.

I accepted the mug she handed me, the warmth seeping into my palms. "I appreciate it," I said, meeting her gaze evenly.

Mandy sat across from me, her smile unwavering. "So, you and Jake, huh?" Her tone was casual, but there was a sharpness to her words.

"Sorry?" I asked, knowing Jake hadn't told her about us.

"Working together. After all this time."

I sipped my coffee, considering my response. "Yeah, me and Jake."

She leaned forward, her elbows on the table. "He's a great guy. Been through a lot, you know?"

I nodded, the unspoken implication hanging in the air between us. "He is. And yes, he has."

Mandy's eyes flickered with something that wasn't entirely friendly. "Just... it's been tough on him, with Lexi and everything. He needs someone who understands."

The underlying message wasn't lost on me. "I understand him more than you think," I replied, my voice steady.

Mandy's smile faltered, then she recovered, laughing softly. "I'm sure you do. I just mean, it's good he has someone to come home to. Someone to take care of him. It's not like you can come home with him after work to have some beer and watch TV together."

My grip on the mug tightened, but I kept my expression neutral. "He takes care of himself. We take care of each other."

There was a pause as we both sipped our coffee.

"Well, I'm just glad he's not alone," Mandy said, her tone sweet as syrup but with a bitter aftertaste. "After all, who knows what could happen, right?"

I set my mug down, the clink of ceramic on wood sharp in the quiet room. "That's right, Mandy. Who knows."

She stood, her movements a little too quick. "More coffee?"

I shook my head. "No, thank you. I should get going." As I stood up, ready to leave, a question tugged at the back of my mind. "Mandy, before I go, did you know Jude well?"

Mandy paused, her back still to me as she placed our mugs in the sink. "Already grilled Jake about him, didn't you?"

"Yeah, but you might remember something he didn't. Anything could help."

She wiped her hands on a dish towel, leaning against the counter. "Like I told Jake, Jude was bad news. Even in high school, he was scary."

My brows shot up. "High school? I thought you all went to college together?"

"Did I say high school?" Mandy's laugh was hollow, her smile forced. "Sorry, I misspoke. College, of course."

I nodded slowly, watching her. She was fidgeting, a clear sign of nerves. "It's okay. If you remember anything else—"

The Rookie's Second Chance

"I'll tell Jake," She cut in quickly.

I appreciated her offer, but as I walked to my car, I couldn't shake the feeling that Mandy was holding back. It was the way her eyes darted away when she mentioned high school, the way her hands trembled slightly.

Driving home, I turned the radio off, needing silence to think. Mandy's slip of the tongue about high school and Jude and her quick correction didn't sit right. I was sure she had information, but for whatever reason, she wasn't willing to share it with me.

The more I thought about it, the more I realized that Mandy would never open up to me about Jude or anything else that could help. But Jake... she might talk to him, especially if she thought it would bring them closer.

I pulled into my driveway, the house too quiet. Every creak of the floorboards as I moved through the rooms felt louder than usual, echoing the turmoil in my mind.

I needed to talk to Jake, to tell him about Mandy's reaction, but it would have to wait. For now, I had to focus on what I could do alone. But damn, it was frustrating to think that an answer was being held just out of reach, guarded by someone whose motives I couldn't trust.

The early afternoon streamed into my living room as my phone buzzed on the coffee table. Seeing Jake's name light up the screen sent an unexpected rush of warmth through me.

"Hey," I answered, trying to sound casual.

"Kayla, you up for a late lunch today?" His voice, even over the phone, had that gravelly edge that tugged at me.

I hesitated, a flicker of uncertainty crossing my mind. "Wouldn't that be a risk, though? We're still supposed to be keeping a low profile, right?"

"We can head out to the ranch and have a picnic there. Keep it quiet. I doubt the stalker will come back again, and if he does—we'll be there to catch him." A hopeful note in his voice made it hard to resist.

A smile crept onto my face, the idea appealing more than I wanted to admit. "Okay, sounds nice. I'll grab some takeout."

"I'll pick you up in an hour?" he suggested.

"Perfect. See you then."

I ended the call and took a moment to savor the silence before getting ready. The thought of an afternoon away from the chaos under the vast expanse of the open sky felt like a much-needed reprieve.

I drove to pick up our favorite dishes from a little family-owned restaurant downtown, the smell of seasoned meats and fresh bread filling the car, promising a feast.

True to his word, Jake was at my door an hour later, a soft smile on his face that reached his tired eyes. I hadn't seen that smile in what felt like ages.

"Got everything?" he asked as I locked my front door.

"All set," I replied, lifting the bag of food.

The drive to the ranch was quiet and comfortable. The tension that had been winding tighter in my chest began to ease as the town fell away behind us, giving way to open fields and a golden sky.

We laid out a blanket in a secluded corner of the ranch, the late afternoon enveloping us in a cocoon of privacy. Jake popped open a bottle of wine, pouring each of us a glass as I set out the containers of food.

"To us," he toasted, raising his glass.

"To us," I echoed, clinking my glass against his.

We ate and talked, the conversation meandering from light-hearted banter to the case that had consumed our lives. Every so often, Jake's hand would brush against mine, sending a jolt of electricity through me.

As the sun began to dip, Jake lay back on the blanket,

pulling me down beside him. We lay side by side, looking up at the endless heavens.

"It's beautiful out here," I murmured, feeling a peace I hadn't known in too long.

"Yeah, it is," Jake agreed, his voice soft. He turned his head to look at me, and our eyes locked. For a long moment, we just gazed at each other, the rest of the world falling away.

I leaned into him, resting my head on his shoulder. His arm came around me, pulling me closer, and I could feel the steady beat of his heart against my cheek.

The afternoon had been perfect, almost like a dream, but as the evening crept in, I could see a restlessness creeping into Jake's demeanor. His gaze kept drifting off, a frown flickering across his features now and then.

"What's eating you?" I finally asked, nudging him with my elbow.

He shook his head, trying to brush it off with a half-hearted "Nothing."

I raised an eyebrow, not buying it for a second. "You're a terrible liar, you know that?"

He let out a chuckle, the sound a bit strained. "Yeah, you got me there. I was just thinking... about the house. I 'haven't really checked it out since Lexi went back to the safe house, and then with Mandy..."

I felt a twinge of irritation at the mention of Mandy, but I pushed it aside. This wasn't about petty jealousies. "And you're worried you missed something?" I pressed, keeping my tone even.

"Yeah, I guess so. It's been nagging at me," he admitted, his eyes meeting mine. There was an earnestness in them that pulled at me.

I smiled despite the gravity of his concern. "And here I thought you were just overwhelmed by my charm."

He grinned then, a genuine, Jake-like grin, and leaned in to kiss me, a soft press of lips that was reassuring in its familiarity. As he pulled back, he glanced toward the house, the gears clearly turning in his head.

"I hate to ruin the moment, but... would you come check out the house with me? Just to be sure?" he asked, his voice tinged with a seriousness that matched the set of his jaw.

I laughed despite the odd romantic pivot. "What a way to woo a girl, Barrows."

He stood, offering me his hand with a playful bow. "I promise to make it up to you."

I took his hand, letting him pull me to my feet. "You'd better," I teased, but inside, my heart was racing with anticipation and dread.

The chill of the early evening crept up my spine as Jake and I approached Luke and Lexi's house. The place stood silent, its windows like dark, watchful eyes. Even with Jake's steady presence beside me, an uneasy feeling had begun to twist in my gut.

"We should check around the outside first," Jake suggested, his voice low as if the night could overhear us.

"Lead the way, detective," I replied, trying to keep the mood light.

We started with the perimeter, Jake's flashlight beam adding just a touch more light to highlight anything out of the ordinary. I trailed slightly behind Jake, my gaze darting between the ground and the looming structure of the house.

"There," I pointed out when I noticed smudges on the lower corner of a windowpane as Jake's beam of light fell on them. "Fingerprints."

Jake crouched down, examining the marks. "Good

catch," he murmured. "Looks like someone was trying to be careful, but they slipped up."

I knelt beside him, the cool air nipping at my cheeks. "Too bad for them," I said, though the satisfaction of the find was dampened by the implication of what it meant.

We continued our sweep, the beam of Jake's flashlight methodically exposing more signs of intrusion—a scuff mark on the siding, a few strands of hair caught in a thorny bush.

"Let's check inside," Jake said after we completed a full circuit around the house. His voice held a firmness that belied the concern I saw in his eyes.

The front door creaked ominously as we stepped into the foyer. The silence inside was oppressive, the faint echo of our footsteps a stark reminder that we were in a space recently violated by unknown intentions.

Jake led the way to the window we'd inspected from outside. He pulled out a fingerprinting kit from his jacket pocket and looked at me sheepishly.

"You really are well prepared for this date, aren't you?" I teased.

He grinned as he dusted the sill, revealing a clear set of prints. "Look similar to the ones outside, but we should get them to the lab to make sure," he noted, his brow furrowing. "Let's bag these."

While he worked on collecting the prints, I scoured the room. A few loose fibers on the back of a chair, a slight disarray in the placement of the cushions—subtle hints that someone had been there, searching, waiting.

"Anything else?" Jake asked, glancing up from his evidence bag.

"Maybe. It's hard to say without knowing what it looked like before," I said, frustration lacing my words.

We moved through the house methodically, the familiarity of the procedure a thin veil over the raw nerves and heightened senses. In the kitchen, Jake found a broken glass of water beside the counter, a slight red stain on one of the sides where it had cut someone.

"How did they miss all this?" I asked.

"My guess is that since Lexi was safe, they just assumed we'd be by to do a sweep ourselves. But anyway... that glass could be nothing, something Lexi just dropped in fear, but let's take it in," he said, already reaching for another evidence bag.

The living room gave up a few more clues—a disturbed stack of magazines, a lampshade slightly askew. It was nothing definitive, nothing that screamed 'stalker,' but it was enough to keep the unease simmering in my chest.

"We'll need to bring the team in for a full sweep," Jake concluded, his voice grim. "There's more here than we can process alone."

As we stood there in the dimly lit living room, surrounded by the ghosts of the day's revelations, I felt a surge of anger. Someone was playing a twisted game with Lexi and us, and I was tired of it.

"We'll find them," I said, the promise as much for myself as for Jake. "We have to."

He reached out, his hand finding mine in the semi-darkness. "We will," he assured me, and I felt his conviction.

Chapter Twenty-Nine

JAKE

Driving through the darkening streets with Kayla, I could feel the tension rolling off her in waves. It wasn't just the case eating at her; something else was on her mind. I snuck a glance her way.

"Spill it, Kayla. What's got you twisted up?" I finally asked, breaking the silence.

She hesitated, then let out a sigh, "I visited Mandy today."

I raised an eyebrow. "You did? Why the hell would you do that?"

"To thank her for the flowers," she replied, her voice flat. "But Jake... she was very... off."

"Off how?" I prompted, my curiosity piqued.

Kayla turned to face me. "She knows about us, Jake. Or at least, she hinted at it—like she was marking her territory."

A grimace twisted my features, my grip tightening on the steering wheel. "How would she—" I started, but Kayla cut me off.

"Just the way she talked, the things she said. It felt like a warning, like you were... hers." Her voice trailed off.

I reached over, taking her hand in mine. "Not a chance," I said firmly, squeezing her hand for emphasis. Relief flickered over Kayla's face, but it was quickly replaced by a frown.

"And there's something else," she added, "She mentioned Jude... being a nightmare back in high school."

"Not college?" I clarified.

Kayla shook her head. "She said she misspoke, but... I don't know, Jake. I think she's holding back. She knows more than she's saying."

The car hummed beneath us as we drove, our conversation hanging in the air. Mandy's odd behavior, her apparent slip-up about Jude—it all added to the growing list of questions without answers.

I kept one hand on the wheel, the other entwined with Kayla's, as I navigated the roads back to her place. The night was quiet, too quiet. I could sense Kayla's mind working overtime next to me, piecing together the fragmented clues.

"We'll get to the bottom of this," I said, breaking the silence. "Starting with Mandy. If she knows something, we need to find out what it is."

Kayla nodded, her gaze fixed on the road ahead. "She's scared, Jake. Whatever she knows about Jude, it's got her terrified."

The revelation sent a shiver down my spine. If Mandy, who always seemed so calm, was scared, then we were definitely missing a piece of the puzzle—a piece that could very well be the key to unlocking this whole mess.

We drove on, the silence between us now a shared resolve. Whatever was waiting for us in the shadows, we would face it together. I could feel Kayla's presence beside me, a steady force in the turmoil of our investigation. We would figure this out for Lexi, Kayla, and all of us.

As we pulled up to Kayla's place, I let out a long breath I hadn't realized I'd been holding. "Mind if I come in for a minute?" I asked, not ready to be alone with my thoughts just yet.

Before she could answer, my phone rang, cutting through the car's silence. Lexi's name flashed on the screen. "It's Lexi," I said, thumbing the answer button. "Hey, Lex, you okay? It's pretty late."

"As okay as I can be," her voice crackled through the speaker, a tired edge to it. "Have you guys found out anything? I just want this nightmare to be over."

"We found some evidence at the ranch," I told her, watching Kayla's face for any sign of discomfort. She just nodded, encouraging me to continue.

"Anything useful?" Lexi's voice held a flicker of hope.

"Maybe. We're taking it to the lab first thing in the morning," I said, trying to sound more confident than I felt.

Her tone shifted, "We? You and Mandy?"

I frowned, confused. "Why would you think that?"

"Because Mandy made it sound like there might be something between you two," Lexi said, a hint of irritation seeping into her words.

"No, no," I hastened to correct her misunderstanding, "I meant Kayla. We're... together. But it's got to stay under wraps for now, you know, with work and all."

From the corner of my eye, I saw Kayla's lips curve into a smile, a hint of blush coloring her cheeks.

There was a moment of silence before Lexi's laughter bubbled through the line. "Thank God! I always knew you two were meant to be. Hang on, Luke wants to talk to you."

Before I could protest, Luke's voice boomed over the speaker. "Congrats on finally getting your head out of your ass and getting back with the girl you should've never let go in the first place."

I rolled my eyes, a grin spreading despite myself. "Thanks, Luke. Your blessing means the world to me," I said, my voice thick with sarcasm.

Kayla snorted a laugh, and I winked at her. "Hey, I've got to go, but we'll keep you both updated. Stay safe, alright?"

"We will, Jake. And... be good to her," Lexi's softer voice returned on the line, her words a gentle warning.

"I will," I promised, a sincerity in my voice I hadn't expected.

"Wait, before you go... one more thing." I held the phone close, my brows furrowing. "Do you remember a Jude Paulsson?"

The line was quiet for a long stretch, the silence expanding like a bubble ready to pop. "Lexi?" I prodded, anxiety clawing at my gut.

"Why do you ask?" Lexi's voice was cautious and tinged with something I couldn't quite place.

"Someone mentioned Jude might've been involved in Garrett's disappearance," I said, glancing at Kayla as I spoke. She was leaning against the doorway, arms folded, her expression serious.

"What? Garrett left school on his own..." Lexi's voice trailed off, disbelief evident.

I shook my head, even though she couldn't see it. "I don't think so, Lex. I think something happened to him." I explained the missing person's report and the John Doe, the details spilling out in a rush. "And the officer in both cases... might be Jude's father."

There was a sharp intake of breath from the other end. "Jude was bad news, I knew that... but to think he might have killed Garrett..." Lexi's voice cracked with horror.

"If he's your stalker, that might have been why he killed Garrett—to get to you." The words felt like lead on my tongue, heavy with implication.

Lexi's sob broke through the line, a sound that twisted something deep in my chest. "If it weren't for Mandy, I never would've been brave enough to break up with him."

That caught me off guard. "Was Mandy able to help because she knew Jude before college?" I asked, my voice tight, recalling Kayla's earlier suspicion.

"What? No. We all met at the same time in college." Lexi's confusion was apparent.

"Oh, okay, thanks." I tried to keep my tone even, but questions were piling up like cars in a traffic jam.

After a few more words of comfort, we said goodbye, and I ended the call. I let out a sigh, turning to face Kayla. Her eyes, usually so full of fire, were clouded with concern.

"Kayla," I started, my words slow as I pieced together the conversation with Lexi and what Kayla had told me earlier about Mandy. "Mandy said something about Jude being scary back in high school, but Lexi just confirmed they all met in college. Something's not adding up."

Kayla pushed off from the doorframe and came closer. "I knew she was holding something back," she said, a note of vindication in her voice. "We need to confront her, Jake. She knows more than she's letting on."

"Yeah, we do. But not yet. We need to be careful how we approach this. Talk to Jude first." The last thing I wanted was to tip off Jude—if he was involved—by making it obvious we were onto him.

Kayla nodded, her face set in determination. "Let's go over everything we know first thing in the morning, map it out. Then we decide our next move."

"Sounds like a plan." I agreed, but a heavy feeling settled in my stomach. I knew that whatever was coming next wouldn't be simple or clean. But with Kayla by my side, I felt like we could face anything—even the truth about Jude.

Kayla's gaze lingered on me, a silent question hovering between us. "It's been a long day. You want to go to bed?" she asked, tilting her head slightly.

I flashed her a lopsided grin. "Don't you remember what happened the last time I let you convince me to sleep?" I teased, recalling the avalanche of missed calls and regret that had sat on my shoulders when I woke up.

She laughed softly, the sound easing some of the tension from my frame. "Well, why don't we just relax then?" she suggested, moving to the fridge to pull out a six-pack of beer. "I heard this helps you relax a little?" she said, holding up the cans with a playful quirk of her eyebrow.

Watching her, a warmth spread through me, the kind that had nothing to do with the alcohol she was offering.

"Oh, yeah? Where'd you hear that?" I leaned back against the counter, arms crossed, amusement dancing in my eyes.

"I have my sources, officer," she retorted, a mock-serious expression on her face.

I laughed, the sound bubbling up from somewhere deep inside, a place that had been quiet for too long. Pushing away from the counter, I closed the distance between us and pulled her into a kiss.

With a shared smile, we settled onto the couch, the movie playing a distant second to the company we kept.

The six-pack sat between us, an unspoken agreement that we'd share the burden and the comfort it provided.

As the opening credits rolled, I felt Kayla's head rest against my shoulder, her body fitting against mine like she was made to be there. The tension of the day, our investigation, it all began to fade into the background as we lost ourselves in the simple act of being together.

Occasionally, she'd pass me a beer, our fingers brushing, a silent exchange that spoke louder than words. We laughed at the same scenes, our mirth mingling in the space around us, cocooning us in a momentary reprieve from reality.

The movie rolled on, but my focus was on the woman beside me, the rise and fall of her chest, and how her laughter seemed to chase away the shadows. For the first time in what felt like forever, I let myself just be, my guard down, my heart open.

This was what I needed—not sleep, not answers, but this: a quiet night with Kayla, where the world outside could wait, where the only thing that mattered was the here and now. The cases and threats would still be there tomorrow, but tonight, they had no power over us.

The movie had been over for an hour at least. Kayla's breaths were even and deep, her chest rising and falling in the rhythm of sleep as she lay beside me on the couch. Her head rested against my shoulder, her face peaceful. Watching her, something inside me clicked, a realization settling with certainty. I was in love with her. Hell, she was the one. She always had been.

I didn't want to wake her, but there was something I needed to say, something I couldn't hold back anymore. Gently, I nudged her awake, her eyelids fluttering open to meet my gaze.

"Kayla," I whispered, my voice low but filled with an emotion I could no longer contain. "I'm all in."

Her brows furrowed in a drowsy confusion. "What do you mean?"

"I mean I love you," I said, the words spilling out with an intensity that felt like it could light up the darkened room. "And I'm ready to go to the chief's office, make it official, and stop hiding."

Her eyes widened, surprise and happiness dancing within them. "Really?" she asked, her voice a soft echo of my resolve.

"Yes," I affirmed, my heart pounding with the declaration. "I don't want to spend another day pretending."

She leaned in, her lips finding mine in a kiss that held the promise of a future together. But then she pulled back, a sudden seriousness replacing the earlier warmth. "Wait. Not yet."

I felt a jolt of disappointment. "Why?" I asked, a frown creasing my forehead.

"Because we need to finish this case first," she said firmly. "We need to be able to work together without anyone questioning our methods or our ability to do things right."

I hated the idea, hated the thought of waiting even a moment longer to shout from the rooftops that she was mine. But deep down, I knew she was right. "Okay, that makes sense," I conceded, the words tasting bitter even as I spoke to them.

She kissed me again, her lips soft and insistent. "But that doesn't mean we can't enjoy being together right now," she murmured against my mouth.

I couldn't help the smile that spread across my face. "I love you," I said again, the words a vow, a promise for what was to come.

"I love you too," she replied, her voice steady and sure. And with that, I stood, gently guiding her to her feet.

Hand in hand, we walked to the bedroom, leaving the chaos of our world behind. It was a declaration that no matter what the days ahead might bring, we had each other. And for now, that was enough.

And if I had my way, it always would be.

Chapter Thirty

KAYLA

Jake walked me across the house to my bedroom and led me inside, his lips never leaving mine. We stumbled into the door as he turned the knob, then fell through it, barely remaining upright. Laughing, he kicked the door to my bedroom shut behind us, his hands exploring my body with an intensity that left me breathless.

A gasp escaped me as his hands dipped under my shirt, his fingers dancing over my skin. I reciprocated eagerly, tugging at the hem of his shirt, the fabric bunching in my fists. We parted briefly to shed our clothes, our breaths coming out in harsh pants.

God... if you'd told me two months ago I would have been working with Jake Barrows and sleeping with him, too, I'd have had you taken in for a psych hold.

His gaze met mine, a burning desire in his eyes. I married it as I closed the distance between us, my hands trailing up his torso, moaning at the feel of the hard muscles underneath. A low groan resonated in his throat as he pushed me against the wall, his lips returning to mine with a fiery passion.

The way Jake touched me, the way he kissed me, it was like he had been starved. His hands were everywhere, in my hair, on my hips, trailing down my back. His touch was electrifying, leaving me aching for more.

As his mouth trailed down my neck, a sigh of pleasure escaped my lips. I felt his smirk against my skin, the satisfaction in his touch. He pulled back, his hands gripping my hips as he gazed at me.

"Kayla," he breathed out, his voice husky and filled with emotion. I looked at him, my heart pounding in my chest, my body throbbing with anticipation. "God… I was a fucking idiot to ever let you go."

"Yeah," I said with a breathless laugh. "You were. But I forgive you."

And then we were moving, our bodies entwined as he guided me towards the bed.

His gaze never left mine as he laid me down and hovered above me, a predator circling its prey. His hand descended, tracing a path down my body that set my nerves on fire. I let out a sigh, my hands grasping his muscled arms.

His eyes glinted with amusement, a smirk tugging at his lips. He brushed a stray lock of hair from my face before leaning in, his lips grazing my collarbone. A shudder ran through me at the contact, my heart pounding in my chest.

I took in the sight of him, shirtless, his muscles flexing under his smooth skin. Even through the denim of his jeans, I could see the outline of his arousal, a thrilling sight that sent a pulse of anticipation through me.

His hand, large and warm, descended lower. It was as if he was mapping out my body, committing every inch of me to memory. I squirmed beneath him, anticipation pooling in my belly.

"Jake," I murmured, a silent plea.

His name seemed to be the trigger he needed. With a swift move, he shucked off his jeans, and now there was nothing between us but the thin material of my underwear. The sight of him in all his naked glory made me gasp, heat pooling between my thighs.

"Kayla," he responded, his voice a deep rumble that vibrated through me. "You're so damn beautiful."

His fingers hooked onto the edge of my underwear, tugging them down my legs. There was a glint in his eye, a promise of pleasure that had my heart skipping a beat. Before I could even anticipate what was about to come, his mouth descended on mine again, his body pressing against mine. The world faded away as his hands explored, his fingers touching, teasing, driving me wild with desire.

His cock was stiff and throbbing in my hand as I reached between us and stroked him, every flex of my fingers earning a sharp intake of breath from him. It was empowering, knowing that I could elicit such reactions from him. I found myself wanting to hear more of those breathless whispers, wanting to see him lose himself in the pleasure I could give him.

"Kayla," he groaned, pressing closer to me, his length sliding through my fingers. His mouth descended onto my nipple, his tongue flicking it teasingly before he took it into his mouth. I shivered, my breath hitching as pleasure coiled tighter within me.

I leaned back, one hand still on him, the other clutching at the sheets. His lips and tongue created an exquisite torture that sent jolts of pleasure coursing through me. His touch was like fire, burning, consuming, leaving me in a haze of desire.

"Jake," I gasped, my voice shaking. He moaned around my nipple, the vibrations making me shudder. My grip tightened around his cock as I pumped him in time with

The Rookie's Second Chance

the rhythm of his mouth on my nipple. His hips bucked into my hand, chasing the friction.

Suddenly, he released my nipple with a pop, his eyes meeting mine. There was a hunger in Jake's gaze that made my heart pound. "Kayla," he breathed, his voice rough with desire. "I need you."

His words lit a fire within me, intensifying the ache between my legs. "Then take me," I whispered, meeting his gaze.

And with that, he moved, sliding a condom on and positioning himself between my legs, his cock brushing against my folds. His gaze never left mine as he pushed forward, inch by slow inch, until he was fully seated within me. I let out a soft moan as I adjusted to his size.

Opening my eyes, I found him watching me, a look of pure adoration on his face. "You okay?" he asked, concern coloring his tone.

I nodded, wrapping my legs around his waist, urging him to move. He did, slowly at first, but soon our rhythm became faster, more frantic. His mouth found mine again, swallowing my gasps and moans as we undulated together, the world around us forgotten in our shared pleasure.

He thrust into me with an urgency that made my heart pound in my chest. Each hard, powerful stroke sent me spiraling closer to the edge. My hands clutched at his broad shoulders, my nails digging into his skin, marking him as mine.

His name slipped from my lips in a breathless plea. "Jake," I gasped out. "Oh God, Jake."

His rhythm became erratic, his breath ragged. He buried his face into the crook of my neck, his teeth grazing my skin. The sensation sent a jolt of pleasure down my spine, and I cried out.

"Kayla," he groaned against my skin. His grip on my

hips tightened, his movements becoming desperate. I felt him swelling inside me, and I knew he was close. The thought of him coming undone because of me, inside me, sent a rush of heat pooling low in my belly.

I met each of his thrusts, our bodies moving in perfect harmony. The tension inside me coiled tighter, tighter. "Jake, I'm—"

He cut me off with a desperate kiss, swallowing my words. His hand slid between our bodies, finding my clit. His thumb circled it, the pleasure so intense that I saw stars. I screamed his name as I came, my body arching off the bed.

He followed me over the edge moments later, his hips stuttering against mine as he released within me. His name echoed in the room as he rode out his climax, his body shuddering against mine.

As our breathing slowed, he rolled off me, pulling me into his arms. His heart thumped wildly against his chest, matching the erratic beat of my own. We were a tangled mess of limbs and sheets, the scent of sex heavy in the air.

For a moment, we just lay there, panting and sweaty, the silence only broken by the occasional sigh. Jake's fingers traced idle patterns on my bare skin, sending shivers down my spine. It was intimate and tender, a side of him I had never seen before.

"I've… loved you… for a long time, Kayla," he whispered into my hair, his voice soft and raw with emotion.

I looked up at him, surprise flickering in my eyes. "You have?"

He nodded, kissing my forehead gently as my eyes closed. "I never stopped."

. . .

I woke up to the soft rustling of fabric and the muted clinks of a belt buckle. Jake was getting dressed, his back to me as he pulled on his shirt. The sunlight streaming through the window cast a warm glow across his broad shoulders, highlighting the contours of his muscles. I propped myself up on one elbow, watching him for a moment, admiring the way he moved with a quiet confidence.

"What's going on?" I asked, my voice still thick with sleep.

He turned to me, a smile playing on his lips. "It's my day off," he said, shrugging into his jacket. "A buddy of mine from my rodeo days is in town and wants to grab lunch."

A pang of disappointment tugged at me, but I masked it with a smile. "Rodeo days, huh? That was what, like a year ago?"

"Yeah," he chuckled, running a hand through his hair. "Feels like a lifetime ago, though."

I sat up, pulling the sheets around me. "Well, have fun. I'll miss you, but I guess I can get a head start on digging more into Jude and Mandy's connection."

He paused, looking at me with concern. "You sure you're okay with me going?"

I nodded, trying to sound more enthusiastic than I felt. "Of course. Go, catch up with your friend. I've got plenty to keep me busy here."

He leaned down and kissed me, a soft brush of lips that lingered just long enough to make me wish he didn't have to leave. "I'll miss you too," he murmured against my mouth. "But I'll be back before you know it."

As he headed out the door, I lay back down, letting out a long breath. It was just lunch, nothing to be worried about, but I couldn't shake the feeling of wanting to hold on to him a little longer.

Shaking off the feeling and pushing the thought aside, I rolled out of bed, determined to make the most of my day. I had a mystery to unravel, and every minute counted. I went to the kitchen, brewing a strong cup of coffee before settling at my makeshift workspace.

My laptop hummed to life, and I began to sift through the information I had on Jude. The more I dug, the more I realized how little we actually knew about him. There were the arrests Jake mentioned, but nothing concrete tying him to Garrett's disappearance or the stalking incidents.

I leaned back in my chair, rubbing my temples. And then there was Mandy. Her connection to Jude seemed tenuous at best, but something in her behavior nagged at me. Why did she lie about knowing Jude in high school? What was she hiding?

I opened a new tab, deciding to delve deeper into Mandy's background. Maybe there was something there, a clue that we'd overlooked. But where to start? Her social media profiles were a dead end, nothing but surface-level posts and smiling selfies.

I glanced at the clock. Hours had slipped by, and I was no closer to finding anything substantial. With a sigh, I closed my laptop, frustration knotting in my stomach. This was going to be harder than I thought.

But I wasn't one to back down from a challenge. As I stood up, stretching the stiffness from my limbs, I resolved to keep digging. There was a story here, and I was going to uncover it, piece by painstaking piece.

Chapter Thirty-One

JAKE

The moment I stepped into Rosie's Diner, the familiar scent of coffee and fried food hit me, grounding me in a sense of normalcy that had been rare these days. The bell above the door jingled, announcing my presence, and a few heads turned my way, offering nods and smiles of recognition.

I scanned the diner, spotting Chris at our usual booth by the window. He hadn't changed much since I last saw him, still wearing his trademark cowboy hat and a grin that could light up a room. I made my way over, feeling pleasant anticipation at seeing an old friend.

"Jake! You son of a bitch, look at you all cleaned up!" Chris exclaimed, standing up to pull me into a firm handshake that quickly turned into a back-slapping hug.

I laughed, clapping him on the shoulder. "Yeah, well, the chief's badge requires a bit less dust and a bit more polish."

We settled into the booth, and Rosie, the ever-present waitress, ambled over with two mugs of coffee. "On the house, boys. Good to see you, Jake."

"Thanks, Rosie," I said with a smile, taking a sip of the steaming coffee.

Chris leaned back, his eyes scanning the diner before settling back on me. "So, how's the new gig? You catchin' bad guys now or what?"

I shrugged. "Yeah, something like that. It's been... intense, to say the least."

He raised an eyebrow, a silent prompt for me to elaborate, but I wasn't in the mood to dive into the complexities of the case. Instead, I redirected the conversation. "How about you? Rodeo life still treating you well?"

Chris chuckled, running a hand through his hair. "You know how it is. Same old dust, same old bulls. But damn, we miss you out there. You were one hell of a rider."

I felt a pang of nostalgia, a reminder of simpler times when my biggest worry was staying on a bull for eight seconds. "I miss it too, sometimes. But this... this feels right. Like I'm where I'm supposed to be."

We talked about old times, the rodeo circuit, and the people we knew. It was a conversation that flowed easily, filled with laughter. Chris had a way of making everything seem straightforward, a welcome break from my current life.

Just as I was about to tell him about a particularly memorable rodeo in Cheyenne, the bell above the door jingled again. I glanced over and saw Mandy walking in. She caught my eye and waved, a bright smile on her face.

"Shit," I muttered under my breath. I hadn't expected to see her here, and suddenly, I felt a twinge of unease.

As Mandy approached our table, Chris nudged me with his elbow, an amused smirk on his face. "That why you're so content to settle down, huh?"

"No, no," I said quickly, shaking my head. "She's not

my girlfriend. She's my sister's friend. Staying with me while we sort out some issues with Lexi."

Mandy arrived at our table, her smile widening as she looked at me. "I was wondering where you were. You didn't come home last night," she said, her tone laced with a hint of something I couldn't quite place.

I avoided her gaze, focusing instead on the coffee mug in front of me. "Ah, yeah, just got caught up with work stuff," I replied, trying to keep my voice even.

Mandy leaned against the table, her eyes lingering on me a second longer than necessary. The air around us grew heavy, charged with an odd tension. I thought about the information she might be holding back that could help Lexi. But I kept my face neutral, unwilling to tip her off that we suspected anything.

After a few moments of awkward small talk, Mandy finally excused herself, heading back out of the diner. As she walked away, Chris leaned in, lowering his voice. "That's why you don't stick your dick in crazy."

I shot him a surprised look. "What are you talking about?"

Chris snorted, shaking his head. "Man, she's got stage five clinger written all over her."

I frowned. "I never slept with her," I said firmly. "She's just a friend."

Chris raised his eyebrows, a teasing glint in his eyes. "Are you sure about that? Because she acts like it."

I opened my mouth to reply, but the words stuck in my throat. Chris's observation, though crude, wasn't entirely off the mark. Mandy's behavior had been increasingly possessive, and it was starting to worry me.

The conversation was interrupted as Rosie came over to refill our coffees, and I used the moment to collect my thoughts. I needed to figure out Mandy's angle to understand her connection to all of this. But for now, I'd keep playing it cool, not giving away any signs that I was on to her.

Chris's frown lingered as he glanced towards the door where Mandy had exited. "Something up?" I asked, eyebrows raised.

He hesitated, scratching his beard. "Nah, it's nothing. Just... she looks familiar, that's all."

I leaned back in my chair, puzzled. "Familiar? No, you wouldn't have met her before. She's new to Silver Creek. Lexi never brought her around."

He shrugged, still looking uncertain. "Must be my imagination then."

But his comment stuck with me. Was it possible Mandy had been around before, and I just didn't know it?

After finishing our lunch with some more chit-chat about the rodeo days and current town gossip, I said my goodbyes to Chris. I wasn't ready to head home yet, not with all these thoughts swirling around in my head about Mandy. I needed to talk to Kayla and see if she had made any progress.

I drove to Kayla's place. The Silver Creek streets were familiar, yet I felt different under the pressure of all these mysteries. When I arrived, her car wasn't there. I pulled out my phone, seeing a text from her: "Went to meet a friend. Back later."

A sigh escaped my lips. The timing couldn't have been worse. I leaned back in the driver's seat, staring at the empty house. It was too quiet, the kind of quiet that lets your mind run wild. I tapped my fingers against the steering wheel, considering my options. Going home didn't feel right. Not yet.

I ended up driving around town, the streets slowly filling with the orange glow of the setting sun. My mind was a whirlwind of theories and questions about Mandy, Jude, and this whole messed-up situation. Every corner I turned seemed to bring more questions than answers.

As the sky darkened, I pulled into the parking lot of Rosie's Diner again. Maybe a coffee would clear my head. I walked in, the bell above the door chiming my arrival. Rosie gave me a knowing look as I approached the counter.

"Rough day, officer?" she asked, pouring me a cup of her strongest brew.

"You could say that," I replied, taking a seat at the counter. "Just a lot on my mind."

I sipped the coffee, the bitterness somehow comforting. Rosie left me to my thoughts, busy with her other customers. My eyes drifted over the diner's interior, and my thoughts kept circling back to Mandy. Chris's words echoed in my mind. What if she was more involved in all this than I'd thought?

I finished my coffee and thanked Rosie, stepping back out into the cool night air. The sun was slowly falling from the sky as the afternoon slipped away, a silent audience to my turmoil.

Chapter Thirty-Two

KAYLA

The morning light poured through my window, casting long shadows across my desk, where I sat hunched over, squinting at my laptop screen. I was trying to dig up anything I could on Mandy, but every search led me to a dead end. It was like she was a ghost before arriving in Silver Creek. Frustration gnawed at me —I knew I'd have to pull some strings at work to get any real info, but that would have to wait.

Needing a break, I picked up my phone and scrolled through my contacts, stopping at Sarah's name. It had been ages since we last caught up. Sarah was one of those friends who drifted in and out of your life, not because of any falling out, but just because life got busy. She had five kids and lived in the next town over, while my life was a constant whirlwind of work and now, this case.

I dialed her number, half-expecting her to be too swamped to talk. To my surprise, she answered on the second ring.

"Kayla? Is that you? It's been ages!" Sarah's voice was a

welcome change from the tense tones I'd grown accustomed to lately.

"Hey, Sarah. Yeah, it has. Look, I was wondering if you're free for lunch today? I could use a change of scenery," I said, trying to sound casual.

There was a moment of shuffling on the other end, probably Sarah managing one of her little ones. "I can make it work. Let's do it. There's that new cafe just off Main Street in my town. Meet you there around one?"

"Perfect, see you then," I replied, a smile tugging at the corner of my lips. It felt good to make plans that didn't revolve around the case.

I spent the rest of the morning half-heartedly scrolling through social media, trying not to think about Jake, Mandy, or any of it. But as the clock neared one, I grabbed my keys and headed out, eager for a distraction.

The drive to the cafe was short, and I found Sarah already waiting at a table outside. Her face lit up when she saw me, and I felt a wave of nostalgia hit me.

"Kayla! You look great, but tired. Are you okay?" Sarah asked as we hugged.

"Yeah, just work stuff. You know how it is," I said, sliding into my seat.

We chatted about this and that—her kids, the latest town gossip. I steered clear of anything related to the case. It was a relief to talk about normal things for a change. When the waitress came to take our order, I opted for a chicken Caesar salad while Sarah went for the quiche of the day.

As we waited for our food, I found myself venting about the frustrations of work, carefully omitting any details about the case.

"You always were the hardworking one, Kayla. Don't

forget to take a break now and then," Sarah advised, her eyes filled with genuine concern.

"I know, I know. I'll try," I replied, offering her a wry smile.

The quiche and salad arrived, the aroma of fresh herbs and baked crust mingling pleasantly. For a moment, I was distracted from the swirling thoughts in my head. Sarah's eyes, however, were locked on mine, full of curiosity and concern.

"So, tell me about this case," she prompted, cutting into her quiche.

I hesitated, picking at my salad. "It's... complicated. There's this person who might have information we need for the investigation. But I can't shake the feeling there's more to it."

Sarah leaned in, her voice dropping. "Do you mean they're a suspect?"

"Not exactly," I replied, swirling a crouton around my plate. "More like they might know something crucial. But there's a catch."

Her brows knit together. "What's the catch?"

I sighed, fiddling with my fork. "This person... they've shown a clear interest in Jake."

Sarah's eyes widened. "Wait, Jake? As in the same Jake who—"

I cut her off with a nod. "Yeah, that Jake. We're... back together."

She whistled softly. "Wow, Kayla. But what does this have to do with the case?"

I took a deep breath, my salad suddenly unappealing. "The thing is, this person, Mandy, she's been really possessive over Jake. And now she might be tangled up in all this mess. I don't know if I'm being paranoid because of our history or if there's actually something to it."

Sarah chewed thoughtfully for a moment. "That's a tough spot. Jealousy can cloud judgment, sure. But your gut feeling in cases like this... it's usually not wrong."

"Yeah, but what if I'm just scared of losing him again? What if I'm seeing things that aren't there?" The words tumbled out, laced with doubt and fear.

Sarah reached across the table, placing her hand over mine. "Listen, Kayla, you're one of the sharpest people I know. If you think there's something off with this Mandy, then there's probably a reason for it. But you need to separate your personal feelings from the professional ones. Hard, I know."

I nodded, taking a small bite of my salad. "I know you're right. It's just... hard to know where the line is sometimes."

She squeezed my hand reassuringly. "Just be careful, okay? And remember, you and Jake have something solid now. Don't let insecurities from the past ruin what you have."

I smiled, grateful for her support. "Thanks, Sarah. I needed to hear that."

After lunch, we took a walk through town. I was torn between the comfort of confiding in my friend and the professional boundaries I was trained to uphold.

"Kayla, what did you mean about Mandy being possessive?" Sarah's question broke through my thoughts.

I hesitated, glancing at the passersby, ensuring our conversation remained private. "I shouldn't say," I started, but Sarah's encouraging look nudged me further. "It's just that... there's something off about her involvement in all this."

Sarah's expression was curiosity and concern. "Involvement? With what exactly?"

I sighed, weighing my words. "Jake's sister, Lexi, she's

being stalked. Mandy, she's Lexi's friend from college, visiting from out of town. She's been staying with Jake since Lexi and her husband had to leave their house for safety reasons."

"And Mandy and Jake?" Sarah prodded gently.

I looked down, kicking at a loose pebble on the sidewalk. "She's been... a good friend to Jake. Taking care of him, you know? After long days at work, during this whole mess."

Sarah raised an eyebrow. "You don't sound entirely convinced."

I chuckled despite the seriousness of the conversation. "You know me too well. It's just... it's obvious Mandy has a thing for Jake. I'm trying not to be jealous, but there are inconsistencies in her stories about Lexi's past and the stalker."

"That sounds tough," Sarah empathized.

I nodded. "Yeah, and I've been keeping tabs on her through social media. I haven't used official resources because I don't want to seem petty."

Sarah stopped, turning to face me. "Kayla, if this is about safety, not jealousy, maybe you need to use all your resources. There's only one way to make sure this Mandy isn't involved or in danger herself."

I exhaled deeply, knowing she was right. "You're right, Sarah. I just... I need to be sure I'm doing this for the right reasons."

Sarah smiled warmly, placing a reassuring hand on my shoulder. "You're one of the most honest people I know, Kayla. Trust your instincts."

As we resumed our walk, my mind was a whirlwind of thoughts—the complexities of the case, my relationship with Jake, and now Mandy's potential involvement. I knew what I had to do, but the path forward was fraught with professional and personal risks. For Lexi, Jake, and justice's sake, I had to tread carefully but decisively.

Chapter Thirty-Three

JAKE

Waking up to Kayla shaking me awake, I found myself momentarily disoriented, the dimming light of the sunset filtering through the windows.

"Hey, how was lunch?" she asked, her tone light but curious.

I rubbed my eyes, sitting up on the couch. Part of me wanted to tell her about Mandy appearing unexpectedly at the diner, but another part hesitated. Kayla already had enough reasons to feel uneasy about Mandy, and I didn't want to add fuel to the fire, especially if there was an innocent explanation for Mandy's behavior. Instead, I opted for a simple response.

"It went well," I said, offering a half-smile.

Kayla sat down beside me, her eyes searching mine. "How was your lunch?"

I stretched, trying to shake off the remnants of sleep. "It was great. We haven't seen each other in months. Just caught up on things."

She nodded, seemingly satisfied with my answer.

"Sounds nice. I met up with a friend too, Sarah. We had lunch at a cafe near her place."

"Sarah?" I echoed, trying to place the name.

"Yeah, we became friends after... you know, when we were apart. She has five kids and lives in the next town over."

I could sense there was more to her meeting with Sarah than just catching up, but I didn't press. Instead, I asked, "How was it?"

"Good, it was nice to step away from all this craziness for a bit. We talked about everything and nothing. It's weird, you know, how life goes on outside of our little bubble here."

I knew exactly what she meant. Sometimes, it felt like our lives had been reduced to this case, to the endless cycle of leads and dead ends.

I stood up, stretching my arms above my head. "I should probably head to bed soon. I'm wiped."

Kayla's expression shifted, a hint of concern flickering in her eyes. "Everything okay?"

"Yeah, just... a lot on my mind with the case, and Mandy, and... everything."

She reached out, her hand briefly squeezing mine. "We'll figure this out, Jake."

I nodded, appreciating her faith in us, in me. "I know we will."

There was a pause, a comfortable silence that settled between us. I wanted to tell her everything, to share the burden of my thoughts, but I held back. This case, our relationship, Mandy's odd behavior—it was all a tangled web, and I needed to tread carefully.

"Thanks, baby," I said, breaking the silence. "For everything."

She smiled, her eyes softening. "Always."

I grabbed my jacket, ready to face the evening chill. As I headed towards the door, I felt a sense of unease. Mandy's presence in my house, her growing possessiveness, and my feelings for Kayla were all converging into a storm I wasn't quite sure how to navigate.

The following day, the station was eerily quiet, the usual hum of activity reduced to a near-silence that prickled at the back of my neck. In a small town like Silver Creek, we only had just over a dozen officers, but Kayla and I seemed to be alone. I was flipping through reports, trying to make sense of the connections tying Jude, Mandy, and this whole damned mess together. That's when the doors burst open.

Jude stormed in, Mandy in tow, his arm wrapped around her neck, a gun pressed against her temple.

He was of average height, with a lean build that spoke of someone more wiry than muscular. His hair was unkempt, a dark mess that looked like it hadn't seen a comb in days. There was a wildness in his eyes, a sort of frantic energy that flickered between desperation and madness.

He wore a plain jacket that had seen better days, its fabric frayed at the cuffs, and his jeans were just as worn, clinging to him like a second skin. Despite his disheveled appearance, there was something unnervingly deliberate about him, as if his every move was calculated to instill fear. The way he held Mandy, his arm tight around her neck and the gun pressed against her head, was both menacing and controlled.

But it was his eyes that caught me the most. They were a piercing blue, but there was no warmth in them. They were the eyes of someone who had lost touch with reason and fallen too far down a rabbit hole of his own making.

They darted around the room, taking in every detail, every potential threat, never settling, never resting.

Kayla, seated beside me, leaped to her feet in an instant, her hand inching towards her gun. "Jude, let her go!" she shouted, her voice sharp and commanding.

Mandy's eyes were wide with terror, flicking to me, pleading silently for me to do something. I could see the fear etched into every line of her face, and something inside me twisted. Despite our awkwardness, she was in danger, and I had to help her.

"What do you want?" I asked, my voice steady despite the adrenaline coursing through me.

Jude's eyes, wild and unpredictable, darted between Kayla and me. "You know what I want. I want this all to end."

Kayla edged closer, trying to talk him down. "No one needs to get hurt, Jude. Let's talk this out."

But Jude wasn't listening. He was ranting about betrayals, conspiracies, and being hunted. It was hard to follow, his words a jumbled mess of paranoia and anger.

I tried to move closer, to find an angle, but Jude was watching me like a hawk. "Stay back, or I swear I'll shoot her!"

It was then that Kayla made her move, lunging at Jude with the speed of a panther. But he was ready, twisting away and snatching her gun from its holster in one fluid motion. Now he had two guns, one pointed at Mandy and the other at Kayla.

"Choose, Jake!" he screamed, his voice echoing off the walls of the station. "Who's it gonna be? The girlfriend or the hostage?"

My heart pounded in my chest, every beat a thunderous roar in my ears. I wanted to choose Kayla, to save her, but with every eye in the station on me, I knew I couldn't. I was a officer, sworn to protect the public. Choosing Kayla would make me look like a crooked cop.

"Jude, please," I begged, my voice cracking. "Don't do this."

But he only laughed, a sound that chilled me to the bone. "Time's up, Jake!"

And then he pulled both triggers.

I woke up with a start, my body slick with cold sweat, my heart racing. It was just a dream, a fucking nightmare. I lay there, trying to catch my breath, the images from the dream still vivid and haunting.

Jude, who I had only known through research, had infiltrated my subconscious, turning my fears into a twisted reality. He didn't know me, didn't know Kayla, but he knew Mandy. Or did he? His words had been a contradiction, a confusing mix of timelines that didn't add up. College or high school? Which was it?

I sat up, rubbing my face with my hands, trying to shake off the remnants of the dream. It had felt so real, so terrifyingly real. The choice Jude had forced on me, the look in Kayla's eyes, Mandy's silent pleas for help—it was all too much.

Lying back down, I stared at the ceiling, the shadows dancing in the dim light of the room. I needed to get a grip and focus on the case and the facts. But as I lay there, the dream continued to haunt me, a vivid reminder of the stakes we were playing with.

I couldn't let it happen, not in my dreams, not in reality. I had to protect them, both of them, no matter what it took.

Chapter Thirty-Four

KAYLA

As I sat at my desk, buried in the computer screen's glow, I couldn't shake off a gnawing suspicion about Mandy. It gnawed at me like a dog with a bone. "Fuck it," I muttered under my breath, my fingers hovering over the keyboard. It was time to use police resources to dig deeper into Mandy's past, though I wasn't about to tell Jake how far I was willing to go.

My search led me down a tangle of public records and legal documents. That's when I stumbled upon something that made my heart skip a beat—a restraining order filed by Jude, but not against him. This one was to keep Mandy away.

"What the hell?" I whispered, leaning in closer to the screen.

The details were sparse, but it was clear that Jude had gone to great lengths to keep Mandy at bay. Why would Jude need a restraining order against Mandy? What kind of relationship did they have? It didn't add up.

I dug further, tapping into the case file, but it was like trying to read through a fog. The injunction was dropped, and the signature at the bottom of the document made my blood run cold—Officer Kilkenny. The same man entangled in this twisted web we were unraveling. The same man who was apparently Jude's father.

"Why would Kilkenny kill his own son's restraining order?" I murmured, rubbing my temples.

I leaned back in my chair, my eyes burning from the screen's glare. The clock on the wall ticked steadily, a reminder of the time slipping away as we hunted for answers. I pulled up Mandy's file again, looking for any clue or connection that could explain this bizarre twist.

But the more I searched, the more elusive the answers became. Every lead seemed to end in a dead end or a new question. Frustration gnawed at me, mixing with a growing sense of urgency.

I glanced at my phone, half expecting Jake to call and ask what I had found. But the screen remained dark, the silence of the device echoing the silence in the room. I was alone with this, at least for now.

With a deep sigh, I turned back to the screen, my fingers resuming their dance across the keyboard. I had to be missing something, some thread that would unravel this whole mess. I was determined to find it, no matter how deep I had to dig.

And I knew there was one more step I had to take to get there.

I dialed the number for Miami PD, my heart pounding a rhythm against my ribcage. "Miami Police Department, how may I assist you?" a dispatcher answered professionally.

"Hi, this is Detective Kayla Green from Silver Creek chief's Office. I need to speak with Officer Kilkenny," I said, trying to sound as official as possible.

There was a pause on the other end. "Officer

The Rookie's Second Chance

Kilkenny? He retired and moved down to Key West a few months ago."

A chill ran down my spine. The timing was too perfect, aligning with when Lexi's stalker reemerged. "Do you have a contact for him? He's a person of interest in an ongoing investigation," I pressed, my mind racing with possibilities.

The dispatcher sounded surprised. "Officer Kilkenny? But he was such a great guy, a good cop, a real family man. He loved his kids more than anything."

I perked up at that. "Kids? As in plural?"

"Yeah, he was a foster parent. Took in loads of them, mostly teens. Even his own nephew, Jude, was with him for a while."

My head spun. Jude wasn't his son. The 'kid' at Lexi's college wasn't him. It could be any of Kilkenny's foster kids. "Can you send me his contact info and any details on the foster kids? One of them might be involved in our case," I said, barely able to conceal the urgency in my voice.

The dispatcher's tone shifted to one of concern. "Of course, Detective. I'll send it over right away."

I hung up, my mind a whirlwind of thoughts. If Kilkenny was the stalker, it changed everything. And if it wasn't him, we had a whole roster of potential suspects from his foster kids.

I leaned back in my chair, feeling every second ticking by. This was big, bigger than anything I'd expected. My phone buzzed with the incoming email from the Miami PD dispatcher, and I opened it with trembling hands.

I scrolled through the list of names, each one a potential lead, a potential threat. There were so many of them, each with their own story and possible motive.

I was hunched over the computer as I scrolled through

the list of names when Jake's voice startled me. "What you got there?"

I spun around, nearly knocking over my coffee. "Shit, Jake, you scared me," I said, my heart racing.

He leaned against the desk, his brow furrowed. "Sorry, didn't mean to. What's up?"

I hesitated for a second, then decided to spill it. This wasn't about Mandy, so there was no reason to keep it from him. "I called Miami PD about Kilkenny. He's retired, moved to Key West around the time Lexi's letters started up again."

Jake's eyes narrowed. "Kilkenny? The cop tied to Jude?"

I nodded. "And get this – he was a foster parent. Took in a bunch of kids, including Jude, who's apparently his nephew, not his son. We've got a list of potential suspects now."

Jake whistled low. "Damn, that's a hell of a development."

We spent the next hour diving into the backgrounds of Kilkenny's foster kids, now all adults. None of the names rang a bell, but we knew any one of them could be our stalker.

"Alright, I'll run background checks on these names," Jake said, scribbling notes.

"Meanwhile, I'll try calling Kilkenny," I said, reaching for the phone. I dialed his number, but it went straight to voicemail. I tried his wife's number, too, but no luck.

"Voicemail?" Jake asked, looking up from his screen.

I nodded, frustrated. "Both of them."

Jake's gaze was intense, his mind clearly working overtime. "We need to figure out if one of these kids is in Silver Creek. Any of them could be our guy."

The Rookie's Second Chance

I leaned back in my chair, my mind racing. "I can't shake the feeling that we're missing something obvious."

Jake stood up, stretching his back. "Let's keep digging. We're onto something here."

I shifted in my chair, glued to the screen as I dove into the digital world. The list of names from Kilkenny's foster children was long and varied. I started with social media, hoping to glean anything that might point us in the right direction.

"Here we go," I muttered as profiles began to pop up. One by one, I scanned through them. Most seemed to be leading pretty normal lives. I noticed that a lot of them were still connected to Kilkenny, but there was a glaring absence on their friends lists – Jude. It was like he was the black sheep of this makeshift family.

"Find anything?" Jake asked, his voice tinged with curiosity.

"Just checking their social media," I replied. "Most seem well-adjusted, but it's interesting that they're not connected to Jude."

Jake leaned over, peering at my screen. "That is odd. Anything else?"

I scrolled through more profiles. "Here's one – Michael Donovan. Works in IT, lives in Atlanta. Seems to have a pretty tight-knit group of friends, including Kilkenny, but no Jude."

"And this one," I continued, clicking on another profile, "Tara Henderson. She's a nurse in Seattle. Volunteering, lots of outdoor activities. Same story – connected to Kilkenny, not to Jude."

Jake scribbled down the names. "Good. We can look deeper into them. Anyone else?"

I clicked on another profile. "Lucas Grant. This one's interesting. He's a freelance photographer, travels a lot.

Photos from all over, but none in Silver Creek. Again, Kilkenny's there, but no Jude."

I clicked through a few more profiles, noting details. Some were married, some had kids, their lives splayed out in photo albums and status updates. "Seems like Kilkenny really was a father figure to these kids," I observed.

"Yeah, but what about Jude?" Jake asked, his eyes not leaving the screen.

"Either he's distanced himself, or they have," I said, closing another profile. "There are a few who don't have social media. We'll have to wait for your checks on them."

I leaned back, rubbing my eyes. The screen glow was starting to blur together. Jake was still furiously typing away, his focus unwavering.

"Keep at it, Kayla," he said without looking up. "We'll crack this."

Jake's phone buzzed suddenly, slicing through the hum of focused silence in the room. I watched him glance at it, his expression shifting from concentration to annoyance. His fingers hovered over the screen before he set the phone down, face-up, without responding.

"What's wrong?" I asked, my curiosity piqued by his reaction.

"It's nothing," he muttered, but the crease between his brows deepened.

I waited, watching him as he chewed the inside of his cheek, a clear sign he was wrestling with something. Finally, he sighed. "Okay, fine. I didn't want to show you because I didn't want you to worry or get jealous or anything."

My heart thudded in my chest, a mix of nervousness and anticipation. "Show me what?"

He hesitated, then slid the phone across the desk to me. I picked it up, my eyes scanning the screen. Texts from

Mandy flooded his inbox, each one more forward than the last. Pictures of food, messages like "Missed you last night" and "Can't wait until you get home," all adorned with heart emojis. My stomach knotted.

"What the hell is going on, Jake?" I asked, unable to keep the edge out of my voice.

He ran a hand through his hair, a gesture of frustration. "I was just trying to be nice, you know? But I didn't realize how much she didn't seem to understand that I just want to be friends. Not until Chris pointed it out."

I scrolled through the messages, noting he hadn't responded to any of them. Relief and discomfort swirled inside me. "Chris pointed what out?"

"At lunch," he explained, "Chris noticed how she acted when she showed up unannounced. He said she seemed... clingy. Like she thought there was something more between us."

I handed the phone back to him, feeling a tightness in my chest. "And is there?"

"No!" he said immediately, his eyes meeting mine with a sincerity that I felt deep in my bones. "Absolutely not. I mean, I've been friendly, but I never led her on or anything. I swear."

I believed him, but the situation was messy. "Jake, you're going to have to say something to her. She clearly thinks there's more to your relationship than there is."

He nodded, his jaw set. "I know. I'll talk to her. I just... I didn't want to upset her. She's been through a lot with all this stuff with Lexi."

I reached across the desk, touching his hand. "I trust you, Jake. I do. But this isn't fair to any of us. Not to you, not to Mandy, and not to me."

"You're right," he agreed, his voice firm. "I'll handle it."

We sat in silence for a moment, the conversation settling around us. Then, almost as an afterthought, Jake added, "I'm sorry, Kayla. For all of this. I never wanted to make things complicated."

I squeezed his hand. "I know. And I appreciate you being honest with me. Let's just... let's focus on the case for now. We'll deal with the rest later."

He nodded, and we turned back to our screens. We were in this together, no matter what. And together, we'd see it through to the end.

Chapter Thirty-Five

MANDY

I sat at the dining room table, my fingers drumming a restless rhythm on the polished wood. My phone lay before me, its screen a litany of my unreturned messages to Jake. I tried not to let frustration and anger boil over. This was Kayla's doing. She'd come back into Jake's life and just swept him off his feet, like some sort of femme fatale. But I wasn't going to let her win. Not this time.

I sighed, standing up to clear the dinner plates. It was just me tonight. Jake was out somewhere, probably with her. The thought left a bitter taste in my mouth, but I pushed it aside. I had to focus on the bigger picture. Jake and I had a connection; I could feel it every time he looked at me and was kind enough to let me stay.

As I rinsed the dishes, I found myself lost in thought. I had been in this situation before with someone else, and I knew how to turn things around. It was all about patience and understanding, showing Jake that I was the one who truly cared for him, who really understood him.

I wiped my hands on a towel and went upstairs, my

steps light. I hesitated in front of my room, then, with a determined breath, I turned toward Jake's door. He might not be home yet, but I wanted to feel closer to him, to be surrounded by his presence.

I opened the door quietly, almost reverently, and stepped inside. His room was a reflection of him - orderly, strong, and safe. I walked over to his dresser, running my fingers over the objects there. A watch, a rodeo belt buckle, some loose change. Each item felt like a small piece of him.

I sat on the edge of his bed, the fabric of the sheets cool under my fingers. It wasn't the first time I'd been in here, but tonight, it felt different, like a statement of intent. I lay back, staring at the ceiling, imagining Jake beside me. The room felt comforting, filled with his essence. It was as if he was there with me, telling me everything would be alright.

My thoughts drifted to Kayla. She was a thorn in my side, but I was convinced she was just a phase, a fleeting moment in Jake's life. He needed stability, someone who could be there for him, who could take care of him. And that person was me.

I closed my eyes, breathing in the faint scent of his cologne that lingered in the room. A small smile curved my lips. Kayla might have won this round, but the game was far from over. I had played this game before, and I knew patience was key.

I'd wait, bide my time. Jake would come around; he had to. We were meant to be together. I just had to remind him of that, gently, subtly. It was only a matter of time.

The mattress was soft and inviting, with cushions and blankets that seemed to engulf me in a cozy hug. I settled into the bed, feeling a sense of ease and tranquility wash over me, accompanied by an unfamiliar sensation I hadn't experienced in so long, I questioned if it was even real.

My fingers trailed up and down my body, enjoying the sensation of my smooth skin heated beneath the blankets. My nipples became firm, and my core ignited with an intense warmth.

In my mind, I envisioned Jake—I pictured him coming inside in his uniform, finding me in his bed and smiling. "I'm sorry," he would say in my imagination, offering a remorseful glance. "I shouldn't have kept you waiting. I'm glad you're here. You're all I want."

I imagined pulling him onto the bed, our bodies intertwined as he ran his hands up my sides and caressed me, eliciting soft sighs.

Clasping my breasts, I played with the sensitive peaks, each touch sending ripples of delight through my body. I yearned for more, for the sensation of him covering me entirely.

I envisioned him shedding his shirt, our bare chests meeting as he continued to kiss me deeply, his hand gradually descending…

My left hand wandered between my legs, my fingers gently teasing my clit. In my fantasy, I urged him to do the same, imagining his self-assured grin as he gazed down at me. I pictured what it would feel like to have him between my legs, his tongue exploring every inch.

A tremor ran through me as I inserted one, then two fingers inside, feeling my arousal spill out into the surrounding water. A small wave of orgasmic pleasure washed over my skin, leaving me sighing contentedly.

Visions of Jake penetrating me, claiming me, filled my thoughts.

"Oh, yes…" I whispered softly. "Make love to me. Please, I beg… just make love to me."

"Oh, I intend to," Jake replied in my daydream. "I've craved your sweet, tight body since I first laid eyes on you."

"Oh god, yes."

I was now stimulating my clit with my thumb while fervently moving in and out, eyes shut, head tilted back, repeatedly murmuring Jake's name.

I fantasized about his mouth lavishing attention on my nipples, teasing and circling them with his tongue. My beautiful, perky breasts, I imagined, would drive him wild with desire.

In my daydream, I reached down, grasping him firmly. He was impressive, and I delighted in the sensation of his size in my hands. He responded to my touch, signaling my readiness for him.

"I need you, Jake," I declared. "Right now."

Fantasy Jake chuckled, replying, "As you wish." He aligned himself with me and entered slowly, filling me completely.

"God…" I whispered aloud. I focused on my most sensitive spot, continuing to envision Jake moving above me, eliciting these sensations himself.

My climax was quickly approaching, and I concentrated on the imagined feeling of Jake's powerful thrusts, each one sending waves of pleasure through me.

"I'm about to come," I told him in my fantasy.

"Good girl," he responded, intensifying his pace. The combination of mental and physical stimulation pushed me over the edge into a powerful orgasm.

"Jake!" I exclaimed as the climax overwhelmed me, leaving me in a euphoric state of bliss and satisfaction.

Regaining my composure, I realized how vocal I had been. Embarrassed, I hoped Jake hadn't come home and heard me.

Then again… maybe if he did, my fantasy could become reality…

I lay in bed, still tingling from the pleasure of my own

The Rookie's Second Chance

caress. My mind wandered through memories, each one like a scene from a movie I'd directed. I always got what I wanted. Always. It was just a matter of being smart about it, of playing the game better than anyone else. Jake would be no different.

The room was dark, the only light a sliver from the streetlamp outside, casting a dim glow. I turned over, burying my face in his pillow. The scent of his cologne was strong, enveloping me. It felt like a promise, a hint of what was to come.

My thoughts drifted to Kayla. She was a temporary obstacle, a minor inconvenience. I was sure of it. Jake had been so kind to me, so caring. He couldn't possibly have real feelings for her. Not when he was always there for me, always ensuring I was okay.

I smirked in the darkness. Kayla might have history with Jake, but I had the present. I was the one living in his house, sharing his space. Proximity was power, and I intended to use it.

As the clock ticked away, I found myself lost in plans and fantasies. I'd cook for him, listen to him, and be there when he needed comfort. He'd see, eventually. He'd realize that what he needed was right in front of him all along.

Chapter Thirty-Six
JAKE

I walked into my house, my steps echoing in the quiet. The plan was to grab a quick shower and change into my uniform before heading to the station. I had spent the night at Kayla's, trying to steer clear of Mandy. The situation with her was getting too complicated, and I needed space to think.

As I passed by my bedroom, I noticed the bed was unmade. That was odd; I always made it before leaving. Then it hit me - Mandy. She must have been in here. A wave of irritation washed over me. I had to set some boundaries, and soon. But right now, I didn't want to wake her up and start a conversation I wasn't ready for.

I tiptoed past her room, but something caught my eye. There was a picture sticking out from a book on her bedside table. I noticed she was gone, and curiosity quickly overpowered my intention to leave. I leaned in closer to take a look. It was a photo of a younger Mandy, smiling widely, with... Officer Kilkenny. They looked extremely close, almost like family.

My heart pounded in my chest. Was Mandy one of

Kilkenny's foster kids? Was that the connection? It suddenly made sense - her knowledge of Jude, her being in Silver Creek. Everything was starting to click, but not in a good way.

I took a picture of the photo with my phone to print out later, then carefully slid the picture back, making sure not to disturb anything. I couldn't let Mandy know what I'd found until I had more information. This discovery changed everything. If Mandy was somehow connected to Kilkenny, she might be more involved in this case than I had ever imagined.

I quickly changed into my uniform, my mind racing with questions and theories. How deep did this go? Was Mandy just an innocent bystander, or was she part of something darker?

As I drove to the station, my thoughts were a jumble. The sunlight was bright, but my mood was anything but. The picture of Mandy and Kilkenny haunted me. I gripped the steering wheel tighter, trying to focus. I had to tread carefully and play this right. If Mandy was involved, I couldn't tip her off.

I barely acknowledged Kayla's smile as I barged into the station, my phone, with the photograph of Mandy and Officer Kilkenny now saved on it, burning a hole in my pocket. I didn't even say hello. I just handed her my phone, watching her face change from a welcoming smile to stunned disbelief.

"Is that...?" she began, her voice trailing off as she took in the image.

"Yeah, it's Mandy and Kilkenny," I said, my voice tight. "Looks pretty damn cozy, doesn't it?"

Kayla looked up at me, her eyes wide with realization. "But why would she have a picture of him? What's their connection?"

"That's what we need to find out," I said, pacing back and forth. "There's more. I checked the list of Kilkenny's foster kids. There's no Amanda on it."

Kayla pulled up the list again, cross-referencing it with other databases. After a few tense minutes, she let out a soft gasp. "Mandy isn't his foster child," she said, looking up at me. "She's his biological daughter. But she uses her mother's maiden name."

"You think Kilkenny was covering up for her, not Jude?"

"It's possible," Kayla said, her voice laced with uncertainty. "But we need more evidence."

I rubbed my face. "We need to get in touch with Kilkenny. Now."

Kayla dialed Kilkenny's number again, but it went straight to voicemail like before. The same happened with his wife's number. Frustration gnawed at me. We were so close, yet so far.

I grabbed my phone and called the Key West PD, requesting a wellness check on Kilkenny. "I need this, guys," I said into the phone. "It's urgent."

After I ended the call, Kayla and I sat silently, the tension between us thick. The photo of Mandy and Kilkenny lay on the desk.

I leaned back in my chair, running my hands through my hair. "This is messed up, Kayla," I said, shaking my head. "If Mandy is involved..."

"I know," she replied softly. "But we can't jump to conclusions. Not yet."

I nodded, though a part of me felt like I already knew the truth. The pieces fit together too well. Mandy's odd behavior, her possessiveness over me, her connection to Kilkenny. It all pointed to something sinister.

"We wait for Key West PD to get back to us," I said, trying to sound more confident than I felt.

Kayla nodded, her expression serious. "Yeah. We wait."

The clock on the wall ticked loudly in the silent room, marking the passing seconds as we waited for a call that could change everything.

We both jumped when my phone finally buzzed, but it was just a text from Mandy asking where I was. I ignored it.

Kayla and I exchanged a look. We just had to wait for that call from Key West, the call that could answer all our questions or lead us down an even darker path.

As I drove home, my mind was a whirlwind of thoughts, mostly dread at the thought of confronting Mandy. Kayla was right, though; it had been too long that we'd taken the easy route. The gnawing suspicion about Mandy's involvement had become too loud to ignore.

The house was eerily quiet when I walked in. Mandy wasn't there, which was both a relief and an opportunity. I hesitated for a moment before heading upstairs to her room.

Mandy's room was meticulously organized, almost unnervingly so. My eyes were drawn to her desk, where I found a box full of magazines. Something about them seemed off. On closer inspection, my heart sank. There were letters cut out, the same kind of cutouts used in the stalker letters sent to Lexi.

A cold sweat broke out across my forehead as I continued to rummage through her things. Hidden in a drawer, I found a stash of pictures of Lexi from college. They were taken from afar without her knowledge. But what was more disturbing were the photos from the past year. Mandy had claimed she wasn't around during that time. The photos told a different story.

I felt sick, but the most unsettling discovery was yet to come. Tucked away in another corner of the drawer were doctored photos. Pictures of the meals Mandy had made, photoshopped to show us eating together and cuddling. She'd created a fantasy life with me as the unwilling co-star.

The last straw was the photos of me sleeping. They were recent, and there were many. The violation of my privacy, the sheer creepiness of it all, made my skin crawl.

I sat back on my heels, still holding a photo of me asleep. The room felt like it was closing in on me. Mandy's obsession, her delusions, had been right under my nose, and I had been too blind to see it.

How had things spiraled so out of control?

I glanced at my watch. I had to get back to the station, to Kayla. We needed to piece this together, to understand the full extent of Mandy's involvement.

I stuffed the most incriminating items into a bag, evidence that needed analysis.

As I stood up, ready to leave the room, my phone buzzed with a text from Mandy: "Hey, where are you? Can't wait to see you tonight."

Tonight? What was she planning? I pocketed my phone without responding.

I needed to talk to Kayla. We had to figure this out before it was too late.

I was about to leave and head back to the station with my evidence when the slightly open closet caught my eye. It was just enough that I couldn't leave without looking, without peeking inside…

I stood frozen in the closet, my heart pounding against

my ribcage. The closet was a shrine to a twisted obsession, but not just with me – with Kayla. Photos of her, some normal, but others... Jesus, others were defaced, marked with violent scribbles. It chilled me to the bone. Mandy's obsession with me was one thing, but this? This was downright dangerous.

I fumbled for my phone, my hands shaking. First, I tried calling Kayla. It rang and rang, then went to voicemail. "Kayla, it's me. Call me back as soon as you get this. It's urgent." My voice was tight with panic.

Then, I heard it – footsteps outside the room. Light, quick steps, the kind of steps that knew they'd been caught. I lunged for the door, but I was too late. The front door slammed shut, the sound echoing through the empty house.

"Shit!" I hissed, sprinting down the stairs and out the door. But it was useless; Mandy was gone, her car missing from the driveway. She knew. She saw me going through her things.

I needed the evidence, so I ran back upstairs and took pictures of everything, then ran back out the front door.

Adrenaline coursed through me as I bolted to my cruiser, throwing the evidence bag into the passenger seat. I had to find Kayla before Mandy did. The thought of what she might do and what she was capable of terrified me.

As I drove, I called Kayla again, each ring sending a new wave of dread through me. It went to voicemail once more. "Kayla, please, you need to call me. It's about Mandy – she's not who we thought she was. Please, be careful."

I pushed the cruiser to its limits, my mind racing as fast as the engine. Every possible scenario played out in my head, each worse than the last. The realization of how blind I had been, how I had misjudged Mandy so completely, gnawed at me.

Mandy's obsession, her fixation on me and her hatred for Kayla, whatever her reason was for stalking Lexi to begin with, it all made a twisted kind of sense now. I needed to get to Kayla to protect her and end this before it went any further.

"Please, Kayla, be safe," I whispered to the empty car, pushing it even faster. The roads blurred past me as I sped towards the station, hoping someone there might have some answers, my mind racing just as fast as the car.

"Come on, Kayla," I muttered, redialing her number, hoping she'd pick up this time. But again, it went straight to voicemail.

Frustrated and worried, I called the station. The chief picked up after the second ring. "chief, it's Jake. Have you seen Kayla?"

"Hey, Jake. Yeah, Kayla just left a few minutes ago," he replied, his voice casual.

"Where did she go?"

"To meet you, I thought," the chief sounded confused. "She seemed in a hurry. Said something about meeting you at a location."

"What? No, I didn't..." Realization hit me like a ton of bricks. Mandy. It had to be her.

"You alright, Jake? What's going on?" The chief's voice was laced with concern now.

"I think Kayla's in trouble. Mandy Pennington—she's been staying with me, a friend of my sister's—I think she's behind Lexi's stalking. Behind all of it. I gotta go." I hung up abruptly, my mind racing.

I floored the accelerator, pushing the cruiser to its limits. The winding roads blurred past me, each turn taken with a precision honed from years of driving these routes.

But today, each curve felt like an eternity, each mile a marathon.

As the station came into view, my heart was hammering in my chest. I pulled into the parking lot, barely slowing down before I killed the engine. My hands were shaking, the adrenaline coursing through my veins.

"Come on, think, Jake," I muttered, trying to piece together Mandy's plan. Where would she take Kayla? What was her endgame?

I knew I had to act fast. Every second counted, and I couldn't afford to waste any. With a deep breath, I prepared to face whatever lay ahead, the situation bearing down on me. Kayla's life might depend on what I did next.

I got out of the car, determination steeling my resolve as I headed towards the station, ready to piece together the clues and find Kayla before it was too late.

Chapter Thirty-Seven

KAYLA

As I delved deeper into Mandy's history, the pieces began to fall into place. The sealed records I managed to access were a goldmine. Mandy, born Amanda Kilkenny, was a person of interest in both Garrett's disappearance and the unidentified body case where Officer Kilkenny, her father, was the lead. But there were no arrests, no charges, just a string of interviews, and then... nothing. It was as if she'd been wiped clean from the cases, her involvement just a ghostly echo.

I kept digging, finding her birth certificate with Kilkenny clearly written as her last name. Yet, when she enrolled in college, she was Amanda Pennington. The change of name was deliberate, a way to distance herself from her father, or perhaps a deeper, more sinister reason.

Her connection with Jude was vague, scattered across social media with limited interaction. They appeared close in some photos, almost intimately so, but then there would be long stretches of no contact, no acknowledgment of each other's existence.

As I was piecing together her college life, trying to find

the link between her, Jude, and Garrett, my phone rang, jolting me from my focus. I glanced at the caller ID – it was an unknown number. My heart skipped a beat. This could be the call that shed light on all the shadows Mandy had cast.

I answered, my voice steady but my mind racing. "This is Detective Green."

The call was from an officer in Key West PD. Their voice was somber, weighed down by the news they had to deliver. They had conducted a wellness check on the Kilkenny residence, and what they found was a scene straight out of a horror story.

The Kilkennys and their nephew had been found dead, their bodies in a state of advanced decomposition, suggesting they had been lying there for months. The officer detailed the scene – signs of a struggle, the positioning of the bodies, the nature of their injuries. It was a gruesome tableau.

As the officer spoke, I scribbled notes, trying to make sense of the chaos. The injuries, as they were described, bore a striking resemblance to those found on the unidentified body from the John Doe case – the one Officer Kilkenny had been in charge of. The similarities were too much to be a coincidence.

The officer mentioned they had tried to contact the next of kin, the Kilkennys' daughter, but to no avail. Mandy. They couldn't reach her. My mind raced with possibilities – was Mandy the perpetrator or another victim?

I thanked the officer for their information as I hung up.

If Mandy was behind all of this, she had orchestrated a complex web of deception and violence. But why? What was her endgame? And if she wasn't, then who was pulling the strings?

I pondered the possibility that Mandy knew Jude was the stalker and had killed him to protect Lexi. But that theory crumbled under recent evidence – the letters, the threats, they all continued long after Jude would have been dead.

I knew I had to talk to Jake to share what I had found.

I texted him and spent the next half hour staring at the blank screen. I couldn't shake the feeling that something was off. Taking a deep breath, I went to the chief's office, determined to get the ball rolling on an arrest warrant.

"chief, we need to talk," I said as I entered his office. His eyes met mine, instantly registering the seriousness in my tone.

"What's going on, Kayla?" he asked, setting aside his paperwork.

I explained everything – the deaths in Key West, the connection to Mandy, the similarities in the injuries. The chief listened intently, his expression growing graver with each detail.

"Jesus, Kayla," he muttered, reaching for his phone. "I'm calling this in. We need warrants, now."

I nodded, feeling a surge of adrenaline. "I'll get all the info printed off. We need to be ready."

As I turned to leave, my phone buzzed. It was a text from Jake. My heart skipped a beat as I read his message.

"Kayla, I found something BIG. Meet me at the ranch ASAP."

"Why not the station?" I texted back, my fingers trembling slightly. "This is official now."

His response came quickly, "It's way bigger than we thought. But you have to come FAST."

Hesitation gnawed at me. Something about this felt wrong. Why the ranch? Why the urgency? But it was Jake, and I trusted him implicitly.

"Okay, I'm on my way," I replied, trying to push aside the nagging doubts. Then, I turned toward the chief's office and said, "I have to go. Jake needs me at Dalton Ranch."

"Be careful, Kayla," the chief called after me as I hurried out. His concern was evident, mirroring my own.

I walked briskly to the police cruiser, my mind a whirlwind of thoughts. What had Jake discovered? How did it tie into everything we knew? And why did I have this sinking feeling in the pit of my stomach?

As I climbed into the cruiser, I took a deep breath, trying to steady my nerves. This was it, the moment we had been working towards. But as I started the engine and pulled away from the station, I couldn't shake the feeling that we were heading into uncharted territory.

As my cruiser rolled to a stop at the ranch, unease crept up my spine. The sprawling property, usually bustling with life, lay eerily still under the brooding sky, the midday sun blotted out by clouds. I scanned the surroundings, noting the absence of Jake's familiar truck. A knot formed in my stomach. Something was off.

I reached for my phone, fingers tapping out a quick message to Jake. "At the ranch. Where are you?" The air felt heavy, charged with a tension that made my skin tingle. I watched the screen, willing a reply to materialize.

After what felt like an eternity, the phone vibrated. "Stalker's here. Lexi's in trouble," Jake's message read. My heart skipped a beat. Lexi? Here? A million questions buzzed in my head, each more frantic than the last.

I fired back another text, "Why is Lexi here?" but the only answer I got was the sudden scream that shattered the silence coming from inside the house. It was a harrowing sound, filled with fear and desperation.

Instinctively, I pulled my gun from its holster, feeling

the familiar weight of the weapon in my hand. My training kicked in, guiding my movements as I approached the house. Each step was measured, cautious, my eyes scanning for any sign of movement, any hint of danger.

The ranch house, once a symbol of safety and warmth, now loomed like a malevolent entity. Its windows, dark and unyielding, gave nothing away. The faint sound of sobbing reached my ears, and I paused at the door, listening intently. The sobbing continued, a low, mournful sound that seemed to seep through the cracks.

Was it Lexi? Or Mandy?

With a deep, steadying breath, I readied myself. Gripping my gun with both hands, I nudged the door open with my foot, prepared for whatever horror lay on the other side.

I pushed the door open wider, stepping into the dim interior of the ranch house. My boots made almost no sound against the wooden floor, a testament to years of careful steps on similar assignments. My eyes darted around, adjusting to the low light, every sense heightened.

The living room was a maze of draped furniture and plastic sheeting, remnants of the renovations Luke and Lexi had started. My gaze swept across the room, checking every potential hiding spot. The faint smell of paint lingered in the air, mixing with the scent of old wood and dust.

I moved slowly, methodically, my gun leading the way. Shadows clung to the corners, playing tricks on my eyes. Every creak of the floorboard underfoot made my heart race. I paused, listening intently, but the only sound was the faint whistle of the wind outside.

Stepping through a plastic curtain, I entered the dining area. The table was covered with a cloth, specks of paint dotting its surface. Chairs were stacked against the wall, their silhouettes ominous in the half-light. I scanned the room, but it was as deserted as the rest.

I proceeded to the kitchen, my movements precise. The renovation had left its mark here, too—cabinets stood open, and tools lay scattered on the counters. I checked behind the door, in the pantry, anywhere someone could hide. Nothing.

The silence was oppressive, a heavy blanket. I couldn't shake the feeling of being watched, yet there was no sign of Jake, Lexi, or anyone else.

I continued down the hallway, past the bathroom, its mirror covered in a dusty film. Each step felt like an eternity, my mind racing with possibilities, scenarios playing out in rapid succession.

Finally, I reached the bedrooms. The first was empty, its bed stripped bare, the closet door ajar, revealing an empty space. The second room was much the same, a ghost of a space once filled with life.

I paused at the door to the master bedroom. My hand rested on the knob, hesitating. Taking a deep breath, I pushed it open and stepped inside. The room was in disarray—bed unmade, drawers half-open. But like the rest of the house, it was devoid of life.

Finally, I stood in the center of the master bedroom, my gun still drawn, its metal cold and reassuring in my grip. I listened, the silence echoing around me.

Then, the realization hit me hard – I was standing in a trap. My heart pounded as I pulled out my phone, fingers tapping a quick message to Jake. "Where the hell are you?" I typed, urgency knotting in my stomach.

That's when I heard it—the faint buzz of a phone nearby. I turned sharply, my eyes scanning the room. There, on the windowsill, lay a phone, one I knew wasn't Jake's. I picked it up, my mind racing with possibilities.

The screen lit up to a gallery of photos, all of me, taken from angles I wasn't aware of. Each image was a violation, a silent watcher documenting my movements. My grip on the phone tightened as I swiped through the pictures.

Then, I came across a letter similar to those left for Lexi, but this one was addressed to me: "Surprise, Detective Bitch!" The words taunted me, mocking my failed attempt to catch the stalker.

I realized it then. Mandy, with her crazy crush on Jake. She was even crazier than I'd realized.

A noise behind me snapped my attention away from the phone. I whirled around, but it was too late. Something hard struck my arm, sending my gun clattering to the floor. I reached out blindly, but my assailant was quick and agile.

The next instant, a bag of concrete powder burst open, a cloud of dust engulfing me. My eyes stung, my vision obscured by the thick haze. I coughed, trying to clear my lungs, my thoughts racing.

Desperately, I tried to regain my footing, to orient myself in the blinding cloud. My mind screamed for action, but my body was slow to respond, disoriented by the sudden attack.

I knew I had to act fast to find a way out of this, but the dust swirled around me, a tangible barrier that clouded not only my vision but my thoughts. The fear of what might be lurking in that cloud, waiting to strike again, sent a surge of adrenaline through me.

I reached down, fumbling for my gun, my fingers brushing against the cool metal. As I grasped it, I forced myself to focus and strained to hear over the cacophony of my own coughing. Another scream pierced the dust-filled air, morphing into a laugh.

The Rookie's Second Chance

"Mandy? Is that you?" I shouted, my voice hoarse with dust and tension.

The laughter grew louder, more sinister. I couldn't see her, but I could feel her presence lurking somewhere in the haze. Then, without warning, there was movement—a rustling through the cloud of dust.

Before I could react, a solid hit struck my arm, knocking my gun out of my grasp. I swung wildly toward the attack, but my fist met only air. Panic and frustration surged as I tried to orient myself in the chaos.

Mandy was quick, and she seemed to know the layout of the room better than I did. I kept stumbling over debris and furniture, each fall a painful reminder of my disadvantage.

I tried to fight back, to defend myself, but it was like battling a shadow. The attacker was always just out of reach, always one step ahead. I could feel the balance of the fight tipping against me. With every missed swing and every trip, my situation grew more desperate. I needed to gain the upper hand.

I gasped for air, the dust clogging my lungs and clouding my judgment. I couldn't let this be the end. I had to find a way to fight back, to overpower my unseen opponent. But as the struggle continued, with me losing ground, I couldn't shake the sinking feeling that I was running out of options.

The metallic scraping of metal against the rough wood flooring set off alarm bells in my head. Panic surged through me as I realized Mandy had somehow managed to grab my gun. My heart pounded against my ribs, echoing the fear coursing through my veins.

A gunshot shattered the tense silence, its proximity causing my ears to ring. Instinctively, I ducked, feeling the air shift as the bullet whizzed past my head, narrowly missing me.

"Shit!" I cursed, adrenaline surging through me. My hands trembled slightly, the reality of the situation hitting me hard.

From somewhere in the dust-filled room, Mandy's laughter, cold and maniacal, pierced the air. "Don't worry. I'm not going to kill you... here," she taunted. "Too easy for me to get found out, especially with Daddy gone."

I whirled around, scanning the room for any sign of her. Panic and frustration swirled within me. Realizing I needed backup, I fumbled for my phone. I dialed the station, knowing I could get to Jake or the chief without the middleman of a dispatcher, my fingers shaking.

The call connected almost instantly, Jake's familiar voice coming through. "Kayla? What's happening? Are you okay?"

"Jake, it's Mandy! She's here, and she's got my—" My warning was cut short as a sharp, excruciating pain erupted at the back of my skull. The room spun wildly, a carousel of blurred colors and shapes.

I heard my own voice, distant and faint, "Jake—"

Darkness crept in at the edges of my vision, my knees buckling beneath me. The phone slipped from my grasp, clattering to the floor as I tried to grasp onto consciousness.

"Mandy..." I managed to mutter, the world around me fading into nothingness. The last thing I heard was Jake's voice, filled with panic and confusion, calling my name through the phone before I succumbed to the darkness.

Chapter Thirty-Eight

MANDY

Waking up in Jake's bed, the sheets still smelling of him, my heart twisted in frustration. He didn't come home last night. Didn't he see? I've been showing him, trying to be everything he could ever want. But no, he's still out there, probably with her, Kayla.

I sat up, pushing the blankets away, feeling a surge of anger. It wasn't fair. I did everything right. Just like with Lexi... I was always the perfect friend, always there for her. When Garrett was in the picture, I took care of that problem and made sure he was out of the way. He had to go. He was standing in the way of what was meant to be mine. And then, there was Jude. My cousin. I convinced him to date Lexi, to treat her poorly, so I could swoop in and be her hero. But Lexi, she never saw it. She never realized I was the one she needed.

I stood up, pacing the room, my mind racing. All those years, all that effort, and for what? Lexi got married and moved on without a second thought for me. But when I came here, to Silver Creek, it was like a sign from the universe. It led me to Jake, the real prize. Lexi was just a stepping stone.

My hands clenched into fists. I've been too passive, waiting for Jake to see what's right in front of him. But it's clear now. Waiting isn't going to get me what I want. It never has. It's time for action, just like with Garrett. I can't let Kayla or anyone else stand in my way.

I started getting dressed, each movement deliberate. I needed a plan, something to make Jake see that we were meant to be together. To show him that I'm the one he should be with, not Kayla. I glanced at the clock. Time was ticking, and I couldn't waste another moment.

With every piece of clothing I put on, my resolve hardened. Jake was mine; he had to be. I'd make him see it, one way or another. I couldn't let this slip through my fingers. Not again. This time, I'd take control. And nothing, and no one, would stand in my way.

As I walked out of the room, the determination set in my stride, I knew this was just the beginning. The end game was in sight, and I was ready to play.

I grabbed my phone and opened the app I'd cleverly installed. It let me keep tabs on Jake and Kayla's phones. Thanks to a little hacking and their phone numbers, I was in control. I smirked, swapping their contact numbers in each other's phones to redirect to mine. This way, any communication between them would actually come to me.

Satisfied, I slipped the phone into my pocket and headed out. I drove to a secluded part of the woods, where my van was parked, hidden from prying eyes. As I drove, I remembered that night in this very van, the night I almost had it all.

I'd knocked Kayla out cold right there in the back of the van. The plan was perfect, simple but effective. I would get rid of her, and then Jake would have no choice but to turn to me. I'd be his comfort, his savior. But damn it, Jake had to show up just in time, ruining everything. He'd stopped me before I could finish the job.

I clenched the steering wheel, my knuckles whitening. It was so frustrating. If only he hadn't gotten there when he did, everything would've been different now. I would have Jake all to myself, and that meddling Kayla would be out of the picture.

But now, I realized I could use Kayla to my advantage. She could be the key to getting what I wanted. I could use her as leverage over Jake. The thought excited me, a rush of adrenaline pumping through my veins. I could make Jake choose and force his hand. He'd have to see that we were meant to be together.

I took a deep breath as I reached the van, hidden amongst the trees. This was it—the moment when everything would come together. I'd been planning, waiting, manipulating for so long. It was time to put everything into action.

I opened the van door, the familiar creak sounding like music to my ears. Stepping inside, I ran my hand along the interior, feeling the cold metal and the remnants of my previous plans. This van had been my sanctuary, my operation base. And now, it would be the catalyst for my final move.

I sat in the driver's seat, feeling a sense of power and control wash over me. With a twist of the key, the engine roared to life, a beast awakening from its slumber. It was time to bring my plan to fruition.

I pulled out of the hiding spot, my eyes set on the prize. Jake would be mine, one way or another. The only downside to my plan was Daddy wasn't here anymore to bail me out if things went south. He'd always been my safety net, pulling strings and using his influence to keep me out of trouble. But now, I was on my own. I had to be careful. There was no room for error.

I was sitting at the kitchen table in my parents' house in Key West, the ocean breeze wafting through the open window. It was supposed to be calming, but nothing could soothe the storm inside me. I was trying to focus on my writing, the book I had been working on for months, but the publishers kept rejecting it. They said it wasn't good enough, but what did they know? Their rejections were just fueling my anger, a fire burning inside me, growing stronger each day.

My dad walked in, holding a stack of forwarded mail from my old apartment. I'd been evicted for not paying rent, but that was a minor setback. I was living with my parents because I needed "a little extra support," or at least that's what they told me. I knew they thought I was crazy, but I wasn't. They were overreacting. Daddy especially. If he truly thought I was crazy, he would have never helped me cover up what happened with Garrett.

The memory of that night flashed in my mind. Garrett was supposed to get scared, not fight back. It was his fault, not mine. Daddy understood that. He knew it was for the greater good.

I started rifling through the mail, mostly bills and junk, until my fingers grazed something different. An invitation. My heart stopped as I pulled it out. It was an invitation to Lexi's wedding. Lexi... my Lexi. The thought of her getting married to someone else ignited a firestorm of emotions within me.

Lexi was mine. How could she be getting married? The betrayal felt like a physical blow, a sharp pain in my chest.

The Rookie's Second Chance

I'd done everything for her, been the perfect friend. I'd even gotten rid of Garrett for her. And this was how she repaid me?

I unfolded the invitation, my hands shaking. I had to stop this wedding. I had to do something drastic, even if it meant killing this Luke guy before they could say, 'I do.' But as I scanned the invitation, my heart sank even further. The wedding had already happened. It was over. They were married.

I felt my world collapsing around me. All my plans, all my dreams of being with Lexi, shattered in an instant. The invitation slipped from my trembling hands, fluttering to the floor like a fallen leaf.

I couldn't breathe. My chest tightened, and I gasped for air. A panic attack was clawing its way up my throat, squeezing my lungs. I couldn't think straight. Everything was spinning, the walls closing in on me. Lexi was gone, married to someone else. My plan, my future with her, everything I had worked for, was gone.

I slumped to the floor, my back against the kitchen cabinet. Tears streamed down my face as I struggled to breathe. I felt betrayed, lost, and utterly alone. Lexi was supposed to be mine, and now she belonged to someone else.

Suddenly, I couldn't contain it anymore. A primal scream erupted from me, a raw explosion of all the pain and anger I had been holding back. My parents and Jude, who were in the living room, rushed in, startled by my outburst.

In a blind rage, I stood up, overturning my chair with a loud crash. I started throwing whatever I could get my hands on, my emotions a whirlwind of destruction. I didn't even realize what I was doing until I saw my chair hit my mom, knocking her to the floor. Blood trickled from a cut on her forehead, and my heart stopped for a moment. What had I done?

Jude rushed to her side, his face a mask of concern, while my dad tried to approach me, his hands raised in a calming gesture. "Mandy, sweetheart, calm down. Tell me what's wrong," he pleaded, his voice steady but filled with worry.

Through my sobs, I tried to explain, but all that came out was a jumbled mess of words. "I lost the game... someone else got Lexi..." It sounded so petty when I said it out loud, but the pain was real.

My dad's expression shifted to one of deep concern. He murmured something to Jude, a phrase that sounded like a code. Jude pulled out his phone, and I instantly knew he wasn't just calling for help for Mom.

"What are you doing?" I demanded, my voice thick with tears and suspicion.

"Just getting help for Mom," Jude replied, but his eyes avoided mine. I knew he was lying. He was always the one to cover for me, to take the fall when things got messy. And now, he was betraying me, turning me in to the authorities or worse.

A surge of panic and betrayal washed over me. I couldn't let them do this. I couldn't be locked away, not when there was so much left to do. In a moment of desperation, I shoved my dad, hoping to create a distraction, an escape. He stumbled backward, his head striking the edge of the table with a sickening thud.

The room fell silent, save for my heavy breathing. My dad lay motionless on the floor, a growing pool of blood under his head. My mom, still dazed from the blow and lying beneath Jude's kneeling form, looked at me with a mixture of fear and disbelief.

I knew... I knew I couldn't let them live. If I did, they

might ruin everything. I would have to kill them all. Starting with my cousin. My protector.

Quick as lightning, while Jude was distracted, I grabbed the frying pan off the stove. I had one chance to get him down, to at least knock him out, or he would be able to fight back. I raised the pan over my head and brought it down as hard as I could, hearing the crack and watching the red splatters blossom across the room. Jude crumpled to the ground, unconscious, his body motionless.

Next, I needed to deal with Mom. Her eyes were wide, and she whimpered softly as I raised the pan again and brought it down directly on her face. Her skull caved in with a sickening crunch, blood oozing out of her mouth.

Finally, I moved on to my dad. He had regained consciousness by then, watching with detached fascination as I grabbed the knife from the table and sliced his throat open. He struggled weakly, reaching out to grab me, but he was too slow. The sound of his gurgling breath cut short by the cold steel blade in my hand made me feel no remorse, only relief.

I stood there, my heart pounding in my chest, staring at the lifeless bodies of my parents and Jude. They had been my shield, my protectors, but now they were gone, silenced forever by my own hands. The realization was both terrifying and liberating. I had crossed a line from which there was no return.

With a sense of urgency, I knew I couldn't stay. The bodies would eventually be found, but I had time. No one would come looking for them anytime soon. They were recluses, and our home was a haven from prying eyes.

As I pulled up to Jake's house, I felt a surge of adrenaline. This was it, the final stage of my plan. I quietly entered the house, going to my room where I had stored my supplies.

But then, I saw Jake. He was there, in my room, looking through my things. He had found everything - the evidence that tied me to the stalking, the letters, the photos. My heart sank. He knew. Everything I had worked for was unraveling before my eyes.

Panic set in. I couldn't let him arrest me. Not yet. I had to act fast. Without a word, I turned and ran from the room, the sound of my footsteps echoing through the house.

I knew where I had to go - to Kayla. She was my leverage, my bargaining chip. With Kayla in my control, Jake would have to listen to me, to see things my way. I could still turn this around, still make him see that we were meant to be together.

As I drove towards the ranch, I finalized my plan. Kayla was the key to everything. If I could just get to her before Jake realized what I was planning, I could still win this game. I could still have Jake.

The ranch loomed in the distance, a symbol of my final destination. I knew what I had to do. It was time to take control of my destiny, to claim what was mine. Jake, Kayla, Silver Creek - they were all just pieces in my grand design.

I crouched in the shadows of the ranch house, my heart beating a rapid tattoo against my ribcage. This was it, the moment I had been planning for, the culmination of all my efforts. I had lured Kayla here, to this isolated place, away from anyone who could help her. It was perfect.

As I watched her through the windows, her movements cautious and deliberate, I felt a surge of power. She was here because of me, dancing to the tune I was playing. My phone vibrated constantly in my pocket, a testament to my successful deception.

The tension in the air was palpable as Kayla moved from room to room, her gun drawn. She was a predator, but so was I. I waited, biding my time, until she found the phone I had deliberately left on the windowsill. The phone buzzed, a message from 'Jake' - a final lure to draw her into my trap.

As she picked up the phone and scrolled through the photos, I could almost hear her heart pounding. Photos of her, taken without her knowledge, a letter addressed to her in the same style as those sent to Lexi. Surprise, Detective Bitch! The shock on her face was almost comical.

I moved silently, positioning myself just right. As she turned, I struck, knocking the gun from her hand with a well-aimed hit. The element of surprise was on my side. I had the upper hand, and I intended to keep it.

The fight was brief but intense. Kayla was a trained officer, but I had the advantage of knowing the room's layout. I dodged her swings, using her disorientation to my advantage. When she stumbled, I seized my chance.

I grabbed a bag of concrete powder and smashed it, filling the air with a choking cloud of dust. Her coughs and sputters were music to my ears. I watched as she flailed helplessly, trying to clear her vision.

Then, I struck again, this time with the butt of the gun against her head. She crumpled to the floor, unconscious. A wave of triumph washed over me. I had done it. I had bested Kayla, the detective who had been getting too close to the truth—and Jake.

Quickly, I dragged her limp body to the van, heaving her inside. It was time to get out of there, to put as much distance between us and Silver Creek as possible. I had Kayla, and now I had the leverage I needed over Jake.

As I drove away from the ranch, my phone rang incessantly, Jake's number flashing on the screen. I ignored it, focusing on the road ahead. I had a plan, and Kayla was the key to making it all work.

In my rearview mirror, the ranch house faded into the distance, a symbol of the old life I was leaving behind. Ahead lay a new beginning, a future where I would finally have everything I ever wanted.

Chapter Thirty-Nine

JAKE

I burst into the police station, my mind racing. The realization that Kayla was in danger, possibly at the hands of Mandy, hammered in my chest like a relentless drumbeat. The station was a blur of uniforms and activity, but my focus was laser-sharp. I needed to find Kayla, and I needed to find her now.

I made a beeline for my desk and quickly hacked into the system to track Kayla's phone. The digital map flickered to life, pinpointing her location at the ranch. A surge of fear laced with anger shot through me. Why the hell was she there?

I didn't waste a second. Clutching the incriminating evidence I'd found in Mandy's room – the letters, the photos – I headed straight for the chief's office. He looked up as I barged in, his expression surprised and concerned.

"chief, we have a situation," I blurted out, laying the evidence on his desk. "I think Kayla's in danger, and I believe Mandy's behind it."

The chief raised an eyebrow, his gaze falling on a particular photo – one where Kayla and I were holding hands, a moment of intimacy captured unknowingly. "Jake, what's this about?" he asked, his tone heavy with unspoken questions.

"Not now, chief," I snapped, my patience fraying. "I can explain that later, but right now, we need to save Kayla. She's at the ranch, and I think Mandy's got her."

The chief's expression hardened, and he grabbed the radio. "I'm sending backup with you. Let's move."

I nodded, already halfway out the door. In moments, I was in my cruiser, the engine roaring to life as I slammed the gas pedal. The other cops followed suit, sirens blaring and lights flashing. We tore through the streets of Silver Creek, every second feeling like an eternity.

Kayla, alone and in danger, possibly at the mercy of a deranged Mandy. The thought was unbearable. I gripped the steering wheel so tightly my knuckles turned white.

As the ranch drew closer, my heart pounded against my ribs. I was ready to burst through the door and take down whoever I needed to, just to ensure Kayla was safe. Nothing else mattered.

The cruiser skidded to a halt in a cloud of dust just outside the ranch. I was out before it fully stopped, my gun drawn, ready for whatever awaited me. My only thought was Kayla. I had to find her. I had to save her.

And with that single-minded determination, I charged toward the ranch house, the other officers at my heels. The stakes had never been higher, and failure was not an option. Kayla's life depended on it.

I stormed into the ranch house, my pistol drawn and ready. Behind me, a squad of officers followed, their faces set in grim determination. We moved swiftly, clearing each room with practiced efficiency. My heart hammered in my chest, each beat a silent plea for Kayla's safety.

The house was eerily quiet. Room by room, we

searched, but there was no sign of Kayla or Mandy. We were all on edge, anticipating the worst at every turn.

Then we hit the living room, and everything changed. A cloud of concrete dust hung in the air, coating everything in a fine, gray layer. It was clear a struggle had taken place here. My eyes darted around, scanning for any sign of Kayla. A small patch of blood on the floor caught my eye, and my stomach turned. Was it Kayla's? Or Mandy's?

"Shit," I muttered under my breath, crouching down to examine the blood.

Suddenly, one of the officers burst into the room, urgency etched on his face. "Jake, there are tire tracks outside. Looks like someone peeled out of here in a hurry."

I stood up, my jaw clenched. "Can we follow them?" I asked, hope flickering in my chest.

He shook his head, a grim expression on his face. "They lead to the main road. No dirt or gravel there to keep track of the tracks. We've lost them."

A wave of frustration washed over me. We were so close, yet so far. I felt helpless, and that was a feeling I despised.

"Damn it," I cursed, running a hand through my hair. I needed to think, to plan our next move. But all I could picture was Kayla, in danger and alone. My heart ached at the thought.

Without another word, I pulled out my phone and dialed Lexi's number. She needed to know what was happening. As the phone rang, I braced myself, knowing that this call would bring more worry. But she had to be informed. She deserved to know.

I stood amidst the dust and silence, waiting for Lexi to pick up. The ringtone echoed in the empty room, a stark reminder of the urgency and gravity of the situation. We were running out of time, and every second counted.

The phone rang twice before Lexi's voice came through, sounding anxious. "Jake? What's up?"

"I need to know if there was ever anything off about Mandy. Anything at all," I said, my voice tight with urgency. I held the phone close, every muscle in my body tensed as I waited for her response.

"What? No, why?" Lexi's voice crackled through the speaker, confusion and concern mingling in her tone.

I took a deep breath, trying to steady my racing heart. "Look, I don't know how to say this, but... I found evidence at the house. It looks like Mandy might have killed Garrett back in college. And her dad, a cop, might have covered it up."

There was a sharp intake of breath on the other end. "Oh my God, Jake, are you serious?"

"Yeah, I am," I replied, my grip on the phone tightening. "And there's more. It looks like she's taken Kayla. I need to find her, Lexi. Anything you can remember about Mandy might help."

There was a pause, a heavy silence that seemed to stretch on forever. "I'm coming back," Lexi finally said, her voice firm.

"No, Lexi, it's not safe," I protested, panic rising.

"I brought this monster into our lives, Jake. It's my responsibility to help fix it," she insisted, her voice laced with determination.

I wanted to argue, to tell her to stay put where it was safe. But I knew it was pointless. Lexi was as stubborn as they come. "Fine," I relented, my voice heavy. "Just be careful, okay? We don't know what Mandy is capable of."

"I'll be back in a few hours," she said. "Hang in there, Jake. We'll find her."

I nodded, even though she couldn't see it. "Okay. Thanks, Lexi." With a heavy heart, I ended the call.

The Rookie's Second Chance

As I stood there, phone in hand, frustration washed over me. Lexi was on her way back, but a few hours could be too long. Every second counted, and Kayla's life hung in the balance.

I pocketed my phone, my mind racing with what I'd just learned. Mandy, the woman who had seemed so harmless, was now our prime suspect in a twisted game that had gone too far. And Kayla, the woman I loved, was her latest victim.

I glanced around the dust-filled room, the traces of the struggle a grim reminder of the danger Kayla was in. I had to find her, and fast.

I knelt among the concrete dust, my heart pounding as one of the officers pointed out something glinting on the floor. It was a bracelet, a delicate silver chain with a tiny heart charm. I recognized it instantly – the bracelet I'd given Kayla back in high school. She'd started wearing it again recently, a symbol of our rekindled relationship.

The chain was broken, lying discarded among the chaos. If Mandy had taken Kayla, there was no telling what she might do to her. My hands trembled as I picked up the bracelet.

I wanted to tear the place apart, to scream, to do something, anything, to bring Kayla back. But I knew that wouldn't help. I had to be smart about this. I had to think like a detective, not just a worried boyfriend.

"I'm heading back to the station," I told the officer, my voice steady despite the turmoil inside me. "Keep me updated on anything you find here."

He nodded, and I turned to leave, clutching the bracelet in my hand.

When I arrived, I headed straight for my desk, determined to find some clue to help me locate Kayla. I couldn't let my emotions cloud my judgment. I had to stay focused and use every resource at my disposal.

I started by pulling up Mandy's profile again, scanning through the information for any hint of where she might have taken Kayla. I checked her known associates, her recent activities, anything that might give me a clue.

But it was like chasing shadows. Mandy was careful, covering her tracks well. It was frustrating, knowing that Kayla was out there somewhere, potentially in danger, and I was here, seemingly hitting dead ends.

I leaned back in my chair, rubbing my eyes. I couldn't give up. I wouldn't. Kayla was counting on me, and I wasn't about to let her down.

I picked up the phone, calling anyone who might have seen Mandy or noticed anything unusual. But it was all dead ends, nothing that led me any closer to finding Kayla.

I felt useless, stuck here while Kayla could be facing God knows what. I wanted to be out there, searching for her, but I knew I had to be smart about this. I had to use my head, not just my heart.

I looked down at the bracelet in my hand, the silver heart charm a stark reminder of what was at stake. I couldn't lose her, not now, not when we'd finally found our way back to each other.

With renewed determination, I turned back to my computer, scouring through the data, looking for any small detail that might lead me to Kayla. I wouldn't rest until I found her and brought her back safe. She meant everything to me, and I'd do whatever it took to save her.

Chapter Forty

KAYLA

The throbbing in my head was relentless, a drumbeat that echoed through my skull as I came to. My mouth was dry, my lips sealed by a gag, and a blindfold covered my eyes. I tried to call out, but the sound was muffled, useless. I was tied to a chair, my wrists and ankles aching from the tight restraints.

Panic surged through me, but I forced myself to stay calm, to think. I had to get out of this and find a way back to Jake, back to safety.

The blindfold was suddenly yanked away, and I blinked against the harsh light of the cabin. I squinted, trying to make out my surroundings. The place was dingy and abandoned, with peeling wallpaper and a musty smell that spoke of years of neglect. I had no idea where I was.

Mandy's voice cut through the silence, dripping with disdain. "Don't bother, Kayla. No one can hear you scream out here."

I glared at her, trying to convey my defiance despite the gag. "Mmmphh!" I tried to speak, but the words were trapped behind the fabric.

Mandy pulled the gag away, and I took a deep breath, my throat raw. "What do you want, Mandy?"

She laughed. "Isn't it obvious? I want Jake. And I'll never have him as long as you're in the picture."

I shook my head, trying to reason with her. "You're wrong. Jake and I are just partners."

Her expression twisted into a sneer. "Don't play dumb with me, Kayla. I know you two are in love. But if you're out of the way, Jake will come around. He'll see that I'm the one he should be with."

The realization of her delusion was chilling. "Are you going to kill me?" I asked, my voice steady despite the fear gripping my heart.

Mandy's face crumpled, her bravado faltering. "I never wanted to kill anyone," she stammered, her eyes darting around the room.

It hit me then – the truth of her words. Mandy had killed her family and maybe others. She was capable of anything, and I was at her mercy.

I had to keep her talking, had to buy time. "Why, Mandy? Why do all this?"

She paced the room, her hands wringing together. "I wanted Jake to see me, to choose me."

Her words were a twisted echo of every person's desire for love but warped by obsession and madness. I watched her, searching for any sign of the girl she might have once been before all this madness took hold.

But as she ranted, her words becoming more frantic and disjointed, I realized the Mandy standing before me was a shell, a broken reflection of unfulfilled desires and twisted fantasies.

I sat there, tied to the chair, my heart pounding. I had to find a way out, had to warn Jake. But as Mandy's shadow loomed over me, I knew escaping wouldn't be easy. I had to be smart, had to be patient.

But most of all, I had to survive. For Jake, for myself, for the chance to put an end to this nightmare once and for all.

Sitting tied to the chair, I racked my brain for any tactic that could get Mandy talking. I had to be clever and draw out her confessions without alerting her to my intentions.

"Mandy, why did you even come to Silver Creek?" I asked, injecting a hint of curiosity into my voice.

She paced back and forth, her hands wringing together. "I had to come, Kayla. Lexi needed me. She always needed me, even if she didn't realize it."

I probed further, masking my fear with feigned innocence. "Needed you? How?"

Mandy stopped pacing and turned to me, her eyes gleaming with madness and pride. "I was always there for her. When Luke came into the picture, I had to show her he wasn't right for her. I had to scare him off and give Lexi a reason to run back to me. I could have made everything better for her."

My stomach churned at her confession. "So, you were the one stalking Lexi? Trying to scare Luke?"

She nodded, a twisted smile playing on her lips. "Yes, I needed her to see that she belonged with me. I was her best friend, her savior."

The pieces were falling into place, the horrifying truth of Mandy's actions becoming clear. I pushed further, hoping to keep her talking. "What about Garrett? Did you have anything to do with what happened to him?"

Her expression darkened, and she sat down across from me. "Garrett was a mistake. He was getting too close to

Lexi, so I just wanted to scare him, to push him away. But things went too far."

"You mean you... killed him?"

Mandy's voice was a whisper, laced with regret and madness. "It wasn't supposed to happen like that. But yes, I did. And Daddy helped cover it up. Jude too. They always helped me."

My heart raced as the extent of her crimes dawned on me. "Your family... in Key West. Did you...?"

Her eyes flickered with a hint of sorrow. "They were going to turn me in. I couldn't let that happen. I had to stop them."

I swallowed hard, the reality of the situation hitting me like a freight train. Mandy was a murderer, a stalker, a twisted soul who had spiraled out of control.

I kept my voice calm, though inside, I was screaming. "Mandy, you need help. You can't keep doing this."

She laughed, a sound devoid of sanity. "It's too late for help, Kayla. I've gone too far. But it will all be worth it if I can have Jake."

The mention of Jake reignited my resolve. I had to get out of here, had to warn him. Mandy was dangerous, and he was her ultimate target.

"Mandy, listen to me," I said, trying a different approach. "You can't force someone to love you. This isn't the way."

She stood up abruptly, her face contorting with anger. "You don't understand! Jake is mine. He was always meant to be mine. And I won't let you or anyone else stand in my way."

I stared at her, my mind racing for a way out. Mandy was lost in her delusion, and I was trapped in her twisted world. But I wasn't going to give up. Not yet. Not while I still had a chance to fight back.

I watched Mandy closely, trying to gauge her reactions. She was unpredictable, a wild card that made this situation more dangerous than anything I'd encountered.

Suddenly, Mandy's phone buzzed. She glanced at it, and a sly smile crossed her face. "Well, speak of the devil. It's Jake... for you." She taunted, but didn't answer it, instead slipping the phone back into her pocket.

I seized the opportunity, "If Jake doesn't hear from me, he'll get worried. He'll come looking, Mandy."

She scoffed. "Good luck to him. Your phone's somewhere along the highway, thrown out the window. And my VPN is impenetrable. He won't find us."

Her arrogance was my advantage. I needed to outsmart her. I squinted towards the window, feigning to hear something. "Did you hear that? Sounds like someone's outside."

Mandy's expression changed to suspicion, and she crept towards the window, peering out into the growing darkness. "Stay put," she ordered, though I had no intention of doing so.

The moment she stepped outside, I worked furiously at the ropes binding my wrists. They were tight, but my constant fidgeting had loosened them enough. With a final tug, they gave way, freeing my hands. I hurriedly untied my feet.

I made a break for it, adrenaline fueling my escape. But my freedom was short-lived. As I sprinted through the underbrush, my foot snagged on something. I crashed to the ground, a net engulfing me. Mandy had set traps.

Panic set in as I struggled against the net, each movement tangling me further. Mandy's manic laughter echoed through the trees as she approached. I was trapped again, helpless, as she loomed over me.

"Nice try, Detective," Mandy sneered, her face twisted in triumph. "But you're not going anywhere."

I glared at her. I couldn't give up, not now. Not when Jake and the others could be closing in. I had to stall to keep Mandy here.

"Jake will find us, Mandy," I said, trying to sound confident despite my fear. "He won't stop until he does."

Her laughter chilled me to the bone. "Let him try. By the time he gets here, it'll be too late."

I eyed Mandy warily, trying to understand her twisted logic. "Why are you keeping me alive if you're just planning to kill me?" I asked.

Mandy sighed, almost as if she was tired of explaining. "I never wanted to kill anyone, Kayla. And I won't kill you... if Jake sees reason." Her eyes darkened. "But I will if I have to."

I struggled against the coarse net, but Mandy's grip was unyielding as she dragged me back to the cabin. The ground beneath me was uneven, jolting my body with every pull. Once inside, Mandy wasted no time in securing me to an old, moth-eaten bed. The ropes were tight against my wrists and ankles, cutting into my skin.

"You might as well get comfortable," Mandy taunted, her laughter echoing in the hollow room.

A sense of despair washed over me. I was a pawn in her twisted game, a leverage against Jake. I watched helplessly as Mandy sat down at a desk, her back to me, and started typing on her computer. I couldn't see the screen, but her focus was intense.

I turned my face into the musty pillow, trying to stifle the sobs that threatened to overwhelm me. The pillow smelled of damp and decay.

I cry, tears streaming down my face. Fear for my own life mixed with frustration at being so utterly powerless.

Mandy had orchestrated everything so meticulously, leaving me with no way out.

In those moments of despair, my thoughts turned to Jake. I hoped and prayed that he would find me before Mandy could enact whatever twisted plan she had in mind. The thought of him searching for me, of his determination and love, gave me a sliver of hope in the darkness that enveloped me.

I tried to calm my racing heart, to think clearly despite the terror that gripped me. There had to be a way out of this, a way to signal for help or escape. But every movement sent fresh pain shooting through my limbs, the ropes refusing to give even an inch.

I forced myself to breathe deeply, to conserve my energy for whatever chance might present itself. I couldn't let Mandy win. I had to survive this, for Jake, for myself, for justice.

As I lay there, trying to find some semblance of peace amidst the chaos, the chilling thought of what Mandy was capable of haunted me. She was unpredictable and dangerous, a wild card in a game with the highest stakes.

All I could do was wait, hope, and prepare for whatever came next. But deep down, I knew that my fate was no longer in my hands. It was a terrifying realization, one that made the cabin feel even more like a prison than it already was.

The phone in her pocket chimed repeatedly, probably Jake's desperate attempts to reach me. Each chime was a stark reminder of my helplessness, of the danger that loomed over us.

Mandy was unhinged, driven by an obsession that had already led to so much destruction. I needed to find a way out, to warn Jake, to stop her. But how? I was tied up, at her mercy, in a remote cabin in the woods.

I strained against my bonds, trying to loosen them, but they held tight. Mandy continued her work at the computer, oblivious to my efforts. I had to keep trying, had to find a way to escape.

Time was running out, and I knew that Mandy's patience was thin. I needed to act fast, to outsmart her, to survive. But the question remained: how?

Chapter Forty-One

JAKE

I sat hunched over my desk at the station, the glow of the computer screen casting an eerie light across the scattered papers and notes. My fingers flew over the keyboard, desperately trying to piece together any clue that might lead me to Kayla. My phone was a constant companion, buzzing with updates from Key West PD.

The images they'd sent over of the crime scene where Mandy had left her family for dead haunted me. Each detail was a vivid reminder of what she was capable of. The thought of Kayla suffering a similar fate twisted my gut in knots. I couldn't shake the image of her beaten to death with something as mundane as a frying pan. It was too much, too brutal.

I rubbed my eyes, weary from the relentless search. My focus was solely on finding Kayla, but every lead turned into a dead end. I felt helpless and frustrated. The clock on the wall ticked away, each second a reminder of how long Kayla had been in Mandy's grasp.

The chief approached my desk, his expression somber.

"Jake, you need to go home. Get some rest. We're all working on this."

I looked up at him, anger and desperation mixing in my voice. "Rest? How can I rest when Kayla's out there with that... that lunatic? I can't just sit back."

He placed a hand on my shoulder, trying to be reassuring. "I understand, but you're running on fumes. We've got the whole department on this. We'll find her."

I shook his hand off, standing up. "If it was your partner or anyone you cared about, would YOU go home?" My voice was sharp, cutting through the quiet hum of the station.

The chief met my gaze, his eyes softening. "No, I suppose I wouldn't." He sighed, stepping back. "Alright, keep at it. But call for backup the moment you have something concrete."

I nodded, turning back to my computer. The chief left me alone, understanding the turmoil that gripped me.

I slammed my fist on the desk in frustration, feeling helpless. This wasn't just a case anymore; it was personal, a race against time to save the woman I loved.

The station was quiet, the late hour leaving only a few night-shift officers and myself. The silence was oppressive, a constant reminder of Kayla's absence.

I rechecked my phone, hoping for a breakthrough, but it was just more of the same. I leaned back in my chair, closing my eyes for a moment. Images of Kayla flashed through my mind - her smile, her strength, her unwavering sense of justice. I couldn't lose her, not like this.

Determined, I opened my eyes and focused on the screen again. I started retracing our steps, reviewing every piece of evidence we had on Mandy, trying to find a pattern, a clue, anything.

But as the night wore on, my efforts seemed increasingly futile. The situation bore down on me, a heavy cloak of fear and frustration.

I was at a loss, but I couldn't give up. Not when Kayla's life hung in the balance. So, I continued working through the night, fueled by adrenaline, coffee, and sheer determination. I had to find her. I just had to.

The station was a whirlwind of activity when Lexi and Luke burst through the doors. Lexi's eyes locked onto mine, her voice tinged with panic. "Jake, what the hell is going on?"

I ushered them into a quiet corner, away from the bustling officers and ringing phones. Spreading out the evidence on a nearby table, I showed them the photos Mandy had taken of Lexi, stretching back to their college days. "Mandy was your stalker, Lexi. Jude was her cousin and foster brother. She's been orchestrating this whole thing."

Lexi's face crumpled as she absorbed my words. Tears welled in her eyes, spilling over as she clutched at the photos. "I can't believe this. She was in my room... all those years in college. I never saw it."

Luke wrapped an arm around her, trying to offer comfort, but Lexi seemed lost in her own world of betrayal and guilt. She muttered, more to herself than to us, "She came to Silver Creek when the stalker did. How did I not see it?"

I then showed her the pictures of me, the ones Mandy had secretly taken. Lexi's eyes widened in realization. "She shifted her focus to you, Jake."

"Yeah," I said grimly, "and now she's got Kayla."

"We have to get her back, Jake. Tell me what to do. How can I help?" Lexi's voice was firm now, her tears giving way to a determined resolve.

I pulled up a chair for her. "Sit down, Lexi. I need you

to tell me everything about Mandy. Anything at all that might help us find where she took Kayla."

Lexi sat, wiping her eyes, her mind racing. "There were never any signs, Jake. She was just... Mandy. A bit clingy, maybe, but nothing like this."

"But think about her habits, skills, anything out of the ordinary?" I urged, trying to find a lead in the tiniest of details.

Lexi thought for a moment. "She was always good with computers. A bit too good, maybe. Liked to know things about people, sometimes things she shouldn't have known."

Luke chimed in, "She always had a thing for secluded places. Liked the woods, said they were peaceful."

My mind latched onto that piece of information. "Secluded places... that could be something."

"And she had this odd thing about personal space," Lexi continued, her brow furrowing in concentration. "She hated being trapped or confined. Always needed an escape route."

"That's useful to know," I acknowledged, scribbling notes.

Luke added, "She was surprisingly good at fixing things, mechanical stuff. Said it was a hobby."

"Mechanical skills, escape routes, secluded places..." I muttered, trying to piece it together. "Anything else? Anything at all?"

Lexi shook her head. "I just can't believe it. All this time, it was her."

I placed a reassuring hand on her shoulder. "We're going to find Kayla, Lexi. With this information, we have a better chance. Thank you."

Lexi and Luke decided to stay at the station, ready to help with any further information that might be needed. The clock on the wall read close to midnight when my phone buzzed. The screen displayed Kayla's name, but I knew better. The text read, "I'm fine, Jake. Sorry to worry you. Just took a longer nap than I planned."

My heart raced, but I forced calm into my fingers as I typed a response. "That's a relief. Mind if I come over? Just want to see you're really okay."

The reply was almost immediate, a little too immediate. "No, still feeling tired. Maybe tomorrow."

I knew it was Mandy. Kayla would never turn down help, especially not now. I called over one of the techs. "Can we trace these messages?"

He shook his head after a few minutes of trying. "It's like they're bouncing off a dozen locations. Can't pinpoint it."

I cursed under my breath, turning back to my phone. "Okay, rest up then. Call me if you need anything."

I kept the conversation going, each message an attempt to catch 'Kayla' in a slip-up, but Mandy was cautious, giving nothing away.

Lexi came over, reading over my shoulder. "What are you doing?"

"Trying to get her to make a mistake. If she thinks I believe it's Kayla..."

Luke joined us, his brow furrowed. "Any luck?"

"Nothing yet. She's careful," I admitted, frustration mounting.

I continued to message, but with each passing minute, it became clear that Mandy wasn't going to reveal anything. With a heavy heart, I put the phone down, my mind racing for another way to find Kayla.

"We'll keep trying," Lexi promised, her voice uncertain despite her words. "We'll find her."

As I leaned back in my chair, my thoughts turned dark. If Mandy dared to hurt Kayla, there would be no holding back. The badge I wore, the oath I took to uphold the law, it would all become meaningless. I knew if the worst happened, I would cross lines and break every rule I had sworn to follow. I'd become something... very... very... different. The law would no longer bind me.

Chapter Forty-Two

MANDY

In the dim light of the cabin, my fingers trembled over the phone screen, Kayla's muffled sobs echoing in the background. "Shut up!" I snapped, unable to contain my frustration. She was ruining everything, making it impossible to think. I had to make a move, something bold, something that would force Jake's hand.

I switched to my number, abandoning the pretense of being Kayla. My heart raced as I typed a message to Jake. 'Miss you. When are you coming home?' It felt daring, a lure to bring him to me. But his response came too quickly, too alert. 'Huh? What do you mean? I'm at home now. Where are you?'

Panic surged through me. Shit, had I miscalculated? In a moment of hesitation, I didn't reply, my mind racing through possible scenarios. Then another message popped up, Jake's words cutting through me like a knife. 'Look, Mandy. Let's stop fucking around. I know you have Kayla. Where the hell are you?'

I felt the walls closing in on me. He knew. How much

did he know? My fingers hovered over the keyboard. I had to be smart about this. I had to stay one step ahead.

I quickly typed back, trying to regain control of the situation. 'Jake, I just wanted to talk. Kayla's fine. She's here with me. We're just... sorting things out.' I hoped it sounded convincing, desperate as I was to keep him off balance.

Silence followed. The phone lay heavy in my hand, each passing second stretching into an eternity. I glanced at Kayla, tied and gagged, her eyes wide with fear and confusion. If Jake didn't play along, if he didn't come here alone like I needed him to, I had no choice. I had to end this one way or another.

Kayla's eyes met mine, a silent plea in their depths. She didn't understand. She couldn't. This was about love, about destiny. Jake and I were meant to be, and I'd do anything to make that happen. I couldn't let anyone, not even Kayla, stand in the way of what was meant to be.

My grip tightened on the phone, ready to make my next move.

When he finally messaged back, demanding to talk to Kayla, I felt a surge of panic and anger.

'If she's safe, let me talk to her.'

Rage boiled up inside me. How dare he not believe me?

"Listen up," I snarled at Kayla, gripping her face in my hand. "You're going to talk to Jake, and you're going to make it sound like everything is normal. If you give him any hint, any fucking clue where we are, I swear I'll kill you right here."

Kayla's eyes were wide with fear, but she nodded, understanding the gravity of the situation. I dialed Jake's number and held the phone to her ear, watching her every move.

"Jake?" Kayla's voice trembled slightly as she spoke.

"Kayla, where are you?" Jake's voice came through, tense and worried.

"I'm just... enjoying some time with Mandy," Kayla said, her voice barely above a whisper.

Kayla paused, then asked, "How's everything going with the Henderson case?"

Jake hesitated. "Good. I think we almost have it solved. Do you remember where they found the weapon?" Jake asked, his tone urgent but controlled.

"At Godwin's liquor," Kayla answered, her voice steadier now.

"Right, okay, thanks," Jake said, and they exchanged a brief goodbye before hanging up.

As I ended the call, I couldn't shake the feeling that something was off. Jake's questions were too specific, too calculated. He was trying to communicate something to Kayla, but what? I couldn't let my guard down, not now when I was so close to getting what I wanted.

I turned to Kayla, my mind racing. "You did well," I said, though my suspicions still gnawed at me. "But don't think for a second that you're safe. This is far from over."

I tightened the ropes around Kayla, ensuring she couldn't move an inch. Satisfied with my handiwork, I left her there, a heap on the moth-eaten bed, and headed out to the van. My heart was racing. This was it, the moment I'd been preparing for.

The van was a mess, cluttered with my hastily gathered belongings. I rummaged through the bag, finding my makeup kit and a brush. I needed to look perfect for Jake. He had to see me, really see me, as the woman he was meant to be with.

I lugged the bag back into the cabin, setting it down with a thud. The bathroom was a reflection of the cabin's overall state – rundown, forgotten. But it didn't matter. I could transform myself anywhere.

I started with foundation, carefully blending it into my skin. Each brush stroke was methodical, a ritual to calm my racing thoughts. I chose my eyeshadow – a soft, smoky hue. It had to be enticing, not overwhelming. As I applied it, my mind wandered to Jake, his smile, the way his eyes crinkled when he laughed. I'd seen that smile directed at me, even if he didn't realize it yet.

Next came the eyeliner, a precise line to accentuate my eyes. I wanted Jake's gaze to be drawn to mine the moment he saw me. Mascara followed, thickening my lashes.

My lips were last. I chose a subtle shade, nothing too bold. I wasn't trying to shock him, just... entice him. Show him what he'd been missing. I practiced my smile in the mirror – not too wide, just a hint of longing. Perfect.

Satisfied with my appearance, I stepped out of the bathroom. Kayla was still, her breathing steady. She'd finally fallen asleep. Good. Her constant whimpers and pleas were grating on my nerves.

I took a moment to look at her, tied up and helpless. A part of me felt a twinge of guilt. She didn't deserve this. But it was necessary. She was the only thing standing between me and Jake.

As I gazed at her, my mind drifted back to the plan. Jake would come; he had to. And when he did, he'd see me, really see me. He'd realize that we were meant to be together. All this... mess, it was just a means to an end. A way to show him the depth of my love.

The silence of the cabin was my companion as I sat there, waiting, preparing myself for the moment Jake would walk through that door. Every second felt like an eternity, but I knew it would be worth it. Soon, everything would fall into place.

The Rookie's Second Chance

I wanted to share this moment with someone, wanted to tell Jude how close I was to getting everything I ever wanted. But then the harsh reality hit me – Jude was gone. I killed him.

Anger boiled inside me. It was his fault, not mine. He was going to betray me, going to hand me over to the authorities. He was going to ruin everything we had worked for. I didn't want to kill him, but he left me no choice. He forced my hand.

My thoughts turned to my dad. He always had my back, always covered for me. He understood me, understood why I did the things I did. He saw the bigger picture. But he was gone, too. I killed him. It was a moment of panic, a reaction to his and Jude's betrayal.

Sitting there alone, my actions started to sink in. Without Jude, without my dad, who was there to justify my actions? To understand that I had good reasons for everything I did? I wasn't a monster; I was just misunderstood. I was doing all this for love, for a connection that I deserved.

The cabin felt colder, emptier. I wrapped my arms around myself, trying to ward off the creeping chill of isolation. They were supposed to be my allies, my protectors. But in the end, they were just obstacles. Obstacles I had to remove.

I glanced at Kayla, still unconscious on the bed. She was part of the plan, a means to an end. With her out of the way, Jake would see the truth. He would understand that we were meant to be together.

But doubt crept into my mind. What if Jake didn't see things my way? What if he saw me as a monster, too? The thought sent a shiver down my spine. No, I couldn't think like that. I had to stay focused and believe in my plan.

I stood up and paced the room, trying to shake off the uncertainty. I had come too far to back down now. I had sacrificed too much. Jake was mine, and nothing was going to stand in my way. Not Kayla, not the police, not the ghosts of my past.

I stopped pacing and looked out the window into the dark woods. This was it, the final act. It was time to see it through. Time to claim what was rightfully mine. And if anyone tried to stop me, well, they would learn the same lesson Jude and my dad did.

The rustling of leaves outside caught my attention. Footsteps? I couldn't be sure. Tension knotted in my stomach as I slowly approached the cabin door, my hand gripping the handle of the knife I had taken from the kitchen. The night was still, the only sound being the distant hoot of an owl. I stepped out, scanning the dense treeline, my heart racing. Nothing. No sign of anyone. Just the woods, dark and foreboding under the moonlit sky.

I circled the cabin, my senses heightened. Every little noise made me jump, but there was no one there. It must have been my imagination, the stress of the situation getting to me. As I made my way back to the front door, I couldn't shake the feeling of being watched. But the clearing around the cabin was empty. I was alone.

Back inside, the first thing I noticed was the empty bed. Panic surged through me. Kayla was gone. How? I hadn't heard the doors open or close. She must still be inside. The cabin wasn't that big; there were only so many places she could hide.

I began my search, moving from room to room. My heart pounded in my chest, my breaths coming in short, sharp gasps. The silence of the cabin was oppressive, every creak of the floorboards sounding like a gunshot in the stillness. I checked behind doors, under the bed, in the closet. Nothing.

The frustration was mounting. Kayla couldn't have just

vanished. She had to be here somewhere. I retraced my steps, looking for any sign of her. What if she had managed to get outside while I was out? No, I would have seen her. She was still here, hiding, waiting for the right moment.

I returned to the main room, my eyes scanning every corner, every shadow. The tension was unbearable. Where was she? A sudden movement caught my eye, a slight shift in the shadows behind the old sofa. My grip tightened on the knife.

"Kayla," I called out, my voice steady despite the pounding of my heart. "I know you're here. You can't hide forever."

There was no response, just the deafening silence of the cabin. I took a step forward, ready for anything. This was it, the moment of truth. Kayla had to be there, behind the sofa. I could feel it.

With one swift movement, I rounded the corner of the sofa, knife raised, ready to confront her. But as I looked behind it, my heart sank.

It was empty. No Kayla. Just an old, dusty blanket that had shifted when I passed by earlier.

I stood there, my mind racing. She had to be here somewhere. I had to find her, had to bring her back. She was the key to everything.

With renewed resolve, I continued my search, moving through the cabin with purpose. Kayla couldn't hide forever. I would find her. I had to.

Chapter Forty-Three

KAYLA

Lying in the musty bed, I worked on a plan. Earlier, while Mandy was busy on her computer, I had caught a glimpse of a map. It showed the Henderson woods off Godwin Road. I knew I had to let Jake know where I was without alerting Mandy. So, during the phone call, I slipped in the code about Godwin's liquor. It was a gamble, but my only chance.

I heard footsteps outside. My heart leaped. Was it Jake? Or Mandy returning? I feigned sleep, every muscle in my body tensed, ready to act. Then, as the door creaked open and Mandy stepped outside, I knew it was now or never. Desperately, I tried to free myself from the bindings, but they were too tight, biting into my skin.

Suddenly, there was someone else in the room. A hand clamped over my mouth, and I nearly screamed, but it was Jake. Relief flooded through me as his lips brushed mine in a hurried kiss.

"We need to go. Now," he whispered urgently, cutting through my bindings with a knife he had brought.

Pulled from the bed, I stumbled, disoriented and weak.

We were almost at the door when Mandy returned. Panic surged through me. Jake's grip tightened, and he pulled me into a closet. My heart hammered in my chest as we heard Mandy's angry voice, her footsteps heavy as she searched for me.

Jake's eyes met mine in the dim light, a silent communication passing between us. We moved cautiously, shifting from one hiding place to another, avoiding Mandy's frenzied search.

As we crouched behind an old dresser, I could hear Mandy's breathing, ragged and close. Jake's hand found mine, squeezing it gently. It was a small comfort in the face of our peril. We were so close to freedom, yet so far.

Mandy's voice echoed through the cabin, filled with frustration and anger. "Kayla! Where are you? You can't hide forever!" Her footsteps moved away, and Jake signaled it was time to move.

We tiptoed towards the back door, every creak of the floorboards making my heart skip a beat. We were almost there, just a few more steps.

But then, a noise from the other room made us freeze. Mandy was coming back. Panic set in. We couldn't be caught now, not when we were so close. Jake's grip on my hand tightened as we looked for another place to hide.

We found ourselves in a small pantry, cramped and dark. I could barely breathe, the fear and the closeness overwhelming. Jake's presence was the only thing keeping me grounded.

Mandy's voice was getting closer, her footsteps echoing in my ears. My heart was racing, the adrenaline pumping through my veins. We couldn't let her find us, not now. We had to get out, had to escape.

Pressed against the pantry wall, my breath came in short gasps. Jake's hand on my arm was the only thing anchoring me. He cautiously peered out, signaling it was safe to move. I followed, my legs trembling, the taste of fear sharp in my mouth.

But then, in a heart-stopping moment, Mandy's hand clamped around my arm, wrenching me away from Jake. My heart plummeted into my stomach. I spun around to face her, and there it was – the cold metal of my own gun pressing against my temple. Jake whirled around, his pistol aimed, but the sight of me in Mandy's grip froze him.

"Don't hurt her," Jake's voice was a desperate plea, thick with emotion. Mandy's eyes were wild, her grip on me unyielding.

"I have to," Mandy's voice cracked. "Or else we can't be together."

I could feel my whole body trembling, the gun cold and heavy against my skin. Then, without warning, Mandy struck me with the gun. Pain exploded in my head, stars dancing before my eyes. I whimpered, the sound muffled and weak.

Jake's voice was steady, but I could hear the undercurrent of fear. "We can be together."

Mandy's laugh was bitter. "You're lying."

Jake's next move took me by surprise. He stepped forward, closing the distance between them, and kissed Mandy. My heart stopped. Horror and confusion flooded through me. But then, through the haze of fear and pain, I caught Jake's eye. He was looking at me, a silent message in his gaze.

At that moment, I understood. It was a ruse, a desperate attempt to disarm her. All I could do was watch, helpless, as Jake sacrificed his pride, his integrity, to save us both.

The moment Mandy's grip on the gun loosened, my instincts kicked in. Adrenaline coursed through my veins, fueling a surge of desperate strength. I lunged, my fingers wrapping around the gun's barrel, struggling to wrest it from her grasp. Our bodies collided, a tangled mess of limbs and raw desperation.

Mandy was surprisingly strong, her fingers like iron around the gun. Our struggle was chaotic, a whirlwind of pushing and pulling. Every muscle in my body screamed in exertion as I fought for control. The gun wavered between us, its deadly potential a hair-trigger away.

"Let go!" I screamed, my voice hoarse with fear and determination.

But Mandy was relentless, her eyes wild with madness. For a moment, it seemed like she might overpower me. Then, with a twist and a sharp jerk, I managed to wrench the gun free. But in the chaos, my finger slipped. The gun went off with a deafening bang.

"Jake!" The name escaped my lips in a horrified gasp as I spun around. He was clutching his arm, pain etched on his face. My heart plummeted. "Oh God, no," I whispered, aghast.

Mandy was shrieking now, a manic gleam in her eyes. "You shot him!" she screamed, her voice laced with a twisted sense of triumph.

"You're fucking insane!" I retorted, my voice trembling as I pointed the gun at her, my finger trembling on the trigger. I was ready to shoot if she moved.

Just as Mandy seemed poised to lunge at me, the door burst open. Another officer, gun drawn, took in the scene in an instant. Before Mandy could react, he deployed his taser. The electrodes hit her, sending her convulsing to the floor in a heap.

My breath came in ragged gasps as the tension broke. The gun felt like a lead weight in my hand, its cold metal a stark contrast to the warm rush of relief flooding through me. I lowered it slowly, my gaze fixed on Jake, who was still gripping his arm, his face contorted in pain.

"Jake, I'm so sorry," I stammered, my voice breaking with relief and fear.

The officer was already radioing for backup and medical assistance. I rushed to Jake's side, my hands shaking as I tried to assess his wound. The sight of blood, his blood, was a visceral punch to the gut.

"It's okay, Kayla," Jake managed through gritted teeth, his eyes meeting mine with a look that held a world of understanding and forgiveness.

As the cabin filled with the sounds of approaching sirens and shouting officers, I realized the nightmare was finally over. Mandy was down, incapacitated by the taser. Jake was hurt but alive. And I, despite everything, was still standing.

Mandy's eyes fluttered open, confusion etched across her face as she tried to orient herself. The arresting officer, standing firm and composed, began the familiar protocol.

"Mandy Pennington, you are under arrest," he stated, his voice steady. "You have the right to remain silent. Anything you say can and will be used against you in a court of law. You have the right to an attorney. If you cannot afford an attorney, one will be provided for you. Do you understand these rights as I have read them to you?"

Mandy's face crumpled, tears streaming down her cheeks. "No, no, you don't understand," she sobbed, her voice breaking. "My dad will fix this. He always does."

The officer, unfazed by her emotional outburst, continued to secure the handcuffs around her wrists. He looked at her with a mixture of pity and sternness.

"Officer Kilkenny?" he asked, his tone softening. "They found his body, Mandy. Along with your mother and cousin. I don't think he'll be fixing anything for you ever again."

Mandy's sobs intensified, her body shaking as the full weight of the officer's words hit her. Her cries echoed through the cabin, a sound of despair and realization that her world, the one she thought she controlled, had irrevocably shattered.

Lexi and Luke burst into the cabin. Lexi immediately knelt beside Jake, her hands gently assessing his wound.

"Jake, are you okay?" she asked, her voice thick with worry.

"I'll be fine," Jake managed, wincing as Lexi prodded gently at his arm.

Turning her attention to Mandy, Lexi's face hardened. The officer holding Mandy started to lead her away, but I intervened. "Wait, let her have a moment," I said, my voice firm despite the lump in my throat.

Lexi stepped closer to Mandy, her eyes blazing with anger and disbelief. "I can't believe I ever trusted you," she said, her voice quivering with emotion. "You were like a sister to me."

Mandy's eyes, now clear and lucid, met Lexi's. "I did it all for you... for Jake. I love you both. I just wanted to be with you," she said, her voice a desperate, twisted plea.

Lexi shook her head. "Then you should have just been yourself, Mandy. You shouldn't have ever hurt anyone. The minute you did, you lost me—lost all of us."

Mandy's face crumpled, a sob escaping her lips as the reality of her actions and their consequences finally seemed to hit her. But there was no sympathy in my heart for her, only relief that her reign of terror was over.

The officer tugged gently at Mandy's arm, signaling it was time to leave. As Mandy was led out of the cabin, her sobs fading into the distance, I turned back to Jake. His eyes met mine, filled with pain and gratitude.

"We did it, Kayla," he whispered, reaching for my hand.

I squeezed his hand tightly, nodding. "We did," I agreed.

The ride to the hospital was a blur of sirens and flashing lights, but all I could focus on was Jake, sitting beside me, his face etched with pain. Every time the ambulance jolted, he winced, and I tightened my grip on his hand, trying to offer some comfort.

When we arrived at the hospital, the medical staff swarmed around us. A nurse tried to usher me away for a check-up, but I refused, adamant about staying by Jake's side.

"I'm fine," I insisted, even though my body ached from the scuffle with Mandy. "I need to be with him."

Reluctantly, they allowed me to stay, and I watched as they carefully examined Jake's wound. The bullet had grazed his side, leaving a raw, angry mark. The doctor, a middle-aged man with kind eyes, worked with steady hands as he cleaned the wound.

"You're lucky," he told Jake. "A few inches to the left, and we'd be having a different conversation."

Jake grimaced, but his eyes never left mine. "Yeah, lucky," he echoed, squeezing my hand.

As the doctor stitched him up, Jake and I talked softly. We spoke about how close we had come to losing everything and how we couldn't believe we hadn't pieced together Mandy's involvement sooner.

"I love you," I whispered, my voice thick with emotion. "I'm so glad you're safe."

"I love you too," Jake replied, his voice steady despite

the pain. "Nothing's going to change that. Not Mandy, not anything."

After the doctor finished giving Jake instructions for care and a prescription for pain relief, we left the hospital. The night was cool and quiet.

We drove back to Jake's house in silence, each lost in our thoughts. The knowledge that Mandy wouldn't be there waiting, that this nightmare was finally over, was a relief I couldn't quite process yet.

Once inside, we headed straight to the bedroom, both physically and emotionally exhausted. We lay down together, holding each other close. I could feel Jake's heartbeat against my chest, a reassuring rhythm in the darkness.

As I drifted off to sleep, wrapped in Jake's arms, I realized that despite everything, we had each other. And that was all that mattered.

Chapter Forty-Four

JAKE

Sitting across from chief Dawson, Kayla and I exchanged a nervous glance before I started to speak. The moment was heavy; we were about to confess something that could change our careers.

"chief," I began, my voice steady, "there's something we need to tell you."

The chief leaned back in his chair, his expression unreadable. "I'm listening."

I took a deep breath. "Kayla and I... we've rekindled our relationship from high school during this case. It wasn't planned. It just happened."

Kayla chimed in, her voice firm yet tinged with apprehension. "We didn't let it affect our work, chief. We kept it professional."

The chief raised an eyebrow. "You're telling me you two are an item now? After all these years?"

"Yes, sir," I replied. "We realized we still have feelings for each other. It's serious."

He steepled his fingers, considering our words. "And

what about the force? You two are partners. How do you plan to handle that?"

"We've talked about it," Kayla said. "We're willing to do whatever it takes to make this work, even if one of us has to transfer out."

The chief sighed, rubbing his temples. "You two know the rules about fraternization. It's not just about you; it's about the team, the department."

"We understand, chief," I said. "But we also believe we can still be effective as partners. We've proven that we can work together under extreme circumstances."

He looked at us for a long, silent moment. "You're damn good cops, both of you. This case... it was a mess from the start, but you handled it. Together."

"We appreciate that, sir," Kayla replied, her voice soft.

The chief leaned forward, his gaze fixed on us. "I'm willing to make an exception under one condition. You keep it professional. At work, you're deputies, not a couple. Don't make me regret this decision."

We both nodded eagerly. "Absolutely, chief. You won't regret it," I assured him.

"And if I hear even a whisper of this affecting your work..." he warned.

"You won't," I interjected quickly. "We'll be nothing but professional."

He studied us for a moment longer, then nodded. "Alright. Get back to work, and remember what I said."

As Kayla and I stood up to leave, I felt a sense of relief. We had taken a risk, but it had paid off. We could be together, both in and out of uniform.

"Thank you, chief," Kayla said, her voice filled with gratitude.

"Yeah, thanks, chief," I echoed, feeling a sense of hope for our future together.

As we left his office, I reached for Kayla's hand, squeezing it gently. No matter what the future held, we were ready to face it together.

We arrived at my house to find Lexi bustling around the kitchen, the aroma of a home-cooked meal filling the air—one that didn't come with a side of guilt and obsession.

Luke was upstairs in the room Mandy had used, diligently clearing out every trace of her presence. The thought of Mandy being sent back to Key West for trial on multiple charges, including murder, lingered in my mind, but tonight was about moving forward.

"Smells great, Lex," I said, kissing my sister on the cheek. The warmth of family and safety enveloped me like a comforting blanket.

"Thanks, Jake. I just wanted to do something for you guys. After everything you've done..." Lexi trailed off, her eyes glistening with unshed tears.

"Hey, it's okay," I said softly. "We're all safe now, thanks to Kayla and the team. And you, Lex, you were brave through it all."

She nodded, managing a small smile. "Without you and Kayla, I wouldn't be here. Mandy would still be out there, and I wouldn't even know."

In the other room, the sound of rustling bags and the occasional clank of discarded items being thrown out filled the space. Luke emerged, his arms laden with garbage bags.

"That's the last of it," he announced, a note of finality in his voice. "I don't want to see anything that reminds us of her ever again."

We all agreed, the sentiment hanging in the air as we sat down for dinner. The table was a symbol of unity, a place where we could share our experiences and begin the healing process.

As we ate, the conversation was light, avoiding the heavier topics. Laughter and casual banter replaced the tension that had hung over us for weeks. It was a relief to be a family again, without the shadow of danger looming over us.

Every now and then, I caught Kayla's eye, and we shared a silent understanding. We had been through hell and back, but we'd come out stronger, individually and together. The ordeal had forged a bond between us that was unbreakable.

After dinner, Lexi and Luke helped clean up while Kayla and I stepped outside for a moment of quiet.

"Can you believe it's over?" Kayla asked, leaning against the railing.

I wrapped my arm around her, pulling her close. "It doesn't feel real yet. But I'm just glad you're safe. That we're all safe."

She rested her head on my shoulder. "Thanks to you, Jake. You never gave up."

Back inside, the dinner had a warmth that spread beyond the food and the kitchen. Laughter and stories were shared, the sort of familial chatter that had been missing for too long. As we ate, I caught Lexi's eye across the table. She nudged Luke, who offered a knowing smile. It was clear they were in on something, but what?

I grinned, looking back at Kayla. "You're right, you know. I didn't give up. Just like I never really gave up on you, Lex," I began, feeling a surge of emotions. "For over a decade, I compared everyone I met to you. Never found a single person who could measure up. Even when I thought I'd lost you for good, a part of me always hoped we'd find our way back to each other. And here we are."

Kayla's eyes shimmered with unspoken words, her smile lighting up the room. I took a deep breath, feeling the moment settle over me.

Standing up, I moved closer to her. The room went quiet, all eyes on us. I reached into my pocket, pulling out a small velvet box. My heart was pounding in my chest, a rhythm that echoed through the room.

Kayla's hand flew to her mouth, her eyes widening in surprise. I took her hand in mine, feeling the warmth of her skin against mine. Dropping to one knee, I looked up at her, my voice steady despite the storm of emotions inside me.

"Kayla, these past weeks, hell, these past years, have shown me that life without you is incomplete. You've been my partner, my confidant, my rock. You've seen me at my worst and still stood by me. I can't imagine a future without you in it. I want to spend the rest of my life making up for the time we lost, creating new memories, and facing whatever life throws at us together."

I opened the box, revealing a simple yet elegant ring. "Kayla, will you marry me?"

The room held its breath. Kayla's eyes glistened with tears, her expression a mix of shock, happiness, and love. She took a moment to let the question sink in, then nodded vigorously.

"Yes, Jake, yes! A thousand times, yes!" she exclaimed, tears streaming down her cheeks.

I slipped the ring onto her finger, standing up to embrace her. The room erupted into cheers and applause. Lexi and Luke came over to congratulate us, their faces beaming with joy.

"Welcome to the family, officially," Lexi said, hugging Kayla.

Luke clapped me on the back. "You did good, man," he said, grinning.

We spent the rest of the evening in a euphoric bubble, surrounded by love and support. As the night drew to a close and the guests departed, Kayla and I remained, wrapped in each other's arms, lost in the promise of a future together.

It was a perfect ending to a day that had begun with uncertainty and fear. As we headed to bed, the ring on Kayla's finger caught the light, a symbol of our renewed commitment and love. We lay there, holding each other, talking about our plans, our dreams, and the life we would build together. The trials we had faced had brought us closer, solidifying an unbreakable bond.

Her hands rested on my chest as I leaned in and kissed her. I had nearly lost her, and now the only thing in the world that I wanted, now that she'd agreed to marry me, was to feel her against me, to show her the depth of my love by worshipping her body.

One kiss on her neck was all it took for her to arch against me. As I felt her breasts pressed against my chest, her legs wrap around my waist, I moaned softly, unable to control myself any longer. Pulling away from her lips, I buried my face between her thighs, kissing and licking, nibbling and sucking. Her cries of pleasure grew louder, echoing off the walls, as I relished the taste of her, savoring every second of this most intimate of acts. As I licked her and tasted her sweet juices, the sound drove me wild, and I felt my own arousal swelling beneath me.

"Please, Jake... I need you."

Unable to wait any longer, I pulled away, stroking my fingers along her damp cleft. Biting her lower lip, she wriggled under me, trying to get closer, begging me to take her.

Clasping her hips, I thrust hard into her wet heat, my breathing labored.

She clutched my shoulders, her nails digging into my flesh, matching the pace of my strokes. I could feel her tightening around me, the sensations almost too much to bear. I slowed down, wanting to truly worship her, to show her how precious she was to me.

Her body reacted to my every move, and her voice was little more than a series of whimpers. Finally, her inner muscles convulsed, squeezing me tightly, pushing me over the edge, joining her in climax. In an explosion of bliss, our bodies rocked together, clinging to each other, locked in our mutual passion. After several minutes, we collapsed, basking in the afterglow.

With my head nestled against her shoulder, I ran my fingers lightly through her hair. Gently, I kissed her neck. She nuzzled her face against my shoulder, her warm breath tickling my skin. Wrapping my arm around her, I rolled to my side, spooning her against me.

"I love you so much," I whispered.

"I love you too," she replied, kissing my cheek. "Thank you for finding me. For saving me from her."

I smiled. "I had to. I couldn't live without you."

She cuddled into me, and soon, I heard the soft rhythm of her snores. Leaning in, I brushed my lips against hers, tasting the remnants of our combined passion. This was where I was always meant to be, who I was meant to be with. I knew it wouldn't be easy, but I knew, without a doubt, it would always be worth it. Every day. Forever.

And as I drifted off, despite the turmoil of the last few months, I was grateful for it all. I wished more than anything that no one I loved, not Kayla or my sister, not my best friend Luke or even myself, would have had to deal with the fear and tragedy that Mandy had brought. But if we had to go through it, at least we went through it together.

And we were all stronger for it.

About the Author

Jennifer Rivers is an emerging author of contemporary romance novels with a little touch of mystery. Originally from Ireland, she now lives in New England with her husband, kids, and her two crazy pups.

When she's not dreaming up her next enemies to lovers or brother's best friend suspenseful romance. She spends her time out and about with her kids or in the kitchen feeding her cooking passion.

Go ahead and click "+Follow" to be notified of all upcoming releases!

Also by Jennifer Rivers

Straight Up Single Dad

Fireman's Forbidden Flame

Stolen From My Billionaire Boss

The Rancher's Fake Fiancé

Did you like this book? Then you'll LOVE Jennifer's other romantic mystery The Rancher's Fake Fiancé Book 1 of the Silver Creek Series

If you would like to be the first to hear about Jennifer Rivers new and upcoming releases you sign up to her newsletter here

or follow Jennifer on her official Amazon Author's Page

Check out this sneak peek of the Rancher's Fake Fiancé

Lexi

The moment I stepped off the bus, the distinctive scent of Silver Creek enveloped me: a blend of fresh mountain air and the distant horses from the ranches. The general store, unchanged, still stood proudly. Its wooden facade was a silent witness to countless memories. Children's laughter drifted towards me, and, for a moment, it felt like I had never left.

"Feels good to be home," I whispered, my boots crunching the gravel beneath.

I was reaching down for my bags when a familiar voice, infused with a warmth and urgency, called out. "Lexi!"

Lifting my gaze, I found my brother barreling toward me. We met in a tight embrace. "I've missed you more than you know," he murmured.

Pulling away, I teased, "It's only been two years, Jake. Not a lifetime."

His eyes twinkled with mischief, though an undercurrent of concern was evident. "Still, you've changed. College did wonders."

I grinned. "Just enough to dodge your playful banter."

Jake chuckled. As we began the journey home, I couldn't help but notice the subtle weight in his steps, his occasional glances over his shoulder, as though expecting something—or someone. "Alright, Jake," I probed, "you've got that look. What's going on?"

He hesitated, seemingly gathering his thoughts. "Remember Luke Dalton?"

At the mention of the name, a familiar shiver raced down my spine, a cocktail of memories and suppressed feelings. "Luke? Of course, how could I forget?" I replied, hoping my voice didn't betray my flood of emotion.

Jake, seemingly oblivious to my reaction, continued, "He's... different now, Lex. More intense. And it's not just him. There are new people in town. They've been snapping up properties left and right, and they're... different."

"What does Luke have to do with these newcomers?" I asked, trying to keep the conversation casual while my heart raced.

Pulling into the driveway, Jake got out and unloaded my bags.

We walked inside, and the familiar feeling of home washed over me.

But before I could truly settle into the comforts of home, Jake gripped my arm, his face etched with urgency. "We need to talk, Lexi."

Taken aback, I met his gaze, seeing a depth of worry I hadn't noticed before. "Alright, what's the matter?"

He motioned me to follow him to the living room, still filled with brown leather and old books. "It's Luke's ranch," he didn't bother to sit. "It's under threat."

I frowned. "Threat? How?"

Jake paced, each step heavy with tension. "The damn local council, alongside some big-shot corporations, have taken an interest in his land. Rumors are, they're planning to turn it into a luxury resort."

My heart raced, anger boiling within me. "That's bullshit. That land has been in Luke's family for generations!"

"I know, Lex," Jake shot back, his face strained. "But here's the twist. To change the tide of opinion, to present the ranch as an integral part of the community, we've got a... plan."

Suspicion crept in. "What kind of plan?"

Jake glanced at me as if gauging my reaction in advance. "We need Luke to be... engaged."

My heart missed a beat. A barrage of memories with Luke, all hidden from the world, flashed through my mind. "Engaged? To who?"

Jake met my eyes squarely, a hint of desperation in his voice. "To you, Lexi."

I felt the blood drain from my face. "What? Are you out of your freaking mind?"

"It's just a ruse, Lex!" Jake exclaimed. "We think tying Luke to a known local, especially a Barrows, might just be the push we need. It'll strengthen the ranch's stance."

My thoughts spiraled. He had no idea about the clandestine nights, the secret meetings, the love that had grown and faltered in the shadows. "Has Luke agreed to this?" I managed to ask, trying to keep my voice steady.

Jake scratched the back of his neck, clearly uncomfortable. "He's out in Helena, getting supplies. He doesn't know yet. But we're running out of time."

I took a deep breath, trying to align my thoughts. Playing this part would mean reopening old wounds, diving deep into a past I had tried hard to bury. "Jake, this isn't a simple charade. This could change everything."

His eyes softened, the weight of his desperation evident. "I know I'm asking a lot. But it's not just the ranch at stake. It's our history, our community."

I sighed. "Okay. I'm not saying yes. But I am saying I'm hungry. Can we talk more over dinner?"

Click Here to keep reading

Printed in Great Britain
by Amazon